THE WAR OF THE
THREE KINGDOMS

ALSO BY MICHAELA RILEY KARR

The Story of the First Archimage Series
The Allyen

The Desire to Know

THE *War* OF THE *Three Kingdoms*

THE STORY OF THE FIRST ARCHIMAGE

BOOK 2

MICHAELA RILEY KARR

Rye Meadow Press

Published by Rye Meadow Press, based in Emporia, KS.
ryemeadowpress@gmail.com

ISBN (paperback): 978-0-9986065-3-8
ISBN (hardback): 978-0-9986065-4-5
Library of Congress Control Number: 2018903705

Cover Design © 2018: Magpie Designs, ltd.
Photo Credit: Pixabay
Texture Credit: Sascha Duensing
Author Photo Credit: Jordan Storrer Photography
Interior Map © 2018: L. N. Weldon

Printed in the United States of America.
First Edition, 2018.

DEDICATION

For Daphne Evans, my wonderful friend, former roommate, and meticulous grammar nerd. You're the bomb. May your days always be pun-tastic.

NERAHDIS

TREDENO

JOSHUUA'S TREE

LEONAR

THE KINGDOM OF
MINERALTIR

CADEN'S

MINERALTIR CASTLE

DEMORA

TRANINI

THE
GREAT DESERT

IONDRIA

RHYDIN'S TOWER

IVANN'S DELTA

N

★ CAPITAL
● CITY
■ CASTLE

CHAPTER ONE

The battlefield was quiet. The mountain faces stared down in judgment like pale ghosts, and the river ran silent, its gurgling hushed. The thick, emerald grasses of spring had been trampled down over and over by hundreds of soldiers, leaving no hope of ever standing tall again.

The fog began to clear, revealing the bloody aftermath, but the sword in my hands had become heavy. No matter how hard I tried to muster my remaining strength, my sword point felt like it'd been filled with lead. My ears were ringing. I was alone. Almost.

Sam's eyes stared unseeingly up at me, their brown dulled. A rugged, crimson gash reached from his temple to his cheekbone, dripping profusely. There was no shaking the iron grip of failure that gagged my throat.

His tall frame lay sprawled unnaturally on the ground next to me, my fingers buried in the front of his tattered uniform. His Kidek bandana sat to the side with a gaping hole in its threads, crumpled and dirty. I looked down at my beloved husband, tears leaking from my eyes before my ears registered a chuckle that I would never forget.

Rhydin leered over me, his amethyst eyes like fire with a smirk pasted onto his face. He reached forward with his thin, pale hand, and, in heartbroken fury, I screamed, dashing forward. I swiped my sword through his lean arm.

To my horror, the blade passed right through just as it had with Duunzer nearly a year ago. Ice slid down my spine as my sword shattered to pieces like glass, and I could not stop myself from falling to the ground and cowering like a child.

"You will never defeat me, Allyen Linaria," Rhydin said in a low voice, but his grin disappeared. He leaned down and ripped my locket from my neck before glaring at me, deep into my soul. "Nerahdis is *mine*."

I sprang forward out of the nightmare as if I had been stabbed, which was how I always woke up from it. It was always right as Rhydin killed me. I choked on my sobs and flung the tears from my cheeks as if they were poison, holding myself tightly.

My hand fumbled for the warm, Allyen locket hanging around my neck. It was safe. Our room was still dark, cool, and dank. Shortly before dawn, I knew, from my frequent midnight awakenings.

I rolled over quickly and put my hand on Sam's shoulder. He was in the exact position he had fallen asleep in last night, flopped forward on his stomach with his face in a sad, lumpy pillow. As I noticed the light rising and falling of his ribcage, I relaxed slightly. It was always the same dream, and even though Sam was fine every time I awoke, it still haunted me. It felt so real.

Terror was replaced by dread as I ardently hoped that this dream would not come true like the one of Duunzer had. Last year, I'd had a dream about Duunzer, Rhydin's dark, magically-created dragon that attacked Nerahdis, long before we even knew that was what Rhydin was planning.

Rachel had explained to me that Allyen dreams were sometimes visions of the future. Sam also knew about this ability, but he didn't know about these new, repetitive nightmares. I couldn't bear to tell him. Even with all the times I had awakened with a shriek in a cold sweat, not even a noise loud enough to wake the dead could raise this man, especially during harvest.

Whimpering noises began to come from the foot of our bed, and I leaned forward onto my knees, my locket falling forward out of the front of my tunic. With a couple of creaks and crunches of our straw tick, I probed with my tiny fingers for the small basket. Light was only just beginning to brighten the horizon, much less penetrate our dark little house.

As the cries grew steadily louder, my fingers finally touched the rough threads of the wicker. Habit took over, and my hands easily found the small, warm bundle inside the basket. I hoisted the little weight to my shoulder and cradled him in my arms. I wasn't worried for my slumbering rock of a husband but for the neighbors in our compound.

As more light came through our tiny window, I could make out the chubby face of our son. Long lashes framed his little brown eyes, and his downy hair was becoming visible. I smiled at him as he quieted, and I remembered holding him for the first time several weeks ago in Late Autumn. Now, it was Middle Winter, and Kylar Samton Greene was only just beginning to get a good look at this crazy world of ours.

I held Kylar tightly and padded barefoot into the next frigid room. I felt more comfortable and "at home" than when we got married and first moved here, but I was still getting accustomed to this house. After all, I had spent all of twenty years in the house I'd lived in outside of Soläna before Rhydin ruined everything.

This house was smaller with no upper chamber and only a blanket partition between our room and the living room/kitchen. That was the truly strange part. Growing up, we'd had four people in our house, which felt like it was bursting at the seams. Now, with Mama, Papa, Rosetta, and even Keera all missing, it was hard to call this place "home."

Sam, Kylar, and I lived in a compound now, many miles north of Soläna where Lunaka was uncharted. The nearest town was Lun, over twenty miles away. This was necessary, seeing as we lived with other Rounans now.

Since Sam's records were taken when Rhydin killed my family, he decided it would be easier to simply live with his persecuted people seeing as Soläna was too dangerous for us anyway. Now, Sam was more accessible as leader, although the Rounans mostly governed themselves and only brought big issues to Sam's attention.

I looked down at my infant son and turned his flabby little arm over, my eyes soaking in the geometric mark. The diamond and square on the inside of his wrist, and the point stretching to his barely defined elbow. It was the birthmark that made my husband and tiny baby Rounans, the special magic users who were hunted by King Adam and Rhydin. Someday, my little Kylar would be Kidek, just like Sam before him, and the idea thrilled me and terrified me at the same time.

We watched as the world awakened around us. Outside our window, the prairie was covered with ankle-deep snow, which had fallen last week. The air was so freezing that the top layer of the snow had frozen solid, producing a satisfying crunch when stepped upon. Almost one hundred people lived in this little gathering of houses with us, and by looking at them, you would never guess that Lunaka was at war.

Men were treading forth from their warm houses, stomping around in the snow as they tended to their animals. We were self-sufficient out here. There was no need to ever go to town, so the animals always came first. Through the glowing yellow windows, I could see women and children enjoying their breakfast, the former trying to wrap the latter in their warmest cloaks before allowing them to enter the winter wonderland outside. I clutched Kylar tighter, trying to hold his warmth close, glad that I didn't have to worry about letting go of him yet.

Outside, our glinting wind chime began its usual song as the fingers of the icy wind twirled it around. It was made from Ranguvariian feathers, known to hide presences. They allowed our entire compound to be invisible from Rhydin's view.

Rachel, Luke, and James gave it to us, but they were still home with their grandfather, Clariion of the Ranguvariians, discussing this horrendous war and Rhydin's involvement in it. He had to have his hands in it somehow. After all, the fight struck itself into a full-fledged fire after the initial sparks his Einanhi dragon, Duunzer, stoked up.

Every time the sun rose, its rays cast along the wreckage left behind from Duunzer. Collapsed buildings, missing livestock, ruined fields and livelihoods. The worst part? While most people awoke from the Darkness unaffected, its dark power had a strange affinity for infants and the elderly. Not a single child under the age of two, nor adult over the age of sixty, in all of Nerahdis ever woke up from their dark slumber.

The hundreds of deaths caused the people to backlash

against their magic-possessing rulers, demanding them to reveal who had brought Duunzer upon them. King Adam of Lunaka was one of Rhydin's Followers, as well as Queen Jasmine of Mineraltir, who was conveniently sole ruler now that King Morris died in the Darkness. Xavier seemed to believe that he was murdered, but I wasn't quite sure. Therefore, the two were able to create a magnificent falsehood blaming each other as well as my ally, King Daniel of Auklia.

All three kingdoms now believed that its neighbors committed the atrocious crime of unleashing Duunzer, despite Daniel's attempts to warn about Rhydin, the dragon's true creator. Yet, nobody could prove who did it, convinced that their power-hungry Royals had betrayed them, so the war kicked itself into motion within a season of the attack.

Now, hour by hour, Lunaka was dredging itself deeper into war with the rest of Nerahdis. Hour by hour, soldiers were killed and innocents were slain fighting over something that they would never find the answer to. Rhydin was the true criminal, yet he was still keeping his existence a secret for whatever reason.

Many Lunakan men had volunteered to fight in the war with the idea that either Queen Jasmine or King Daniel had tried to control Duunzer thoroughly ingrained in their heads, but the volunteering was beginning to taper off. I feared every day what King Adam might do to fix this and refused to even imagine that it could lead to my nightmare.

"You're up early today... Again."

I jumped at the sudden sound, my mind brought back from its ramblings. I turned to see a very tired-looking Sam, and it did my heart well to see him standing upright with his eyes open. His reddish-brown hair was sticking in every which direction, his bandana not tied on yet, and he was wrapped rather tightly in the deer fur blanket from our bed.

It reminded me of how my toes were turning into blocks of ice in our cold house. After all, the mud chinks filling in the cracks in the walls only did so much to keep the snowy wind out. I cleared my throat, my eyes falling to the floor as I lied. "Sorry, Kylar woke me up. I didn't want to wake you when I fed him."

Sam shrugged and struck a match to light the small lantern on our table. It illuminated our tiny living space, only inhabited by a short kitchen counter with some crude wooden bowls, bent tin plates, and a couple glass jars. Being the Allyen and savior of Nerahdis had some marvelous living conditions, didn't it?

Sam bent down and placed the blanket around my numb shoulders, kissed my forehead, and took Kylar from me, hefting him into the air. The baby smiled and gurgled, and it was a joy to see the love on Sam's face for this miniature human that was only just beginning to assert some sort of personality. I couldn't imagine being one of the parents who suddenly woke up and found their baby dead after Duunzer.

As I dwelled on that thought, I stood and pulled out some of our chickens' eggs to make breakfast. My cooking skills had improved somewhat since marriage, but if Sam ever wanted something beyond eggs or stew, he'd have to fix it himself.

Once our meal was ready, Sam chitchatted with me for a little while about what he was going to do today between bites of egg. Winter was the farmer's time to do all the things he couldn't do during the growing season. Since we had only farmed this land one time, there was a lot of fence building in Sam's mind. I had taken my retirement from the farming profession mostly well, although I couldn't help jumping in to assist Sam anytime I could.

As Sam downed the last of his water and handed Kylar back to me, he cleared his throat. "So, are you going to visit the Royals today?"

I grimaced. "You really shouldn't call them that. It's a mean word."

My husband looked back at me innocently, playfulness in his eyes and the set of his angular jaw. "Oh, you know what I mean. After all, they're still Royals compared to the rest of us. You should go. We haven't seen them in a while. Who knows, they may have an update for ya." His joking mood disappeared.

Sighing, I tucked Kylar close again. I had avoided them as much as possible ever since my nightmares began, which was shortly after our son was born. I knew Prince Frederick would be able to pry it out of me. Somehow, I felt that if I didn't say it out loud, it wouldn't come true.

"Are you sure you're fine? I never heard Kylar cry." Sam's eyes were measuring me up. The bags under my eyes, my bony limbs, my pale face.

I did my best to conjure up a smile, an image of him dead on the ground with the gash on his face flashing in my mind. "You never hear anything, Mr. Dead-to-the-world. I'm fine, I promise."

Sam's eyebrow quirked, not quite believing me. After all, he knew me better than anyone. But, he said nothing. He went back through the curtain partition for a few minutes and reappeared fully dressed in his warmest clothes, his hair somewhat straightened now with his Kidek bandana in its proper place.

He walked over to the door and grabbed his thickest cloak, one that was several years old. I knew it didn't keep him that warm and made a mental note to keep that in mind for a birthday present next year when he turned twenty-three. I stood as he wrapped his moth-eaten scarf several times around his neck and face, and I pulled his hood over his head for him.

He looked at me seriously, his lopsided grin gone. "Go see the Royals, Lina. Let Kylar play with Dominick. No use being cooped up in here. We're not that paranoid."

He gave me a quick kiss and disappeared out the door before he could see my shoulders slump. If I didn't go now, I'd never hear the end of it.

It was light outside now, so I watched Sam for a few moments out the window as he walked toward the barn and chicken coop, measuring his gait to see how deep the snow was. Northern Lunaka acquired a few more inches of snow than I was used to down in Soläna.

I turned around from the window and set about bundling up Kylar against the cold, putting about every piece of his clothing on. After putting on my own cloak and wrapping myself with a shawl, I tucked Kylar in close, took a deep breath, and opened the door into the freezing world.

The sun blinded me upon my entrance, my eyes adjusted after a minute or two, and I wondered at the white scenery. The mountains were closer here, and I loved watching their caps fill with snow for the winter then go bald for the rest of the year. All around us, the mid-sized Rounan community was coming alive.

For the freezing temperatures, more people were outside than you would think. There were small children building snow animals and using their Rounan powers to levitate the balls of snow onto their respective stacks. Some of the older children would sometimes start lifting one of their little siblings, resulting in a scolding from their mother. That was the number one rule of the compound: Don't use magic on other people.

I didn't really fit in with this gathering of people, seeing as I was the only non-Rounan here. I was the only person of Gornish descent, who belonged to the group of people actively persecuting and hanging them. No big deal.

Every once in a while, one of the women would smile at me as I passed by, but most of the time, they turned the other way. Sometimes, my anxiety would start wondering if they only put up with me because I was the Kidek's wife, which only added to my fear of losing Sam.

I followed Sam's deep footsteps to the barn, though I was only able to put my feet in them half the time because his legs were so much longer than mine. Kylar gurgled from inside my shawl, and I smiled as I realized he was discovering the snow. I never wanted him to get older.

Sam was imploring our goat to give him milk when I entered the short, drafty building, but upon seeing me, he stood promptly and went to pull our old plow horse from his stall. We only had one horse at the moment, but Sam was hoping to expand to two next spring with any extra money we had left over from buying seed.

He helped me mount the horse's tall back, and there was no denying the sly smile on his face as he patted my leg. "Go have fun, Mrs. Greene." He winked.

I laughed against my will. I had found it hilarious the first time he had twisted our old childhood joke of calling each other "Mr. Greene" and "Miss Harvey" into my married name, and now he tried to use it every time he knew I wasn't up to snuff.

With a new idea, I playfully pushed my wet boot against his shoulder to move him away from the horse and squeezed the horse's sides. "Whatever you say, Old Mr. Greene."

"Old?" Sam scoffed, confused at my new addition to the joke, "I'm not old! Why do you say that?"

I faced him and winked back. "Because Young Mr. Greene is currently sucking his thumb." I laughed and urged the horse quickly away from Sam. It had taken me *way* too long to come up with that. Teenage Lina would be disappointed.

The miles opened up in front of us, and I pushed the old plow horse into the fastest run he was willing to go. Our old friends didn't live with us in the Rounan community, but they didn't quite live in Lun either to keep their presence here a secret.

Xavier and Mira had been the first to move out here since Nerahdis's uproar at discovering they were still alive. King Adam and Queen Jasmine had lied about their deaths shortly before Duunzer's attack in order to cover up the Darkness's strike upon Mineraltir, and the people's discovery of the massive lie only fed their hatred of Royals in general. Frederick and Cassandra soon followed suit as they began their own family, and Princess Cornflower was sent along to keep her safe from King Adam, their not-quite-so-loving father.

At first, when we were all getting married and starting new chapters in our lives, it was really nice to live so close, but as soon as my nightmares began, I had slowly stopped visiting. I wondered what they would say when I showed up unannounced today. My mind zoned out for those ten or so miles of barren, white land, and it felt too soon to see the quaint, stone cottage come into view.

I could sense them before I had even tied up my horse, my eyes fluttering closed. Even with snow all around me, I could smell the roses of Mira's presence and feel the hyperactivity of Princess Cornflower. I felt Frederick's bravery and Xavier's fire.

Dominick, Frederick and Cassandra's season-and-a-half-old, was no exception, His presence was faint, but as his magic developed, so did his presence even though it didn't feel like anything in particular. If I could sense them, they could sense me, which meant it was too late to turn around and run home.

The bolted, wooden door opened before I reached it. Frederick, the future king of Lunaka, stared me down on the doorstep with his deep blue eyes. He had aged a bit since our days trapped in a livery basement. He was my age, but he was starting to look several years older. His blond hair was beginning to recede slightly, as well as lighten in color from the bright goldenrod it had been.

My mouth went dry. I licked my lips. "Hi, Frederick. Um, sorry, it's been so long."

Frederick shook his head abruptly, and a weary smile found its way to his face. "Oh, Lina, it's perfectly fine. Come right in, I am glad to see you."

He turned and led me into the entryway, which didn't match up with the outside of the house at all. What had seemed like a boring, stone house on the outside was, on the inside, as immaculate as Lunaka Castle had been. There was carpeting on the floor, paintings of Lunakan scenery on the walls, and countless valuable trinkets and books lining every shelf. It made Sam and I's house look like pure squalor, so I tried not to look too hard as Frederick led me into the main living room.

Mira was sitting on a plush sofa with thirteen-year-old Princess Cornflower, a long piece of tapestry stretched between them as the two stitched away on it. They looked up at me with confusion, their faces echoes of each other aside from Mira having dark hair and Cornflower having the color of straw. The elder smiled warmly at me while Princess Cornflower returned to her stitching. After all, we didn't know each other that well.

My old schoolmate, Cassandra, was sitting on the floor, her long, midnight tresses wrapped in the hands of a young boy. While Kylar had been pretty much bald at birth, Dominick had arrived with a full head of dark hair, which had turned blond like his father's since I'd last seen him. The little prince was sitting up all by himself now, and I smiled at the sight of him. I was glad that he got to grow up away from his grandfather, King Adam.

"Hello, Lina. It's been a while." Cassandra looked up at me happily, without a care in the world as she played with Dominick.

"Yes, it has," I said as I knelt to the floor, my knees sinking into the soft plush of the carpet. I unwrapped Kylar and set him on the floor with Dominick, though I couldn't let go or he'd fall over. He squealed with delight as he looked everywhere. "I really do apologize. Things have been a little crazy recently."

Cassandra gave me a knowing look. After all, Dominick and Kylar had been born within weeks of each other. After that, it seemed that the ice was broken, and my body began to relax. Mira and Cassandra small-talked with me about life in the Rounan community, about which I gratefully didn't feel any need to hide anything from them. We were all Gornish here together, and they felt for me when I said I wasn't sure I fit in.

Frederick asked where Sam was and what he was up to, but all too quickly, the nice subjects melted away. We were left to silence, trying to ignore the elephant in the room that everyone wanted to talk about but no one wanted to bring up.

Suddenly, red-haired Xavier strode into the room, barely dressed in what looked like an outfit for magic training. After all, he was covered in ash and scorch marks. His pale, freckled face lit up at the sight of me, and he walked over to playfully grind his knuckles into the top of my head. "Hey, it's the Allyen! How are you, short stuff?"

As I fingered my scalp, he plopped onto the sofa next to his wife, Mira. I laughed at him. "Just fine, Xavier. Did you have a fireball go haywire or something?"

The Mineraltin prince looked down at his burned, sleeveless shirt and shrugged. "Nah. I just cannot stand this winter you Lunakans have. A prince has to keep himself warm."

I smiled. Only Xavier could think of such things. As the silence slowly began to encroach again, the one I was afraid of seeing most finally spoke up.

"So, Lina," Frederick said from his spot in a comfy armchair, "Why did you seek us out today? Did something happen?"

My thoughts raced to my nightmare, and I felt my heart sink. I knew Frederick would be on to me, but I wasn't ready to share that yet. I didn't want it to become real. I shrugged, trying to play it off as happenstance. "Nothing happened. Just finally found the time to visit, that's all."

The future king looked at me carefully but moved on. "Well, then. I suppose I should announce that I will be leaving shortly for Auklia."

"A-Auklia?" I sputtered, completely caught off guard. "Why? Isn't the border really dangerous right now because of the war?"

"It is because of the war that I have to go. Daniel has

written for my help," Frederick said solemnly, "He is having trouble managing both his kingdom and the Auklian war effort."

The gears in my mind were set in motion. King Daniel was the blue-haired Royal who had helped my twin brother, Evan, discover and develop his Allyen magic. He had become king of Auklia right around the Spring Festival last year when his mother retired, and he was the only ruler who wasn't under Rhydin's control.

We had never known this last year, but the reason Evan and King Daniel were unable to leave Auklia before Duunzer's Darkness attacked was because Daniel's wife, Queen Lily, had just had a baby. That baby didn't even get a name before the Darkness hit, and of course, he died. King Daniel was our age and he'd been dragged into a war so soon after losing his heir. The people of Auklia were furious. I was a little surprised he hadn't needed help before now.

Everyone else in the room looked like they already knew this information, so I piped up. "So, what are you going to do to help while you're there? Lunaka thinks you've abandoned them since you left Soläna."

Frederick acquired a hurt expression, and I apologized almost immediately. He took a deep breath, looking at his hands. "I think this could be beneficial for both Daniel and I. He has mostly asked for my advice, seeing as I cannot overstep my bounds as heir to the Lunakan throne. However, I need to redeem myself in the eyes of my people. I need to show Lunaka that I am trying to end the war, not abandon them to it. Daniel is refusing to attack anyone. He only posts his armies at the border to keep his people safe. The Auklians are becoming skeptical of this because they want him to figure out who was behind Duunzer and he isn't. It does not help that someone is beginning malicious rumors about him, making him out to be a coward. Part of my job will be trying to figure out where the rumors are coming from."

"Rhydin?" I asked, finally breathing his name.

"It's always a possibility." Xavier entered the conversation, and his eyes flickered shut. "I can feel him... He's lurking at the edges of this war, waiting to make his move. I don't know what he's planning, but if he plays his pieces right, we could be in much more trouble than his plan with Duunzer ever put us in."

I sighed and pulled Kylar closer to me on my lap as he squished one of Dominick's wooden blocks between his gums. I fought the urge to grip him tight, and I only wished I could absorb him into my body so that he could never be hurt.

I knew it was coming. I felt it in my bones. The time was going to come where I'd have to choose between going and being the Allyen again or staying with Kylar and forfeiting my people. I dreaded it every second.

Suddenly, new presences popped up in my head on my radar. I nearly stopped breathing as I discovered who they were. They were a different kind of presence than my Gornish friends or my Rounan neighbors, but the three of them were nearly exactly alike. I had only jumped to my feet and put Kylar to my shoulder to go get the door when I heard her voice.

"Hello, Lina."

In excitement and sorrow, I turned on my heel to see my favorite redhead, whom I had not seen in nearly a year. Rachel stood in the hallway flanked by her brothers, Luke and James, in their traditional, Ranguvariian garb. It was bright and colorful with strange patterns and stripes unlike any Nerahdian clothing.

I gasped when I saw that her red hair had been cut short to just a little bit longer than her brothers', and a pale green pinwheel shape had been inked permanently onto her left cheek.

Luke and James were both taller than I remembered, if that were possible, but other than that, they were back. My bodyguards. My *Alyen nou Clarii*. My dearest friends, and I needed them now more than ever. The tears sprang forth as I rushed into Rachel's arms and practically gagged her in a tight hug. No words needed to be said.

When I let go, she looked at me fondly and began to coo at Kylar, whom she hadn't met yet. Luke and James walked forward to greet the others in the room as Frederick moved to join Rachel and I.

He said, "Rachel! It is so good to see you again. What brings you back from your grandfather?"

The smile on Rachel's face faded, and she put her hand on my shoulder. "We finished our planning with the Clariion, and it's been decided that my brothers and I should return to Lina since Lunaka is becoming less safe by the hour."

"Why is that?" Mira asked, and abruptly, the whole room became quiet.

Rachel met each of our eyes, stopping last on her brothers, who both nodded at her. "We caught wind of what King Adam is planning."

CHAPTER TWO

The entire room continued to stare at Rachel aside from two absent-minded infants, and it felt like an eternity before her eyes finally rested upon mine. "King Adam is planning a draft."

"What's a draft?" Thirteen-year-old Princess Cornflower looked up from her stitches, her eyes big, blue, and clueless.

My heart slid into my stomach as Mira turned to her little sister, stating quietly, "A draft is where the king commands every male over sixteen to fight for his kingdom."

"When will this happen?" My tongue felt numb as the words spilled out. My mind was already imagining every detail of Sam being taken, forced to wear the uniform, and ultimately ending up in my nightmare.

Rachel shook her head, her eyes apologetic as she reached out and steadied me. "We're not sure, but we have reason to believe that it will not happen until the spring. We only just heard of it today. That's why we have returned."

"I cannot believe my father is doing this…" Frederick took

a couple steps backward before beginning to pace the plush carpet. "Lunaka has not had a draft in ages. My grandfather even refused to use one during the Quarren War a couple decades ago!"

"Aside from those implications, it shows us one thing," Luke spoke up now. "King Adam *wants* this war to continue. He wanted it to begin when he and Queen Jasmine made the people believe the other was at fault, and now we know that he wants it to continue. After all, the volunteers to join the army are tapering off."

"The question is why," Rachel picked back up.

"The only thing King Adam and my monster of a stepmother have in common is Rhydin. He wants the war to continue, and I have an idea how to find out why." Xavier was instantly on his feet, the gears in his head visibly turning as he walked to a corner of the room. He peeled the burned, ashy shirt off of his pale body and quickly replaced it with a thick, woolen sweater.

"We've been discussing this with our grandfather for days and couldn't figure out a way. What makes you think you've found a way within five minutes?" Rachel's hip jutted out, obviously put off.

"Because, Rachel dear, when they come to Lun pounding on doors, I'll go and let them draft me."

"Are you mad?" Frederick stomped over to Xavier in only two mammoth strides, "They will recognize you instantly and turn you over to Queen Jasmine!"

"Not if I'm in disguise." Xavier grinned that rat-like smirk I remembered so well from our first meeting. "Consider it for a second! What better way to figure out this war than go straight to the front line?"

Frederick locked his arms together, and when I glanced at

Mira, her face had turned whiter than the snow outside. Cornflower took the needle out of her clenched hand.

As Frederick thought, Xavier continued, "You have to admit, it's not like I couldn't get away if I needed to. None of the armies have magic." A fireball materialized in his thick hand, his fingers swirling it around into five separate flames. "I could come home as soon as I figured out any information, and they would never know."

The Lunakan prince with a receding hairline sighed hard and shook his head. "I'm sorry, Xavier. But I cannot allow it. If you were caught, the entire Kingdom of Mineraltir would be lost to Rhydin. You're the only heir the people accept."

Mira visibly slouched very un-princess-like against the back of the sofa, her color beginning to come back.

"But, Frederick!" Xavier whined, his shoulders falling even underneath the thick sweater.

"I am sorry, but no. Another way to discover the purpose of this war will present itself eventually."

"Yeah, and how many more people need to die before that happens?" Xavier's lower lip stuck out in mock irritation.

Frederick only eyed him coolly, and the subject was dropped. "We will need to make preparations for this draft in the spring though."

Ice slid down my spine once again as I imagined the draft taking Sam from me. I tried not to allow my anxiety to take hold, but it did with ferocity. I struggled to remind myself that no one in Lunaka knew where our Rounan compound was, but the terrifying power of my dream was too much. In my dream, the grass had been newly green. Spring. When the draft was coming. My breaths doubled, and the world began to teeter on edge.

"Lina? What's wrong?" Frederick turned to me as Rachel

gripped my shoulders tighter. "We will make sure that Sam is hidden from the draft as well."

But I didn't see him. All I could see was Sam lying on the ground dead, dressed in the Lunakan uniform that I hadn't recognized until now. The grass painted with his blood. Rhydin leering over me as he ended my life and stole my locket. I stuttered, "I... It's nothing. I-I just need to go home."

I turned to the door, trying to escape, but Rachel still had a hold of me. "I will transport you home. James will bring the horse back."

As I gazed up at Rachel, her eyes betrayed her. She knew. She knew there was something I was holding back from the group. Could I trust her to not tell Sam? Could she help me to do everything in our power to keep my dream from happening?

My arms clenched tight around Kylar, and he began to whimper. I softened to avoid hurting him, but my heart hardened even more. I couldn't live without Sam, and I would not allow my son to lose his father.

Rachel began to wheel me out the door, but before she got very far, Frederick stopped her. "Lina."

I faced him, still wobbly on my feet as I clutched Kylar close.

"I likely will not see you again for some time," he said sadly, before placing a meaningful hand on my shoulder, "Take care of yourself. If you need anything, Rachel can get letters to me."

Nodding, I swallowed a lump in my throat and offered the best response I could. Frederick was going to cross the border, and that was about as dangerous as volunteering for the army right now. I closed the distance between us to give him a quick hug. Frederick was my magic teacher, my mentor, and my friend. It would be heartbreaking if anything happened to him.

When we separated, Rachel finally pulled me out the door, giving me interrogating looks before linking arms with me. I waited for her transportation magic to overtake me, hoping that the feeling of weightlessness would take the manacle off of my heart. It had been a long time since I had experienced transportation magic, not since before Duunzer attacked. After all, only Ranguvariians and Rhydin could wield it.

Rachel's beautiful, shard-like wings sprouted from her back, the feathers flashing in the sunlight, and they folded around us. The snowy world faded away into nothing but pure whiteness, my ears rang in the silence, but it was only seconds before the whiteness redefined itself into snow, mountains, and clear blue sky once again. Not nearly long enough.

The quaint cottage had disappeared to be replaced by the small shack that I called home, but I knew Sam wouldn't be here right now. No farmer would find himself indoors in the middle of broad daylight. I tucked my baby deep into my shawl once again and tried to begin trudging away toward the house. I had crunched through maybe two steps of snow before I felt Rachel's rock-hard hand grab my shoulder.

"Lina, what's going on?" she asked, her blue eyes bright underneath her hood, "You know the Ranguvariians and I will keep any soldiers far from the compound."

"I know," I said as I fought to keep my voice steady.

Rachel's brow knitted together. "Then what is it? Tell me the truth, I'm your friend."

I shook my head, my vision blurring, and my body wilted. I couldn't hide it anymore. I couldn't overtly lie to my best friend, so I hoped with all of my being that saying it out loud wouldn't cause it to become more than just a nightmare. I tried to swallow the lump in my throat but failed. "I had a dream…"

Rachel's eyes immediately flew wide, but she waited for the rest of my words to come.

I gritted my teeth as I tried to hold it all together, covering Kylar's little fuzzy head as if it would keep him from hearing. "I've had several dreams...nightmares. And in them, I-... Sam..."

Rachel gripped both of my arms, frozen as she waited intently for my words, looking as if she'd prefer to start shaking me to get my words out.

Looking at her as levelly as I could, I spat the words out. "It's always on a battlefield. Rhydin is there...and Sam's there, in a uniform. And he's dead...then Rhydin takes my locket and kills me."

The words were barely audible and breathy, filled with tears, but Rachel looked as if I had struck her. Her breathing quickened as she looked in multiple directions across the snowy landscape. She rubbed her temple, and suddenly the lime pinwheel shape on her left cheek began to glow lightly. Rachel spoke, her words light and airy, but in no language that I understood. "*Jaspen, lenou L'miiuarthan Alyen Liinariia. Naepren nou naeran ta. Sam briintiin jaenan uny C'pren resten Ntiiyran touna ntae.*"

My ears buzzed with the unknown words, picking out only the names of myself and my husband that I now worried about ceaselessly. I looked at her for any sort of clue as to what she was doing, but I was lost amongst the airy words and accent.

Rachel's eyes darted above my head, concentrating very hard. "*Dey, resten Ntiiyran touna. Prii biipren uvou Bartholomiiu te. Nten Luc prii touna. Dey, nten vii nte. Prii anet uvou Alyen Liinariia nte. Dey dey, nten jaene naeran dii nte.*" Rachel's mark stopped glowing, and when she turned to me, all she likely saw was the look of stark confusion on my face.

I stared at her in slight terror. "What just happened? Were you talking to yourself?"

Rachel chuckled slightly in spite of the seriousness of the situation. "No, of course not! I was using my *matrii*."

"M-... Mah-tree?" My lips formed awkwardly over the strange word.

"Yes." Rachel nodded and pointed to the green pinwheel mark on her left cheek. "This is a *matrii*. Ranguvariian men are born with a unique symbol on their hands, and when they marry, the pattern is copied to their new wife's cheek. We can use them to talk to our spouse from anywhere."

I stared at her mark in awe. Just to think, to be able to talk to Sam from all the way across Nerahdis! Or from the house to the barn for that matter. I realized this was why I had often seen Luke and James only wearing one glove on some days at the livery, because they were hiding their own symbols on their hands. It was amazing and almost too much of a thought for my mind to handle. Then something occurred to me that nearly derailed my anxiety altogether. "Wait, you're married?? And you didn't tell me?"

Rachel sputtered that she had thought she'd told me but also that humans were forbidden from attending Ranguvariian nuptials. She had said only maybe three words about her mate, Jaspen, when I recalled my own predicament with my husband.

I cocked my head. "So, what were you saying? To Jaspen through your mark?"

"I told Jaspen that you'd had a dream and therefore fear for Sam's life, as well as your own. I also told him that when spring comes with the draft, we need to protect Sam too to make sure he doesn't get taken. He'll have his own

Ranguvariian protectors come springtime." Rachel grinned confidently.

"Just… Please don't tell Sam, okay?" I mumbled. "I'm not ready to tell him…and I need to be the one to do it."

Rachel set her hand on my shoulder. "I'll do my best not to. Everything will be fine, I promise. I will stay with you and make sure nothing happens to you. We cannot allow this to happen."

A pitiful flood of relief washed over me. I wasn't quite convinced, but I was more hopeful now. Rachel reopened the discussion about Jaspen, which I was sure she contrived in order to try and get my mind off more despairing things. After so much stress, I began to walk toward the barn, Rachel following as she continued to chat. I needed to see Sam. To be reminded that he was okay.

He had said this morning that he would be working on fence today, although I was sure he hadn't gotten very far in the few hours it'd been since I left. I found the first post of newly set hedge on the south corner of the barn with another about six feet away, continuing on into the oblivion of a white horizon. He had gone farther than I thought, and I wondered if he was using magic to help drive the posts into the frozen earth.

Rachel marched along behind me as we followed the skeleton fence, and when another icy wind ripped its fingers at us, I heard her comment on how much Xavier hates our Lunakan winter. Mineraltir did experience winter, but with their giant trees, there was no such thing as wind chill. He was entirely unaccustomed to our climate, but it was far safer here than in Mineraltir for him. If Queen Jasmine were to ever discover him, he'd likely lose his head on the spot.

After maybe a quarter mile, I began to make out the shape

of a person next to the fence posts, and within only a few more minutes, Sam could see us coming. He had no tools with him, which meant I was right on the magic part. He was covered in snow after being out in the wind all day, and what skin was visible seemed pale, nearly blue. He smiled as we approached, his brow slightly furrowed at the sight of my companion but greeted her anyway. "Long time no see, Rachel. What are you doing here?"

Rachel smiled cordially. "It was time for my brothers and I to return. Unfortunately, the war is worsening."

Sam's eyebrow quirked, but his eyes had already picked up on my expression of fear. "It's getting worse?"

Rachel nodded and mumbled, eyeing me excessively to see what was okay to tell and what wasn't, "We have caught word that King Adam is creating a draft for the spring."

Sam looked back at me, thinking he now knew my feelings. "I see. Why is the king doing that?"

"We don't know," Rachel answered, shrugging. "We can only gather that Rhydin wants the war to continue, so they need more combatants."

A shudder ran through my system. Regardless of Ranguvariian help, the very sound of this draft was too much for me.

Sam sighed. "I wish we could find out why. It would be better for my people if this war would end. Although, you wouldn't believe the story I've heard floating around. Apparently, there's this wanderer who shows up at villages before the armies and warns them that it's coming so they can leave. The villages are always wiped out by the invaders, so all the villagers believe him now when he comes."

My brow furrowed in confusion as I tucked Kylar lower into my warm shawl. "A wanderer? Who knows when the battles are coming? Is this here in Lunaka or in Auklia-…?

"It's everywhere. All three kingdoms. Must just be some group of good-doers or something. I thought it was crazy, too." Sam nodded at the skepticism in our eyes. When Rachel turned to me, I could almost see the same question on her lips. What group of good-doers would help all of the Three Kingdoms aside from the Allyens?

I shrugged. "I guess it's nice to know we're not the only ones against this war."

Sam nodded happily. "Well, Lina, I need to get back to work or I'll never get this fence finished. By the way, I'm headed to Lun tomorrow. The compound is completely out of flour, and if someone doesn't go, someone is going to lose their head. It may take a little longer too, because I am meeting with a Rounan from another compound."

I smiled hesitantly, but I knew the draft wouldn't come for another season. Might as well get supplies while we could. "Be careful. I can't live without you," I added on for good measure.

"I know." Sam grinned that lopsided grin that I loved so much and planted a kiss on my forehead. Then he turned and lifted his fists in the air. The next fence post lifted from the ground, rotated in the sky, and began to hammer downward into a new hole as Sam's fists lifted and fell over and over.

As we began to walk back to the house, Rachel linked arms with me, silent now. I tried my best not to worry, placing my hope in my Ranguvariian protectors that had yet to let me down. Together, we enjoyed a quiet evening at home, and I wished it could be this way forever.

Of course, that's never how it goes. Sam left for Lun the next morning with the buckboard and plow horse, even after my small mention of wondering if he could send someone else. However, Sam was a stubborn man, and there was no stopping him when he'd set his mind to something. He likely would not be back for a week, which made my heart ache. It wasn't until the next day that I really started getting cabin fever. I felt like our goat, constantly penned in the barn because there was nothing outside for it to eat.

In my case, there was no one outside who wanted me here. The Rounan people merely tolerated me because I was the Kidek's wife, but there was never any forgetting that I was the only Gornish person here. I hoped I'd never figure out what would happen to me here alone if my nightmare became true. It was funny really. I was more afraid of Sam being killed by Rhydin than I was myself.

As the days without Sam dragged on, I slowly discovered that it was very handy to have a Ranguvariian lying around. Rachel would help me with the chores in Sam's absence. Feeding the freeloading chickens who had ceased to lay eggs in these short days and coercing the one goat to give us milk.

Rachel was much better at it than I was, amazingly enough, considering I was the one who'd grown up on a farm. She also accompanied me on my one brave sojourn to the grocer for some much-needed food, only to help me escape as fast as possible from all the Rounans' brutal glances and bickering about the lack of flour.

It was nice to have a quiet couple of days with Rachel, but it rapidly began to wear on me. At my mention of feeling cooped up late at night one day, Rachel knew exactly what to do. Within only a second, she had gathered Kylar into her arms while also locking a hand onto my arm. She smiled, "I think we should visit the Royals so you don't fall into another rut of no contact."

I grumbled at her slightly, but before I could protest the

lateness of the hour, Rachel pulled me to my feet and pretty much shoved me out the door. Only seconds passed before the familiar feeling of transportation magic overwhelmed me. The world went white, and the Royals' mountain cottage materialized in front of us, barely to be seen in the night with the curtains drawn shut.

We appeared right outside the front door, which Rachel swept open without a single creak. I started to wonder if Ranguvariians couldn't transport through solid objects just like they couldn't transport through the mountains. My boots sank into the plushness of carpet where only the cold earth had been before.

Rachel took Kylar to lay him down to sleep with Dominick, and I was left alone. My eyes glazed over the tapestries and trinkets that lined the walls and shelves, thinking of the bare walls with gaping holes in the chinking that decorated my home. For the first time in my entire life, I found myself wishing our lot was different. I had done a great service for my kingdom. Why was my budding family confined to just barely scraping by?

I tiptoed along the hallway, still deep in thought as I entered the living room. Mira and Cornflower were sitting on the sofa, still working on the same tapestry they had been doing when I was here a few days ago in the light of a few candles.

Xavier walked through the doorway from the bedrooms, a cup of something being subjected to his fire magic within his hands. The cup itself was blackened on the bottom, so I guessed that this was a common occurrence. A hat covered his red head, and by the looks of his watery eyes and flushed nose, Lunaka's winter had taken its toll on him.

He sat on the lumpy chair with the gilded frame in the

corner, quieter than I'd ever witnessed before. Looking around from person to person, the cottage felt a bit empty without Frederick here. The fact that it was dim and dark didn't help.

Mira looked up, and I noticed the circles around her beautiful, dark eyes. "Hello, Lina. How long have you been here? I did not hear the door."

"Rachel," I said simply, eyeing her carefully. "Not long. You look tired, Mira, are you okay?"

The princess waved her hand. "I am fine. Cassandra has come down with quite the cold, so we are doing our best to care for her."

I followed her gaze to see Cassandra laying behind me on the other, longer davenport. I hadn't even noticed her when I'd come in, she was so covered up. Her face was devoid of color and possessed a slight sheen; her body wrapped several times with an intricate blanket. She seemed to be sleeping, so I didn't move toward her, although I wondered if this would bring Frederick home from Auklia. I hadn't heard whether he was making any progress with King Daniel yet.

"I'm sick too, y'know," Xavier grumbled from his chair, nursing his cup.

Mira shot him a glance. "If you can get up and make fire tea, you are just fine. Cassandra cannot even sit up."

The red-haired prince of Mineraltir rolled his eyes and turned his body the other way in the small chair, reaching for a fur-lined blanket next to the fireplace.

"Anyhow, is there anything we can help you with, Lina? I'm afraid we were planning on heading to sleep soon," Mira said kindly as Rachel returned to the room and took a seat on a feather cushion. Young Cornflower looked at me stoically, her young body perfectly erect in appropriate princess-like posture, but she was silent.

"No." I shook my head. "Just needed to not be the only Gornish person for miles."

Mira's expression wilted, although I caught Cornflower's attention. She probably had no idea of the hatred between us and the Rounans. "Well, you are welcome to stay the night if you'd like."

All of a sudden, I felt a new presence enter the scope in my head. Mira, Cornflower, and Xavier noticed it too, all of them moving abruptly and looking around. Rachel was on her feet almost immediately, headed back toward the foyer and the door.

The presence felt strange. I didn't know how to describe it. It felt archaic, yet unimportant. I didn't have long to wonder, because Rachel returned soon with what looked like a guard, armored from head to toe. He was shorter than Rachel and his silver armor glinted in the firelight. Deep navy fabric hung from his shoulder pads, but I didn't recognize the insignia on his chest plate. It was unlike any of the Three Kingdoms, only what at best could be described as a silver leaf shape with an emerald, sapphire, and topaz embedded in the center.

"Who's this, Rachel?" I asked quietly, after witnessing the downward, respectful looks of the two Lunakan princesses and the arrogant but defeated nod of the Mineraltin heir.

Rachel turned to the guard, her hand ready on her sword. "Here is the Allyen. Please relay your message now."

Hidden by the gilded helmet, it was hard to read the guard, but the urgency and authority in his voice were unmistakable. "The Archimage sends his greetings and commands the presence of Allyen Linaria at his palace at once."

CHAPTER THREE

T he guard only allowed one person to come with me. I
wanted to choose Kylar, but I knew he would be safer
at the cottage so Rachel accompanied me. While I knew
Rachel would have never allowed me to go if it was
dangerous, I couldn't help but be on edge. Especially once the
silver and navy guard displayed his transportation magic.
Only Ranguvariians and Rhydin could do that.

I tried not to be alarmed when the world materialized in
front of me and all I saw were black mountains. It was the
mountain range that Luke and I had scaled in order to get into
Mineraltir a year ago to meet Xavier for the first time,
however, seeing as the mountains completely encircled
Lunaka, I had no idea which stretch we had appeared on.

Was war-torn Mineraltir on the other side? Defensive
Auklia? Or simply the peace of the ocean? There was no way
to know since there was no way to sense places, and the sun
had plummeted beyond the horizon hours ago. There were no
moons tonight.

The guard released my arm from transportation and began to walk toward the mountain in front of us. I watched him warily, letting him get ahead of me a bit so there would be space between us if I needed to escape. Rachel followed him without hesitation, but my paranoia reared its ugly head. I asked, "So, where are we?"

"Confidential." The guard tossed over his shoulder, "Please come along. The Archimage should not be kept waiting."

I began to follow after him once Rachel gave me a look. "Who's the Archimage?"

"All in due time."

I rolled my eyes and groaned inwardly. You'd think now that I was a fully-realized Allyen, people would stop keeping secrets from me. My thoughts changed direction as I finally stepped onto rock. Instantaneously, my magic was stripped from me, and my body began to feel tired and weak. Before becoming alarmed, I remembered how this had happened on our trek to Mineraltir. Magic was useless in the mountains.

With this in mind, after a couple more steps, I decided that I deserved to know where we were going if I was going to be defenseless. "I'm not going another step until you tell me. You come out of the blue to summon me for this Archimage, taking me away from my friends and my infant son. I deserve to know."

The guard's shoulders drooped, likely becoming annoyed with me. He turned around, the jewels on his chest plate reflecting the dim moonlight. "I cannot tell you in the open. Answers will be given once we are inside."

"Inside?" I asked confusedly, beginning to look around for whatever building we were headed for. Rachel remained quiet.

The guard closed the distance between us and took hold of my arm once more but raised his other hand in a gesture toward the mountain in front of us as he pulled me along. He didn't have to force me once I finally noticed that this mountain, embedded within all the others, wasn't quite a mountain.

From far away, it had looked like any other rocky face. But now that we were close and quickly ascending, the stones revealed themselves. Something like a castle had been carved out of this mountain; windows, towers, walls, the whole shebang. I began to wonder who would be important enough to live in such a grand building yet remain in hiding. There was a lot more to this Archimage than I'd thought.

As we approached a plateau, a huge gap between us and the mountain palace, the guard released me. He began placing his hands together in a series of strange contortions lit by bright, cobalt blue every time they touched. Immediately after he finished, a drawbridge appeared out of nowhere, the underside painted and modeled after rock to disguise the wood.

We crossed it with my curiosity mounting every second. Once reaching the threshold, I noticed my magic's return, my strength suddenly invigorated. The palace must have a special charm on it to allow magic even while remaining hidden.

Inside the palace, you would have never known that the outside was nearly indiscernible from the stone faces around it. It was the most richly decorated castle I had ever been in, and I had been in both Lunaka's and Mineraltir's. There was no courtyard, but instead the great, stone front door led us directly into a massive throne room, bigger than either of the other two I'd seen. It had to cover at least ten acres, with its deep, black floor from wall to wall. The columns were made of marble, which reached from the onyx floor and steadily became lighter in color until they touched the snow-white ceiling.

Hanging from the ceiling was an intricate gold and crystal chandelier, but that wasn't what caught my attention. Floating, up at the ceiling, was what almost looked like mist. However, this mist was shaded a light blue color and swirled around and upon itself even though there was no breeze.

My eyes followed the mist all the way to the opposite side of the room where the wall was only stained-glass windows. The guard began leading Rachel and I across the room, treading on navy velvet stretched down the middle of the floor, but my eyes soaked up the stained-glass images.

There were four of them, each one depicting a person; one large round one at the top with three smaller, tall and thin ones beneath it. It didn't take me long to figure out that the three tall windows represented the Three Kings of Nerahdis.

The man on the left was clad in green and had red hair: Mineraltir. The man in the center wore oranges, yellows, and reds while his hair was deep blue: Auklia. The third man, on the right, was dressed in white and earth tones with blond hair, just like Frederick: Lunaka. I began to wonder if the fourth, largest stained-glass window person was the old emperor when Nerahdis was first formed, but I was soon to find out that I couldn't be more wrong.

My attention turned back to the room as I noticed that we were coming upon a table. Seated there were only two people, but I suddenly saw that beyond the table was only one throne. Not two, like Lunaka, or four, as in Mineraltir. Just one, made of the same onyx and marble of the floor and ceiling, twisted together. Who ruled by themselves? And over what?

Abruptly, my eyes took in one of the people at the table,

although I began to wonder if it was even human. Even though it was seated, the creature's height could have easily been seven feet, and there was no mistaking the pointed ears that prominently stood out from its brown hair.

The creature was cloaked in an orange robe covered in strange symbols, and I was reaching for where my sword lurked in my magical sash when it looked at me with piercing, emerald cat's eyes. The creature unexpectedly smiled, and the voice was fluid. "Hello, Allyen Linaria. Am I really so frightening, dear?"

My hand froze. "Who are you? W-...What are you?"

The creature rose to its full seven feet and then knelt so that it was not towering over me and at eye level instead. "My name is Arii. I am Clariion of the Ranguvariians. I am very pleased to finally meet you."

"You're..." I looked at him flabbergasted, then at Rachel who was bowing deeply. The eyes...the ears...the height. I was an idiot. This creature was Rachel, Luke, and James's grandfather; the leader of the Ranguvariians. All this time I had thought I'd come to understand all about Ranguvariians, but I had forgotten that Rachel and her brothers were part human. I had never considered that real Ranguvariians would look different. I began to stutter in my humility, "I-I apologize, I-I've just never seen a real-..."

"I understand." The old man Ranguvariian grinned at me and nodded at his granddaughter. "If we were not frightening, the humans would not have designed folktales about us being 'Giants.'"

"I hate to be rude, but this is an emergency, Clariion."

I turned my head to the other person at the table, who stood and stepped over to us. This man was average in height, shorter than Sam, with such pale skin I worried for his health.

Long black hair draped over his shoulders and high cheekbones while his long outfit and adornments were fit for a king. I noticed that his eyes were a strange shade of midnight blue as he reached for my hand and kissed it. "Thank you for coming on such short notice, Allyen Linaria. It is an honor to meet you, even under these circumstances."

My brow furrowed. Ever the curious one, my questions spilled out of my mouth. "What circumstances? Do you mean the war? I'm sorry, who exactly are you?"

"Why, I am Archimage Dathian! Did they not tell you?" The black-haired man placed a hand on his chest, his navy eyes quite surprised.

I quirked an eyebrow at my loyal escort still next to me. "Nope. He didn't. Would you please tell me what an Archimage is, Dathian?"

A flash of pain entered my ribs, the guard having shoved his armored elbow into them. He hissed at me, "The correct way to address the Archimage is 'Your Excellency!'"

"You are dismissed." Dathian's words turned to iron, and the guard exited the gigantic throne room. Upon his disappearance, the Archimage beckoned me to sit at the table with them. He folded his hands carefully and looked up at me without emotion. "The Archimage is a secret position, so I apologize that you have never heard of it before now. However, it is imperative to Nerahdis that it *remains* secret. Do you swear to never breathe a word of my existence or my title?"

I swallowed hard. This was a lot more serious than I had thought. I nodded, my tongue numb. "I swear."

"Good." Dathian grinned a political smile, not quite real. "The Archimage is a position above the Three Kings. It was created by Emperor Caden before his untimely death in order to ensure that his sons would not tear Nerahdis apart with their squabbles. Let me be clear that I rule over no one except the Three Kings. The people of Nerahdis are theirs to rule respectively in their three kingdoms. I am not another emperor. I exist only to keep the Three Kings in check."

My breath left my body, and I had to force it back in. This was definitely not what I had expected the Archimage to be. Mira, Cornflower, and Xavier's respectful glances downward upon the appearance of the Archimage's guard now made complete sense if he was their superior. I almost couldn't believe it.

I began to imagine what Sam's reaction might be to this information, and I felt surprised when Rachel didn't mirror my shock. The questions came rapidly as I forced myself not to lash out. "If you're in charge of the Three Kings, why has King Adam been able to do so many terrible things? And Queen Jasmine for that matter? Why didn't you stop them?"

"I promise you that I have tried." Dathian's eyes saddened, "However, Rhydin's power is too strong for my own. I was fortunate to be able to help you with Duunzer at all."

The look on my face must have hinted that Dathian needed to explain himself. After all, I didn't see him at Lunaka Castle getting shot with fireballs and stabbed with dragon talons.

"You should remember that Lunaka was the last kingdom to be taken by the Darkness. It is I that kept Lunaka out of the thick of it for so long in order to give you the time you needed to prepare. I am truly sorry that I was unable to stop this war before it began, but some things are impossible even for the Archimage." The sincerity in Dathian's words and his eyes was nearly overwhelming, but when I looked at him, the genuine pain on his face was enough for me to believe him.

Arii nodded at me, and I knew I had no reason to suspect

anything.

Dathian sat back, erect against his chair, and straightened his ornate tunic. "Now, Allyen Linaria, even though your brother has yet to arrive I really cannot put off-…"

"My brother?" I shrieked in shock.

My brother was coming? Evan? I had only ever been told that we were to be kept separate in order to protect us from Rhydin, and therefore had never met him. He was supposed to help me defeat Duunzer, but the Darkness had got to him first in Auklia. Even afterward, we were not allowed to meet to keep us safe. What was so important now that we were allowed to be in the same room together? I had to sit on my hands to keep myself calm, both from fear and excitement.

Just as Archimage Dathian began to speak once more, the huge front door yawned wide with creaks that could wake the dead. Immediately, my magical senses were arrested and held prisoner by one of the figures that walked into the massive room. The guard had returned and was leading a young man and woman, both of whom were rather short.

The man reached to his brown head as if he were feeling the same strange sensation I was, and it was not long before we were standing face to face. My locket, hidden in my tunic, began to burn like fire against my skin, hotter than even when I'd used it against Duunzer now that it was in the presence of my brother. He was only a couple inches taller than me. His hair was the exact shade as mine, and his eyes stared back at me with the same golden specks that inhabited my own. Those specks were the telltale sign that we were Allyens.

Yet, after all this time of desperately wanting to meet him, I found my mouth dry and my words absent. This was the first time I'd seen him since I'd caught a glimpse of him dropping off Keera, covered with a cloak and violin, and I had no idea what to say.

Evan looked at me stoically, before nodding his head. "Linaria."

I gulped. "Um…please call me Lina. I've wanted to meet you for so long, Evan…"

His eyes widened at the sound of his nickname, then he looked as if he remembered. "I, too. How is Keera? I've been anxious to hear about her."

My heart sank into the pit of my stomach. Keera, our young cousin whom Evan had grown up with and sent to me to care for. She had been killed the same day as my sister, Rosetta, when Rhydin tricked us out of our hiding place and murdered my grandmother so that she could no longer teach me how to be an Allyen. Tears threatened to spill forth as my heart ached. I could barely keep my words steady. "Evan… She was killed when Rhydin attacked us last year…along with Rosetta and Grandma Saarah. I'm so sorry, I couldn't save her."

Evan appeared as if I'd slapped him in the face, and I could visibly see him shutting down. The young woman who had come in with him stepped forward and placed her hand on his arm. She was beautiful with shining blue eyes and hair the color of lavender. Her dress was made of the same rainbows of silk as Keera had been wearing when she came to me the first time from Auklia. On her finger, I noticed a wedding ring. Was my brother married?

"This is a wonderful reunion and all, but I really must get to why I have brought you all here!" Dathian was beginning to sound exasperated, so Evan, the woman, and I all silently came to sit at his table. Rachel moved to stand behind her grandfather stoically.

When Evan moved away, the warmth in my locket began

to disappear. Evan wouldn't look at me. He kept his back to me as long as he could, a violin strapped to it once again. Yet, all I could feel was my grief for my dead family, exacerbated by the fact that it may have taken my brother from me forever.

The Archimage eyed the two of us, feeling the tension, and cleared his throat. "I have had a dream this night that cannot be allowed to pass."

My head whipped up to look at him. It was unusual for me to hear about someone else having a dream that could come true in the future. Rachel, likewise, finally appeared surprised.

"In my dream, I witnessed Rhydin's victory over all of Nerahdis!" Dathian suddenly looked scared out of his wits, his flighty nature coming through as he spoke faster and faster. "This is an absolute emergency and cannot come true. I need-...!"

"Your Excellency, please calm yourself and slow down. Tell us what you saw exactly," Arii said quietly, perhaps having already heard what the dream entailed. Dread began to twist itself into my stomach.

With a hand placed on his chest, barely touching the dark blue stone at his throat, the Archimage took a deep breath, and fixed Evan and I in a sonder gaze. "In my most horrid of dreams, I saw Rhydin's plans coming to fruition because the both of you die without leaving an Allyen heir. I need to figure out if this is true immediately, and why, as of this moment, there will be no new Allyens! There will be no one to replace you, so the magic will run out, allowing Rhydin's victory!"

I felt my mouth fall open as my mind struggled to process what Dathian was saying. All that I could continue to come to was...no more Allyens? How could there be no more Allyens?

"Please." The word gagged Dathian as it came out. "Do

either of you know how this could happen? How this changed in the last twenty-four hours that I would have this dream only now?"

Numb, I shook my head. Beside me, Evan's round face looked as worried and vague as my own likely did. The woman who had come with him, likely his wife due to the ring, was beginning to look very anxious. I found myself wondering how much of this that she understood and thanked my lucky stars that Sam was so well-informed on magical things.

Dathian suddenly spurted, leaning forward on the table, "Are you both able to have children?"

A deep crimson flushed Evan's face, and I felt my own dander rising. I spoke before any thought could pass through my mind, appalled that this all-knowing Archimage didn't know. "I recently had a baby, D-... Your Excellency."

"Oh. Yes. I knew that..." The black-haired human gestured slightly to the floating mist up by the ceiling and began running his fingers over his scalp. "What about-...?"

"Your Excellency, you asked me here because you consider me an expert on Allyens, correct?" Arii finally spoke up with his flowing words, his eyes still green. Rachel's stern expression behind him seemed to back up every word he said.

Dathian nodded helplessly.

Arii turned to my brother and I, folding his hands neatly in front of him. "You may not know, but it was I who helped your ancestor, Nora Soreta, to create the Allyen magic nearly three hundred years ago."

"You were the one who helped Nora? How is that possible?" I asked, surprised. Frederick and Grandma had told me all about Nora, the First Allyen, my ancestor who created the Allyen locket in order to defeat Duunzer and Rhydin the first time centuries ago. What was the average lifespan of a Ranguvariian? My thoughts continued on into words. "If you both are so powerful, why does it have to be an Allyen to kill Rhydin? Even if the magic ended, wouldn't either of you be able to kill him?"

"I am three hundred and twenty-seven years old. The title of Clariion allows one to stop aging," Arii chuckled, then he grimaced and shook his head. "It must be an Allyen because of the nature of your magic. The magics of the Allyens and Rhydin are strikingly similar due to the fact that neither are genetic. While Rhydin has stopped his aging, the Allyen magic is physically passed down, rather than inherited. They are both created magics, rather than inherent magics, such as what the Royal families, the Rounans, and the Ranguvariians possess. Ranguvariians in particular, as you remember Lina, cannot be around Rhydin at all. His very presence is poisonous to us because of his unnatural dark powers. Therefore, the two of us, and the rest of the world for that matter, are utterly useless."

"Also, Allyen magic is light. Rhydin's is darkness. Everyone else's is elemental. It only makes sense," Dathian piped up as he quickly stood and began gathering several thick, ancient volumes of books off of a nearby bookshelf. He abruptly muttered angrily, cursing what sounded like a ghost as he checked several places before he found a certain book. When he returned, his tie slightly disheveled, he continued, "Even I was once an Auklian prince. While my aguamage abilities were supplemented slightly when I became Archimage, I can only hurt Rhydin, never kill him."

I looked down at my numb fingers. It had been one thing to realize that I was the only one who could fire the Allyen arrow into Duunzer to save Nerahdis. It was another thing entirely to discover that Evan and I were the only ones on the continent who could kill Rhydin. Stack on top of that that something had been changed to cause no new Allyen after us, and well, things seemed downright grim. How was I going to tell Sam when he got home?

I was about to voice another question when Evan finally asked his own question, "If no Allyen comes after us…what happens? Lina and I are young, it's not like we're going to die anytime soon. What if we defeat Rhydin before we die? Does it really matter?"

Dathian pursed his lips as he stared at one of the open books in front of him. "To begin with, neither of you have any guarantee of dying of old age with Rhydin on the loose. More important, because Allyen magic is created, it must be continually renewed in order to survive. This renewal happens every time an Allyen is born and given the magic."

Arii nodded and turned to us. "Normally, Allyens have plenty of time to reproduce and pass on their magic to renew it. However, there has never been two Allyens in one generation before-…"

"We're depleting the magic faster, aren't we? Because there's two of us?" I gasped as I made the connection. "That's why we need an heir, because otherwise the magic will be gone soon and Rhydin will win."

The human and the Ranguvariian nodded, both unsmiling.

"How long do we have?" Evan leaned forward suddenly, gripping the young, violet-haired woman's hand.

"We would have to run some experiments to find out. But primarily, we need to find out why Linaria's son is not the next Allyen." Dathian's eyes turned quizzical.

Arii, however, appeared deep in thought as he stared at one of the books Dathian had brought to the table. He looked up at the two of us as his ancient eyes fluttered between brown and dark gold. Abruptly, his eyes landed on the young woman next to Evan, and the twinkling ring on her finger. He cleared his throat and said, "Mrs. Harvey, I hate to seem presumptuous, but could you, by chance, be a Rounan?"

All of the color drained from her face. She gave the curtest of nods, barely visible, sensing the importance of this conversation. Evan stared at the purple-haired woman, mumbling, "Cayce?"

"What does that have to do with anything?" Dathian whined, sounding at his wit's end.

"Well, scientifically speaking, according to your vision, neither Linaria or Evanarion can bear an Allyen child, which has nothing to do with their fertility, correct?" Arii said with a calculated tone, turning to Dathian. "There must therefore be something that they have in common to cause this. If you had just seen this vision tonight, while only this morning Evanarion was married, that would mean that both of our Allyens are now married to Rounans."

Cayce hid her face in her hands as the blood left Evan's face, and Arii acquired a hurt expression. Obviously, he had uncovered something that no one else had known, Evan included. Rachel's red brow furrowed.

"This should be tested, of course..." Arii began soothingly, trying to make amends, but was interrupted.

"But, it is something to go on for now," Dathian finished for him, looking Evan and I up and down as if we had committed a treasonous act.

As the room plunged into silence, my mind struggled to keep up with all that was said this night. I had thought nothing of the fact that Kylar was born a Rounan. Hadn't even considered that there was something wrong with that, since

Sam was a Rounan. I had always figured that maybe the next one would be an Allyen, or that the next Allyen would be born to Evan. Obviously, I couldn't have been more wrong.

Arii and Dathian began to draw up plans for the tests and experiments that they could complete in order to determine if our marriages to Rounans were the culprit, and they decided to send Rachel to bring my son to me. Apparently, Evan and I were going to be here in the Archimage Palace for a while in order to discover why the Allyen lineage had been chopped off. I ardently hoped that our marriages weren't the problem. I couldn't even begin to consider what their "solutions" might be.

It also made me wonder once more about the Allyen before Evan and I. If this magic was so obviously dictated by having one Allyen per generation in order to support the magic and not use it up before an heir was born, then why had I still heard nothing about the Allyen before me?

I had wondered about this ever since shortly before Duunzer attacked. That Allyen had to have been one of Grandma's sons, but neither my papa or Keera's father were Allyens. My uncle would still be alive in that case, and I knew without a doubt that my father never had magic.

I glanced at Evan and Cayce next to me, the latter whispering fiercely to my brother as he sat stone cold, staring into space. I started to think about how thankful I was that Sam had told me he was a Rounan and hadn't kept it a secret forever, but I knew that wasn't going to solve our problem right now. I wished that Sam could have been here. I didn't want to have to be the messenger.

As it felt like the world was falling down around me, I stared upward at the stained-glass windows once again. It made more sense now, who the windows all represented. I had been right when I'd thought that the three lower, thin windows were the Three Kings of Nerahdis. Probably even the very first kings considering how old this palace seemed to be; King Joshuua of Mineraltir, King Ivann of Auklia, and King Spenser of Lunaka.

The larger, circular stained-glass window above the Three Kings clicked in my mind now as well; it wasn't the old emperor as I'd thought. Dathian had said that the Archimage was a position above the Three Kings, not a ruler like the old emperor, but a way of keeping checks and balances between the Three Kingdoms. It seemed like a great idea to me, if Rhydin hadn't thrown a wrench in the system to revoke Dathian's authority over King Adam and Queen Jasmine.

The fourth window depicted a pale man with dark hair and strangely colored eyes. Apparently, the stained glass hadn't wanted to make the correct color since that particular part looked like it hadn't melted properly, giving a bizarre twist of blue and red. Although, the man definitely wasn't Dathian, who had dark blue eyes, and there were blues present elsewhere in the windows.

The man was likely the First Archimage, seeing as the others were the First Three Kings. I'd probably never know who he was since, like the Three Kings, he had to be long dead by now.

CHAPTER FOUR

To my dismay, we remained at the Archimage Palace for a week, but Dathian never allowed us to forget the importance of their tests. However, it became very dull extremely fast, and it was not long until I felt like nothing more than a guinea pig.

My thoughts drifted to Sam often, wondering if he had ever returned from Lun, and I wished ceaselessly that I had one of those *matrii* so that I could talk to him. I was thankful to have Kylar brought to me at the least, although I cringed at the thought of Dathian and Arii doing tests on him, too.

One of the few positive things that happened during the week was that I finally figured out the purpose of the floating mist in the ceiling of the throne room. Up here in these mountains, Dathian kept his existence a secret by never stepping foot outside his castle, sealed away until his death would bring a new Archimage to spend their life in this cold, stone building.

However, this mist, which was unique to the Archimage

Palace and had been created by the First Archimage, was his way of seeing the world. Dathian could command it to show him anything he desired.

A lot of the time, it would show nature shots of some of the most beautiful places in Nerahdis. The ocean beating against the shore in Auklia, a view of the great, emerald canopy in Mineraltir, and flowing waves of grain in Lunaka. He could even see a small, island village in Caark, and the gigantic dunes of the Great Desert in the southwest.

While Dathian never admitted to it, I was confident that this was how he kept tabs on the Three Kings as well. Arii had even told me that this was how they had discovered King Adam's draft. They had been watching him and heard him talk about it, although I guess sounds were a little touch and go with this mist.

I shuddered at the thought of being watched every day of my entire life and found myself wondering if Dathian had ever used this mist to view Evan or I. Although I knew it was likely true since Dathian said he'd known about my son. I truly tried not to let this creep me out more than it did.

I wished I could use the mist to see Sam as well. To see where he was and what he was doing. But, the mist only listened to Dathian no matter how many times I cried out to it in the dead of night. It would only churn upon itself, up there by the ivory ceiling, in cruel silence.

The other mostly positive thing that happened during my week at the Archimage Palace was a rather lengthy conversation with Arii. He had sat across from me in the parlor on the western side of the hidden palace as we watched the sun sink beyond the mountains. Arii was not very talkative, but he greatly enjoyed being with other people, often sitting and observing all that went on around him.

I imagined this would be quite normal for someone who had been around for three hundred and twenty-seven years. I had originally asked him if Ranguvariians normally lived that long, but the answer was no. It was only the leader, the Clariion, that was stopped from aging until they stepped down.

My brow furrowed as I quickly became increasingly curious about this culture. I had thought I'd known so much from my time with Rachel, Luke, and James, yet, I was discovering that I knew so little. I lingered over my words, making sure that they came out in a nonthreatening way. "So, Arii... why have you never stepped down? Being Clariion must create a lot of stress."

Arii leaned his head back, the silver crown wrapped around his forehead glinting in the fading light. "It was my desire. I knew that Rhydin was still out there, and I could see the corruption occurring in each of the Gornish kingdoms. The Three Kings wiped him from their histories and resorted to renumbering their dates so that the years Rhydin ruled as emperor would be forgotten. I could never allow that to happen with my people. So, I remained, in hopes that we would be prepared for his return."

"Wait," I breathed, my eyes widening. "Rhydin was emperor? When?"

Arii showed the most animation I'd ever seen as his eyes glinted a bright lemon yellow. "Did we not tell you? Nora arose and defeated him because of his usurpation of the thrones. Emperor Caden was meant to be the last ruler, but Rhydin pushed his leadership into place instead with the help of the first Duunzer, as you likely remember. That is why he wants control of Nerahdis now. To reinstate his former empire."

My fingers trembled as I muttered, "I knew Nora defeated him, but I never realized he was actually emperor at the time. I thought he was doing the same thing he was now. History really has come full circle." I tried to focus on my breathing.

"It is an unfortunate fact that Nerahdis has conveniently written his coup of its history, as I said before," Arii murmured as his eyes began to turn blue. "That is why just as Rhydin has halted his aging to take advantage of an ignorant populace, I have stopped my own to ensure that he cannot."

I could barely keep my head from shaking at the weight of it all. "That had to be so hard, though."

"It was." A faint, sad grin appeared on his lined face. "I could not stop my friends and family from dying as well. Even witnessing Nora's death was almost too much. But, I am grateful. The Ranguvariians were prepared for Rhydin's return, and without it, I would have never met my late wife." He turned to me with a twinkle in his eye. "Emily was born centuries after I was. A Mineraltin princess, actually. That is why my grandchildren appear human. It is the dominant trait."

"Wow," I breathed, for lack of coming up with any better words. No wonder Rachel had red hair. "Does that mean-...?

"That my grandchildren are Prince Xavier's cousins? Yes, it does." Arii smiled.

That's Royals for you, I thought. *Everybody is related somehow.*

In the corner of the dim parlor was a small, tidy bookshelf. Right as I began to open my mouth to ask the world's most patient Ranguvariian another question, there was a thud. Both Arii and I turned to the noise, only to see a book had fallen to the ground by itself. While a look of confusion crossed my face, wondering how it had fallen, Arii chuckled to himself, "I see the ghost is listening to us."

"Ghost? But there's no such thing as ghosts," I said firmly, willing this one thing to be truly mythical.

"Generally, you are correct. Dathian for one refuses to acknowledge the mishaps around this palace as an invisible presence. Often, he will use this 'ghost' as an excuse for his own flighty behavior." Arii began to laugh, obviously having gained years of genuine amusement from Dathian's eccentric attitude.

I remembered back to our meeting a week ago when Dathian couldn't find the book he was looking for and blamed it on a ghost. I smiled at the thought, totally willing to believe that this "ghost" was merely Dathian's scapegoat for being unorganized. My voice was cheery with delight, "He really is a little crazy, isn't he?"

"Well, yes." Arii grinned, but then eyed me carefully, "But that does not change the fact that there is a little more to this palace than any of us understand, whether you call this invisible presence a ghost or not."

I swallowed my jocular tone, staring at the fallen book on the floor for a few moments. I refused to believe it was a ghost. There had to be some other explanation, and for the moment, I didn't dare think about it. In order to change the topic of conversation, I tried to bring up my questions about the Allyen between Grandma and I. Before I could, though, Arii stood and offered his apologies, but that he needed to go check on Dathian and the final tests being run.

I was left alone a little sooner than I would have preferred, but with the coming night, servants soon entered to light the massive chandelier above my head. It was made of real gold, I was told. I had grown quite familiar with this parlor over the last week. The wall of windows, the violet, rosy wallpaper, the sequined furniture. There was a white writing desk in one of the other corners opposite the bookshelf.

I found the femininity of the room interesting. I wondered if Dathian ever had a family, or if there had been female Archimages in the past. How did they decide who would be Archimage? The concept still intrigued me greatly.

Later in the week, I sat in the great throne room once again, staring at the mist above my head. The sound of a door swinging open took me from my thoughts. I turned on the cushioned sofa to see my brother walking toward me, Kylar in his arms to my surprise. Evan had been rather obviously avoiding me for the last week. I tried not to let this bother me, after all he needed his time to mourn Keera and sort things out with his brand-new wife.

But, it was hard. After losing Grandma, Rosetta, and Keera from Rhydin along with my parents from the Epidemic, I was desperate for any sort of familial relation. Evan, Sam, and Kylar were my last chance at that type of bond. I'd wanted to meet Evan for so long, and now that he stood here in front of me, he felt like nothing more than a stranger with an unfortunate connection to me.

Upon sight of me, Kylar rotated in Evan's arms and began whimpering, reaching out for me with his pudgy arms. I took him and held him close, wondering if they'd done the same things to him as they'd done to me.

I looked at Evan warily. "Are they done testing him?"

Evan nodded quietly. "Yeah. He's a cute kid. Why did the Archimage and Clariion decide to test him?"

Looking down at Kylar sadly, I was glad he couldn't understand any of this. I hated the feeling that Dathian and Arii somehow saw my son as wrong. As incorrect. I was almost grateful now that Sam had been unable to come. He would have likely flipped his lid.

I sighed, "I guess normally when an Allyen has their first child, the magic automatically moves over as soon as the baby is born. That didn't happen for Kylar, and they want to find out why. Whether it's because he's a Rounan or perhaps it's because there's two current Allyens. None of this has ever happened before. There's no precedent to go off."

Evan looked like he understood, but he remained silent. The division between us was truly palpable. I struggled to come up with another avenue of conversation but failed epically. Shockingly, Evan spoke first, grasping at the only thread of talk he could find. "So, what were your tests like?"

"They were strange. Nothing like I've ever experienced." I shook my head with a slight smile, trying to make light of the situation. "They took my blood with a little needle. I didn't even know that was possible. Arii would put his hands on my head and my heart. I could feel him doing magic, but I couldn't sense it. Only hear his humming."

"Yes, Ranguvariian magic is musical," Evan commented as he ever so slowly came to sit next to me on my cushions.

As he did, my locket began to warm up again just as it had the first time I had gotten close to Evan. Normally, it became warm when I was using magic. Why was it heating up just being near my twin brother? I decided to ask Rachel later, not feeling brave enough to ask Evan.

"Is it really?" I turned to him, surprised. Of course, he had Ranguvariian protectors too. I remembered Rachel singing or humming much of the time she used magic; it made total sense.

Evan only nodded, staring at his hands. His gaze iced over. "What are we going to do?"

My eyes closed, and my body wilted. "I don't know."

"If it's truly because we have married Rounans, what will

you do?"

I stared at Evan in disbelief, feeling heat rise up in my chest. "I'm committed to Sam! He's the only one I've ever loved. I can't even..." My words broke off. The idea was too terrible.

"I know what you mean," Evan said quietly. "Cayce never told me. I had no idea. All I knew was that I loved her. And still do, even though I will never understand why she lied."

I rolled my eyes and chuckled grimly, remembering the Rounans' hatred for me, "You should come with me to the Rounan compound sometime. You'll figure it out pretty quick."

Evan's forehead crinkled in confusion, but he let it go. A few moments passed in silence as I tried to think of something else to talk about. A change came over Evan as he looked at Kylar beginning to fall asleep in my arms. His voice suddenly became hard. "I never knew you had a baby."

My brow furrowed, feeling my brother turning into steel beside me. I retorted more quippy than I intended, "I never knew you were getting married."

Evan abruptly stood, beginning to walk away from me.

I didn't move, but I reached after him with my voice desperately. "I'm sorry about Keera! I did everything I could, and trust me, her death still haunts me, as well as the rest of my family's! Rosetta, Grandma, Mama, and Papa!"

Evan stiffened considerably after my last words and began to quake on his feet, struggling as to what to say. "At least you had one," he spoke over his shoulder, his golden-speckled eyes hidden. "Don't forget, Lina. I'm the one our mother sent to Auklia."

With that, he vanished back through the open door. I felt like I'd been physically struck. It wasn't my fault that we were separated to protect us from Rhydin! It wasn't like I'd convinced our parents to keep me and send Evan away either! He was blaming me for something out of both of our control, yet I wished that I could ask my parents why. Why *did* they decide to keep me? What caused that decision to be made? I would never know, and neither would Evan.

"Lina?"

I didn't even allow myself to hope that it was Evan coming back. Turning in my seat once again, I saw Rachel enter the room trailed by Dathian. She was wearing full Ranguvariian garb now, a long, yellow tunic with dark symbols decorating the sleeves and collar, which made her truly look like a flame with her red hair. Dathian was wearing a much more elaborate outfit now, having changed out of the white robes I'd seen him in during the tests, and I wondered who was coming to dinner tonight that deserved the regalia of an emperor.

"How is everything at home, Rachel?" I asked quickly, before she could belabor me with any bad news.

She smiled, knowing my ways. "Just fine. The animals are well taken care of. Sam wasn't home when I checked them though. I may have just missed him."

I nodded slowly, taking in the information. I truly hoped that Rachel had just missed him, I hated thinking he possibly hadn't returned from Lun yet. I turned to the Archimage. "Are the tests finally finished then?"

"Arii is still finishing a few things up," Dathian answered. "However, with the way the results are looking, we shall soon have visitors."

"Visitors? Who?" I asked, confused as to who else needed to be involved in this catastrophe.

"Any Royals who can make it." Dathian stared at me, the weight of the news holding his shoulders down.

"Why?" My arms tightened around Kylar in fear.

"Because it does not look good. You will need more than sheer luck to get through this one, unlike Duunzer." The short, black-haired man sat in a gilded chair across from me.

I opened my mouth to protest that Duunzer was merely luck, but Rachel stopped me. "He's serious, Lina. Whether Duunzer was luck or not, there is much more at stake this time…" Her words trailed off, and for the first time in the many years I'd known Rachel, her blue eyes turned glassy as she worked to keep it together. "You must understand… If Rhydin succeeds, my people and my family will be wiped out of existence. We cannot be around his magic."

"Why? What is Rhydin planning?" I stood numbly to be near my friend.

"I can only imagine that he wants the kingdoms to destroy themselves in this war," Dathian piped up from his chair as Rachel looked away, trying to compose herself. "Once the Three Kingdoms are destroyed, Rhydin can raise a new dictatorship based on his power alone. If he were to go after the Ranguvariians, or even the Rounans for that matter, they would never stand a chance. Once the Royals arrive, we can discuss what needs to be done."

I gulped. My body began to feel weighed down. So many people were riding on Evan and I's success against Rhydin, and if we failed…

What were we going to do?

A few hours later, the black table in the massive throne room was packed. While nearly half of the Royals on our side were unable to come, Dathian had at least managed to bring one Royal for each kingdom.

Frederick sat to my right, the future king of Lunaka, and Mira was on my left in a thick cloak with the mostly healthy

Xavier on the other side, the future rulers of Mineraltir. Another young woman sat next to Evan, her hair the color of tiger lilies with a crown glinting with the cool colors of Auklia. This was Queen Lily, who had come even though her husband, King Daniel, had his hands full with the war. I had only seen her once before at the Spring Festival shortly after I'd been told I was an Allyen.

Cassandra's cold had worsened so Princess Cornflower had stayed behind to nurse her. Also sitting at the table were Dathian, Arii, Rachel, and Cayce. As I looked from face to face, I tried to keep myself from being in awe. I had never seen so many important people at the same table before, yet while the feeling was inspiring, it also held unending dread.

Dathian stood from the table and cleared his throat. All of the Royals immediately silenced and looked up at him, their respect unmistakable. The Archimage revealed a voice full of authority, and I wondered if he began all of his meetings this way. "Thank you all for coming at such short notice. I would not have called you all here if it was not unbelievably important. In an effort to make it as simple as possible, I will turn it over to Clariion Arii."

Arii remained seated at the table, likely not wanting to show off his seven feet of Ranguvariian-ness. After all, a couple of the Royals were already staring wide-eyed similarly to how I had the first time I saw him. He put on a political smile accompanied with impressive speech skills.

"As you all know, only the Allyens can defeat Rhydin because of their similar magic types. However, we have uncovered a problem, tested it thoroughly, and come to a conclusion that must be shared with you all." The old Ranguvariian met eyes with each person around the table, his own eyes a mix of brown and yellow while also narrowed to a slit. "Because the Allyen magic is created, it must be renewed periodically. Every generation, to be exact. This allows the magic to keep up its existence, and this process is crucial for the continuation of the Allyen lineage."

Please no, I thought. *Don't let it be because we've married Rounans.*

"Something has changed this centuries-old process, and after much testing and consideration..." Arii paused, seeming to give an apology as his eyes turned deep blue in sadness. "Because of the entrance of Rounan magic in the formula, no Allyens will ever be born to either Linaria or Evanarion."

The room was full of gasps and wide eyes. Full of panic. Every person in the room glanced at Evan and I at least once, and of all the times I experienced the hatred of the Rounans back home, I had never been made to feel so dirty as I did now.

"How is this possible?" Frederick took control with that king voice I knew so well.

Arii was calm in his answer. "Allyen magic is created, just as I said before. Rounan magic is hereditary and extremely strong in their blood. The two magics are completely incompatible with each other. It is not nearly as malleable as Gornish magic, which while also hereditary is not as evident in their blood. This is why Gornish mages can be aguamages as in most Auklians, aeromages as in most Lunakans, and pyromages as most Mineraltins are. Since our Allyens have chosen to marry Rounans, every child they will ever bear with their spouse shall be exactly that. Rounan. We tried with Linaria's son, Kylar. He would not accept any magic but his own. If there is no Allyen heir, the magic will cease to exist."

"This has never been an issue in the last three hundred years because of the stigma between the Gornish people and the Rounans," Dathian tacked on with no emotion.

I refused to look at anyone but Frederick. He viewed me with pain in his eyes, but I could see that he was the only one who would stick up for my choice to love and marry Sam. After all, he had been there through it all. Frederick took a deep breath, before he said, "When will they run out of magic? How much time do we have before the Allyen magic is gone?"

"A year, at most, if not less," Arii said sadly, leading to another round of gasps and cries. "Because Evanarion and Linaria are both current Allyens, they are going through the magic faster than any other. While losing the magic will not kill them, it will guarantee Rhydin's victory over Nerahdis."

Mira, with her porcelain skin and fluffy cloak, stood from her chair. Her voice was stronger than I had ever heard before. "There must be something we can do."

Dathian intertwined his fingers and leaned his chin onto them. "Of course, the simplest solution would be for one of the Allyens to have a child with someone else who is not a Rounan."

Nausea swept through me. No. I could never. I vowed to Sam until death do us part. Why did the world have to hinge on this? I was about to air these thoughts as Evan spoke, "I realize that the world needs us to provide an heir, but I believe the world can also respect that we are devoted to the ones that we have chosen as our life partners. Doing something like that could possibly only cause more problems. There *must* be another way."

"I expected that very answer." Arii smiled hesitantly upon the two of us and gestured to the Archimage to take over. Evan and I turned to him expectantly, begging him with our eyes to have a different solution.

Dathian's speech was wary and choppy, exuding

uncertainty over anything else. "The Clariion and I have been discussing and researching, seeing as we expected that response. There is an option with the slimmest of chances available to us."

Every being at the table was leaning forward, desperate to hear what came next in this grim, life or death situation.

"The Ranguvariians helped Nora create her Allyen magic three hundred years ago. Before becoming the First Allyen, Nora possessed only vague magical qualities that were completely useless to her, being the daughter of a nobleman descended from Lunakan Royals," Dathian explained. "We are considering that it may be possible for the Ranguvariians to help move the Allyen magic from Linaria or Evanarion to a newborn with low levels of malleable Gornish magical qualities that I mentioned earlier."

"You mean a Royal child, do you not? You do realize that Duunzer caused the death of every child under the age of two barely a year ago, correct?" Queen Lily spoke up, her voice low and full as her teal eyes flashed with anger. "Our own son was taken from us just moments after his birth! I refuse to give up another child of mine to Rhydin!"

All of the color drained from Mira's face, and Xavier gripped her hand, being oddly quiet. Frederick stood stock still. He licked his lips, struggling to comprehend. "My son, Dominick... He is my only heir, but-..."

"He is already too old, Your Highness," Arii said calmly. "We could not use him even if necessary. His magic is already too developed and no longer malleable. It would not necessarily need to be a Royal child. There are plenty of nobles descended from Royals who could possibly produce the child we need."

There was a sudden crash outside the gigantic stone doors

leading to the outdoors. The ten of us turned in our seats toward the entrance, but the doors abruptly swung open. So fast you could hardly see them, two shapes sprinted inside and took flight once the palace allowed them their magic.

Bright, colorful wings threw them forward with every flap, and before a single thought could cross my mind, the two skidded to a rough landing only feet before the table. I recognized Luke and James, Rachel's brothers. They were completely out of breath and disheveled, their wings vanishing fast.

"*Luc, Jems! Cii iiba vunae tenste da?*" The Clariion was on his feet immediately, running faster than any other 327-year-old over to his grandsons.

As James doubled over in exhaustion, Luke gasped as his words spilled out, "*Ry-liire, cii anae'v Kiidek Samton! Iiba 'draft' touna'v!*"

Rachel's hand flew to her mouth. My ears strained, wondering if I had heard Sam's name, but Arii remained stoic, "*Te matenjcat machliis!*"

As Luke and James scurried back out into the mountain air, their wings disappearing as they reached the threshold, Dathian scrambled forward to place his hand on Arii's forearm, his shoulder out of reach. "Clariion, what is happening?"

Arii's lips turned into a thin line. "Kidek Samton has been taken by the draft. It happened earlier than we expected."

My heart dropped into the pit of my stomach, icy cold washing over my shoulders and down my spine. Panic gripped me and shook me. My breaths became ragged.

Dathian's attention turned upward to the mist, and he bellowed louder than thunder, "Show me Samton Greene!"

CHAPTER FIVE

———— ⚬⚭⚬ ————

T he mist obeyed its master's command. The hazy, liquid
blue swirled until it was suddenly saturated with color.
My mind struggled to orient itself, but once I rotated my head
a certain way, the picture fit together. I would recognize that
form anywhere.

There, up in the ceiling, I could see my husband, Sam,
sitting in the back of a jostling wagon. The sunset was shining
through the thick, canvas over top of the wagon frame just
enough to illuminate the stressed, vacant expression on his
face.

My heart broke as I witnessed him sandwiched between
two other men dressed in Lunakan soldier garb, their faces
unseen. His Kidek bandana was nowhere to be seen. I was
sure that while no one else would think Sam looked scared, I
knew him well enough to see beyond his stoic mask into the
scared eyes of the little boy I had grown up with.

I immediately stood from my chair, my voice rasping, "I
need to get to him!"

Frederick put his hand on my shoulder like lightning. "Wait, Lina. I am sure the Ranguvariians have this all under control."

"Frederick is right, Linaria," Arii said calmly, not backing down as Rachel moved instinctually to flank him. "We have people tracking him at this very moment. As long as the army does not discover that he is a Rounan, I do not believe him in any danger."

"Any danger?" I shrieked, putting nails on a chalkboard to shame. "He's been *drafted* into the *worst* war in Nerahdian history, and you don't think he's in any danger?"

"Sam is a Rounan, Linaria, and a very powerful one at that. I believe he will do just fine unless he is discovered. He may even be able to bring us some valuable intelligence from the frontlines," Arii said slowly, still not getting excited.

"No! You don't understand!" Tears began to pool in my eyes, and Frederick's hand tightened on my shoulder. I could barely see Evan across the table from me. It was time to come clean. It was the only way to save Sam. "I've been having nightmares. It is just after a battle, and Sam is in the uniform... Rhydin kills him, and then he kills me as he takes my locket. It's always the same. Every time."

Several expressions changed around the room, but there were a few that did not. I blinked and my tears fell, but I could see when Xavier leaned forward, pressing his large hands together to keep fire from spraying the room. He urged, "I think someone needs to go after Sam-...!"

"I forbid it," Dathian spoke with finality, his face pale and somber. "We are not losing any Royal blood for a Rounan. Not to mention the safety of your locket."

Heat flared through my chest. I snapped, "He's my *husband*!"

"It does not matter!" Dathian growled, "The Royal bloodlines and the Allyen are far more important! If Rhydin were to gain your locket, the game is irrevocably over. Besides, if you are unattached, perhaps you will choose a Gornish husband next time-..."

I slapped him. The most important and powerful man in Nerahdis. And I slapped him.

Dathian's hand went to his cheek as every other person in the room looked on in horror. I hoisted Kylar to my hip, grabbed my cloak off the back of my chair, and began to storm out of the room.

Rachel bounded after me and grabbed my elbow. "Lina, you can't go!"

I looked at her desperately, pleading with my eyes. My legs were shaking as I spoke, my voice breaking, "But I have to save him!"

"Lina, we *will* make sure he's okay," Rachel said firmly, shooting an angry glance back at the Archimage. "Like my grandfather said, we already have Ranguvariians following him. Let's not freak out until we need to."

I nodded ever so slowly, but it was like moving iron. My mind raced a million miles per hour, but no tangible thoughts ever quite progressed.

Around me, the world became a blur. The meeting was disbanded by a rather put off Archimage. Within the hour, Frederick returned to Auklia with a still steaming Queen Lily to continue assisting King Daniel. Mira was tired so she and Xavier decided to stay at the Archimage Palace for the night, although Xavier was very obviously not happy about it.

Whenever I conquered my anxiety enough to surface from my tumultuous thoughts, I would see him stalking around the throne room. Sometimes, a small flame would burst to life within his hand as he stopped to look at something, but he would clench his fist to extinguish it as quickly as it had appeared.

Rachel tried to encourage me to relax before heading off with Arii to assess the situation, but it wasn't much use. Evan and Cayce returned upstairs as fast as they could, and I wondered if they were still talking through the fact that she was a Rounan.

Later, I could hear the faint lilting of a violin, and my ears were drawn to it like magnets. Even though I couldn't hear it very well, I found it beautiful. But, after a few minutes, the melancholy, long notes only made me feel more helpless.

Now, I was alone at the black table, except for my slumbering child. I stared at his sweet face, seeing nothing but Sam. Everything was softened by baby curves, but I could still see the structure of Sam's face, his nose, and his long limbs just waiting to come out when Kylar was older. The only thing he seemed to have gotten from me was my mud-colored hair. No tinges of red in a lighter brown like Sam's.

I wondered if I'd ever get a child that looked more like me, if being a Rounan was so dominant. Regardless of Dathian's intimations, if something happened to Sam, I had no interest in ever being with anyone else, much less having another child. Sam was my world, and Kylar was part of that. As I stroked the downy hair coming in, I hoped that Kylar would have no memory of this whatsoever, and it would be like it had never happened.

Light taps on the onyx floor brought me back to reality. I looked surprised to the vast stained-glass window, no light shining through it. How long had the sun been down?

With a candle in her porcelain hand, Mira approached the table. She was still wrapped in her fluffy, amethyst cloak, which made me finally feel the chill in the air. Winter wasn't over, I reminded myself and held Kylar closer.

"I am surprised you are not sleeping," Mira said airily.

"I'm not tired," I lied. Obviously, it was late enough for people to be asleep. Whoops. "What are you doing up?"

The princess chuckled a bit, "If I have to listen to any more of Xavier's whining, I might actually use magic to blow him out the window."

I gestured for Mira to sit with me and asked, "Why does Xavier not like being here so much?"

"He hates His Excellency," Mira mumbled, staring off into space. "He blames him for not stepping in to stop Jasmine, his stepmother, from locking up his father and ruining Mineraltir."

My shoulders fell as I thought of how Xavier must feel being around the man who could have put an end to the remarriage and ruination before it ever began. Sometimes, I wondered if he could have done anything about Rhydin, too. I could relate.

"May I?"

I looked up to see Mira smiling and holding out her hands, and I gratefully handed over the heavy boy in my lap. The day was approaching when Kylar would be too heavy to just sit and hold. Mira took him gingerly. She had gotten some experience from being around Dominick, her nephew, so much, but she still slightly looked like she was hefting a sack of potatoes instead of an infant.

As she smiled at him in her arms, her black curls falling forward, her voice seemed strangely out of tune with her expression. "Lina, I need to tell you something."

"What is it?" I asked, noticing the solemnity in her tone and the circles under her eyes.

"Earlier, His Excellency and the Clariion were talking about a possible solution to the Allyen problem," Mira said quietly, her words still ringing in the silence. "That if you obtained a Gornish child with magical qualities, they might be able to transform it into the new Allyen."

"Right," I said skeptically, still doubting how it would ever work.

"Well," the Lunakan princess took a very deep breath, "I have not told anyone for fear of something happening...but I am with child."

My mind was immediately ripped into two completely opposite directions. One half rejoiced, thinking that this whole problem could possibly be over, but the other despaired. This was Mira! And Xavier! And their *firstborn*. The *heir* to Mineraltir's throne! How could I possibly steal that from them?

My lips parted and immediately closed. I could not find any words that seemed appropriate. After several moments passed, I found the safest words I could muster. "What are you saying?"

"I don't know," Mira shook her head, her shoulders trembling.

It was then that her hands absent-mindedly came around to cradle a slightly round waistline underneath her massive cloak that had hid it from sight. I wondered how far she was along. The way she spoke made it seem like quite a bit, but she certainly wasn't showing as much as I had with Kylar.

She mumbled quietly, "I was hoping to talk to Xavier about it tonight, but he is in no mood."

"Does he know?" I replied almost instantly this time.

The princess shook her head again.

I turned to her in my seat. "Mira, before you say anything,

you need to talk to Xavier. He deserves to know and have a voice in this. This isn't a simple matter, and I certainly don't want to make this decision for you."

The black-haired woman nodded, her round cheeks flushing.

"Come on," I said, helping her to her feet. "You can sleep in my room tonight."

The two of us tip-toed out of the throne room to the vast marble staircase. The base began at the blackest of blacks and turned infinitesimally whiter until it was pure as snow at the very top floor where Dathian's quarters were. My room was on the fifth floor, at the end of a gold-wallpapered hallway. It was the Allyen's suite, I had been told, and I wondered how many previous Allyens had slept in there.

Being that there had only ever been one Allyen at a time, Evan had chosen a room on the third floor, which was styled after Auklian design. So, Kylar and I had an entire suite of rooms all to ourselves, as well as a more massive and luxurious bed than I'd ever witnessed before.

Mira collapsed almost instantly upon hitting the plush mattress. A crib had been placed in this room, which redeemed Dathian slightly. It was strange to see Kylar in a fancy crib befitting a Royal child rather than his usual wicker basket at home.

As for me, it was hard to fall asleep on something so cushy. I actually missed my simple bed at home; the feel and smell of the straw. The one in the Archimage Palace just wasn't right, although one couldn't argue its comfort.

These were the thoughts that entertained me until my heavy eyelids came to close, my hands outstretched, searching for Sam. I would have tried to fall asleep faster if I had known that our night would be cut short.

"Lina! Wake up!"

I jolted awake, my eyes and mind foggy from sleep. Immediately, the overhead chandelier was lit, casting its fiery light across the room. I craned groggily toward the window. Still black. What was going on? Kylar began to scream.

At the door was my twin brother, his mud-colored hair sticking in awkward directions, but there was no mistaking the worry in his gold-speckled Allyen eyes. I leapt from the plush mattress and scooped up my crying child as Mira slowly blinked her violet eyes into consciousness.

My voice was hoarse with sleep. "Evan, what's the emergency?"

Evan's eyes flicked once to the princess and back to me, his expression genuinely worried. "Xavier is gone."

My heart sank. "What do you mean, he's gone? Where did he go?"

"He left a note." The short man bit his lip. "He went after your husband."

I felt my eyebrows go up into my hairline. Mira had hardly gotten herself stood up before her knees went out from under her to crash back down to the bed. I rushed back over to her, looking over her with my eyes, but aside from her pale face and raspy breath, she looked okay.

"The Archimage is calling everyone downstairs to figure out what we're going to do, so just come as fast as you can, alright?" Evan backed out of the room as quickly as possible, eyeing Mira uncomfortably.

The two of us changed out of our nightclothes as fast as we could, the silence like an ocean around us; unbreakable. Then, we scampered down the stairs as if our lives depended on it. While Mira struggled to maintain a stoic face, my thoughts tumbled over themselves.

Why did Xavier go? He had expressed concern for Sam, which I had appreciated, but it wasn't like they were super close or anything. Granted, Xavier wasn't the most rational person I knew. I couldn't keep myself from glancing to Mira periodically. She never got to tell him.

The few people that remained in the palace from the previous meeting were already gathered around the midnight table, the one piece of furniture in this place that I truly hated. It seemed like only bad things happened around it.

Dathian was standing in a tunic more suited for bed than meetings, but even his night shirt was fancier than any dress I'd ever owned. He fretfully looked around to Evan, Cayce, Arii, and Rachel, sighing in relief when he saw Mira and I finally arrive.

The Archimage cleared his throat. "As you all know, the situation has changed gravely…"

I couldn't suppress my massive eyeroll. Of course, now that a Royal was missing everything changed. I wished I could slap him again. Sam was important too.

"We have already dispatched a larger team to find Prince Xavier and Kidek Samton," Arii said carefully in that melodic voice of his. "They are working on a solution at this very moment."

For the first time in twenty-four hours, I felt some sort of relief. Arii had included Sam. They were looking for him and trying to bring him home. I smiled at the tear-stained face of Kylar in my arms. His papa would be home soon. My happiness filled me up and brimmed forward, and it was hard to keep the smile from my face as I looked up to Arii, a good two feet over my head.

I gushed, "I want to go with them! I want to help bring them home sooner."

Rachel grimaced from her post behind her grandfather. "I'm sorry, Lina, but we can't allow that."

My cheer was killed instantaneously. "Why not?"

The tall redhead shrugged. "It's just not safe. We still don't know Rhydin's plan, so we do not think it's safe for either of you to be traveling."

I glanced at Evan, and his expression seemed as surprised as mine.

"There's another thing, too." Rachel became sad. "I haven't told you this, but the Rounan compound has been going crazy ever since Sam was taken. They need a Kidek."

My shoulders sagged while my anxiety took off full-fledged. I hadn't even thought of the Rounans being without a leader. Sam was gone. He had no other family in the compound. That meant me. The one they all hated. My hands began to tremor.

Rachel came around the table and wrapped her long, lanky arms around my petite frame. "I really am sorry. I swear I'll get you two back together as soon as we can. But for now, we need to go back to the compound. I promise I'll help you."

"Lina?"

I looked up glumly, my mind beginning to shut down from stress.

Evan was sitting in his chair as if perched on a hundred needles. When he hesitated, Cayce delivered a swift elbow to his ribs, so lightning-fast that one could have easily missed it. My brother recoiled from the purple-haired woman's touch, but her round face just beamed innocently.

His words were shoddy, and his eyes landed in his lap more often than on my face. "We would like to come with you…to the compound."

Confusion crossed my mind, but before I could speak,

Cayce's voice chimed like bells, "While my husband may not like to admit it, we are family. I would not leave my sister if she was in your predicament. Besides, I'm sure you need help. Being Kidek isn't easy. Being a Gornish woman trying to lead a bunch of hardheaded Rounans is darn near impossible." She chuckled.

A sudden light appeared. A light at the end of a dark tunnel of leading a people who despised me. I wanted to fall down on my knees and kiss this Auklian's dainty, sapphire slippers, but I restrained myself by simply stretching my short arm across the table to grip her soft, pale hand. I could hardly swallow the lump in my throat enough to tell her thank you.

Some of us attempted to go back to sleep. Mira stayed with me for the rest of the night, too morose to even think of returning to her own room where the man who had threatened to keep her up all night with his pacing and whining now left a gaping hole. There would be no sleep for either of us, however. Not with both our husbands now missing.

When the sun eventually arose, it cast its dim, winter light along the mountain range and vanquished the reflections of the twin moons. I packed my things solemnly, having been here long enough that a lot of my possessions had been strewn across the Allyen suite. Although, more than half of them were Kylar's.

Mira packed the few belongings that she had brought with her, but as she walked slowly to the ornate wooden door to the hallway, she stopped mid-step. The princess took a deep breath, not turning to face me. "Lina, I cannot give you an answer. Not with Xavier…gone."

I straightened from stuffing my bag closed, having almost entirely forgotten in all the chaos. The idea of Mira and Xavier giving us their firstborn to be the next Allyen still made me nauseous.

Pursing my lips, I answered the best I could, "Mira, I wouldn't want you to do anything different. We'll find Xavier. And Sam. And we'll figure it out."

Mira burst from the room, but she wasn't far enough down the hallway before I heard her gasp with tears. The sound tore at my heart, and I lifted my chin high to keep myself from doing the same. I glanced at the suite one last time before leaving, and I hoped that I would never have to step foot in this forsaken, secret mountain palace ever again.

CHAPTER SIX

The days went slowly at first. Each moment, I waited for news of the Ranguvariians' rescue of Sam and Xavier. But each evening, I went to bed disappointed. Soon, a week had gone by. Then two. Then more. Every time I asked why Sam was not home yet, I received the same answer.

It's not the right time. Rachel or one of her brothers would say. *If we don't do this at the exact right moment, the army will discover that Sam's a Rounan. That will put his life in more danger than if we just leave him be.*

As far as Xavier's situation, it seemed that he was always two steps ahead of the Ranguvariians. He was determined not to be found until Sam had been broken out from the army.

Every day, I could sense Rachel's worry. Sam would be fine as long as he didn't use magic. Xavier, on the other hand, would be recognized instantly, magic or no magic, with his bright, Mineraltin red hair. Then, he would be sent back to Mineraltir Castle. Sent back to Queen Jasmine, Rhydin's henchwoman.

However, Xavier actually ended helping more than anyone would care to admit. Being a Rounan, Sam was like a regular person as far as sensing presences goes. No one could sense him unless they were looking right at him. Xavier, on the other hand, could be sensed for miles. If the Ranguvariians ever lost track of Sam, all they had to do was lock their senses on Xavier and know he was near.

In the passing weeks, the Rounan compound thawed in everything but inter-ancestral relations. The snow slowly diminished, revealing short, brown grass underneath. It soon experienced a transformation, blossoming into a vibrant green color as it began to stretch toward the sky. The prairie wildflowers began to bloom, their tiny specks of pink, yellow, and purple making it seem like the ground had been purposely decorated that way.

Middle Spring was soon well-established, but the Rounans' hatred of me only grew now that I was their temporary Kidek. On top of that, each night, my nightmare became incrementally fleshed out. The sky was cloudier, the grass was greener, and the blood seeping from Sam's face was redder. And, the pain was more searing. Before, I would usually wake up with a gasp or a shriek. Now, I woke up screaming.

Rachel was insisting that they had a plan in place, which was put into motion that very day as I came out of the tiny bed-space into the minuscule kitchen area. She had cooked herself breakfast, sitting at the wobbly table forking eggs into her mouth. Cayce sat with her, Kylar in her lap reaching for her amazing lavender curls, but my mind was in a fog. Still entrenched in my nightmare that I hoped every day would never come true.

Evan and Cayce had slept on a straw tick on the kitchen

floor for the first week after we had returned from the Archimage Palace, but after that, they had been able to procure a small home for themselves inside the compound.

I was rather happy when they left. The Rounans loved Cayce. Adored her. Thrilled to learn about Rounans in Auklia and hear her stories, as well as to help her adjust to our climate. After all, Auklia was warm and humid all year round, no seasons to speak of, and she had just moved into the kingdom with the most drastic seasonal changes of them all.

However, in some sort of masochistic kind of way, I felt strangely appeased that the Rounans hated Evan too. They would flat out ignore him when they engaged with Cayce. Although to my chagrin, it didn't seem to bother him one bit.

I never saw Evan talk to anyone for that matter, or even try as I had when I first arrived. This caused me to begin to wonder about the whole twin thing. It seemed like the more I learned about my brother, the more I felt that we were polar opposites. How could we be any more different from each other?

While it angered me that Cayce was so easily accepted, I very quickly thanked my lucky stars that she was here. She was the one Rounan in the whole compound that didn't hate me, and her advice and knowledge came in handy more than once. She bailed me out later that afternoon in the mercantile.

Cayce and I went together since Rachel enjoyed staying as far away from the heart of the compound as physically possible, and I admit, I allowed my thoughts to wander. It was easier that way. If I was a million miles away, I didn't see the glares. I didn't hear the snide comments. I didn't notice the people's anger that the compound was still flour-less since Sam had never returned with it. I could go out about my business and remain emotionally unscathed on most days.

But, today wasn't one of those days.

"Law of *Blutuern*?" I mumbled, repeating the only words I had heard of the entire sentence.

"Yes, Ma'am."

I blinked mindlessly at the overweight, middle-aged man who had suddenly materialized in front of me in the canned-food section of the small Rounan shop. He exuded an air of self-importance and frustration. My eyes darted around the store searching for my sister-in-law, but Cayce was on the opposite side by the sugar, her attention on the shopkeeper's scale.

As this man continued to stare at me, waiting for a response and becoming angrier with each passing second, I looked helplessly around me for any sort of help with this strange word that I didn't understand.

The eyes of other Rounans, men and women alike, stared back with no mercy. I was Kidek now with Sam absent, yet I had no knowledge of any of the populace, their language, or their inner, political workings. Why hadn't I asked Sam to teach me about his culture? Before I didn't have him to help me?

In my stubbornness to not appear to need help and seem like a good leader, I summoned the best confident tone I could. "I see. And what is it you need concerning this 'Law of *Blutuern*?'"

The man's round face flushed and his mustache bristled. His beady eyes focused on the infant in my arms while his fists seemed ready to lash out if Kylar had not been present. "You Gornish idiot! You don't know what the Law of *Blutuern* is, do you?"

My brow furrowed, my magic building up inside of me, but I kept it in check. After all, every person in this store had

Rounan magic and I was vastly outnumbered, even with my Rounan sister-in-law.

At the sound of the man's rising voice, Cayce's ears perked up. She nearly dropped her little bag of sugar as she scurried over to my side, her blue eyes fierce. She held a strong hand in front of her mouth as she whispered into my ear, "The Law of *Blutuern* is one of the most sacred and oldest laws we have. It outlaws the use of magic on another Rounan to control their actions. Punishable by death."

The words rang a bell. Sam had told me before that it was illegal for Rounans to use magic on each other, but he never told me the special name for the law. While I silently wished that Sam would have told me this, I turned back to the wealthy man. "Sir, if you would like my assistance, I suggest that you do not insult me and tell me straightly what your problem is."

The man shoved his thick hands between his suspenders, grumbling and not backing down. "Patrik Henders stole from me this morning! He used his magic to keep me from moving as he went into my cellar and stole my food!"

My mind whirled. While I didn't know most of these Rounans' names, Patrik's was one name that I knew. He lived near us, and he was always so thin that I worried about him every time I saw him. He also had a wife and six children who were not much better off than he was. I considered my answer carefully seeing as I had such an audience at the moment. My tongue took its time between my teeth. "How much food did he steal?"

"Why does it matter??" The overweight man exploded, "Stealing is stealing!! I can see how a Gornish woman would think that a few cans of beans don't matter, but every morsel does in times like these!"

I felt heat on the back of my neck. I handed the baby to

Cayce, and she eyed me. Rachel wasn't even here, but I could almost hear her in my mind saying 'Don't do anything stupid.' Putting my hands on my hips, I straightened, trying to make my five-foot frame as menacing as possible. "Have you forgotten who I am?"

He leered down at me. "Nothing but a Gornish-..."

"Stop!" I yelled, swinging my hands out with a flash of light magic.

All of the onlookers took at least one step backwards, if not more. While there was a flicker in the man's expression of uncertainty, he did not back down.

I closed my hands and the magic disappeared, but I was quickly pacing around the whole room. "I think you all know that Patrik Henders is not an evil man. He is a poor man with a wife and six children to provide for, and while what he did was wrong, I don't believe he deserves to die for it! That won't solve the problem of starvation! We are out in this compound for our safety, why not look out for your fellow man so that we can all truly be safe?"

"You say 'we' as if you are one of us. But you never will be," the overweight man spat, beginning to turn on his heel toward the shop door, a path widening for him.

"And you!" I whirled on him, my words becoming louder. "Are you stuck in the first century? Yes, my ancestors were Gornish. You all, my husband, and my son are Rounan. But we are *all* Lunakans. And while you all are here, men included, in safety from King Adam, the rest of our kingdom is at war! The rest of the Lunakan male population is gone and fighting, and we don't know if they're coming back. Including my husband! *Your* Kidek! You all should be ashamed of yourselves for being so selfish as to not help a starving man and his family when you hardly have to deal with this war!"

While some of the men and women in the room looked down in guilt, their arms still laden with cans and sacks, my opponent threw one last comment before disappearing through the door. "They're Gornish. They deserve it."

If he had still been here, I would have punched him in the face with all the magical ferocity I could. Avoiding any and all eye contact, I grabbed my forgotten crate of groceries from the counter, gave a quick nod to the people who had empathized with my rampage, and stormed out of the store.

Cayce was close behind me with Kylar, and after a few angry paces, she caught up with me and said, "You handled that well."

I looked at her to ascertain whether that was sarcastic or not. She had a small grin on her face, so I began to think she was being sarcastic and thought it was as big of a blow up as I did.

"You should go into public speaking. An Allyen with the speech skills of a king, who would have thought?" The violet-haired woman laughed, swinging Kylar around to make him giggle as well.

I grinned slightly through my anxiety and embarrassment, but it wasn't quite enough to make me feel better. I wanted nothing more than to give this title of Kidek over to anybody else, but I couldn't. It was Rounan law for the Kidek's next of kin to serve while he was away, and there was only me.

As we walked home, I did my best to ignore what I saw around me. I focused on the crinkle of the prairie grass beneath my feet, the smell of maple as we passed the woodcutter's, or even the clouding blue sky above us. Anything but the view of husbands working in their yards or tending their animals while their wives watched from the window or the front step.

The Rounans had received some residual anger from my personal life in my outburst, which I was sure wasn't a good leadership trait. But it was hard not to resent them. That they weren't going through what I, and the rest of Lunaka for that matter, was going through. I wished they wouldn't focus on the divide between Gornish and Rounan and instead see themselves as what we all were. Lunakan.

Seeming to sense my thoughts, Cayce lost her smile and spoke rather tentatively, "I heard they were in a battle yesterday around Spenser's Lake. Lunaka won it, and Rachel said Sam made it through alright."

I breathed a sigh of relief that they had made it through another battle. I hated hearing about them, but I was glad that I was never told until they were over and that Sam was okay. It had been several weeks, and it felt like an eternity with forever still to go. In order to appease my anxiety, I had begun to dream up different ways to leave the compound and find Sam to bring him home myself before he wound up in my deathly nightmare.

It was helpful that Rachel knew of my plight and gave updates whenever she could, but she and I both knew that I would never truly be able to relax until Sam was back in our tiny shack. I envied the lime pinwheel shape tattooed to her cheek that allowed her to talk to Jaspen, her Ranguvariian husband. I hoped with all of my being that whatever plan the Ranguvariians had in place today would be successful.

We rounded the final corner onto the path that led out of the compound, seeing as Sam and I's shack was on the very edge. It had been a mutual decision, really, seeing as the Rounans didn't like me and Sam had never been a fan of living close to other people. He was still my country boy at heart.

My thoughts took a turn when I noticed the tall, bundled

figure standing at our doorstep. Inwardly, I moaned. Great, here was another Rounan with some squabble for me to inevitably fail to solve. I decided I needed a "closed" sign to hang in my window as Cayce and I meandered over to meet the stranger.

Upon hearing our approach, the figure turned and removed the hood. For a moment, my eyes froze on the face. It was structured and colored just like Sam's; olive skin, long face, and prominent nose with reddish-brown hair framing it. But this face was subtly more cherub and paler than Sam had ever been in his entire life with his permanent farmer's tan.

With the fall of an auburn braid out of the folds of her cloak, I swallowed my pathetic hope that Sam had returned. However, this woman's appearance still strikingly resembled my absent husband. I cocked my head to one side, confused as to how I should act. "May I help you?"

"Yes, I hope so. I'm looking for the Kidek?" The woman answered, folding her hands together nicely. She couldn't be more than twenty-seven.

I sighed. Of course, it was another ruffled Rounan. My words came out harsher than I meant to. "I am she. What do you want?"

The woman's brow furrowed immediately, her voice becoming shrill. "What happened to Samton that a *Gornish* woman is Kidek? That's impossible! I'm his sister, the title should have passed to me!"

My face flushed instantly, and Cayce resituated herself behind me at the sound of the fear and anger in the woman's voice. I remembered Sam's elder sister at school, but she had never come back after their move to Stellan and the Epidemic killed their mother.

After stuttering for a few moments, I tried to speak, "I-…

I'm sorry, let's start over. My name is Lina. I am temporary Kidek in Sam's absence. You're his sister? I'm sorry, I didn't recognize you."

The woman looked me up and down with her eyes, sizing up my petite frame in comparison with her Sam-like height. "I am Kelsi Roan. Yes, I am his sister, his only flesh and blood. Where is he? Why didn't he contact me that he was leaving and needed a replacement? And *who* are *you*?"

Today was really not my day. I took a deep breath, trying not to let this woman get under my skin. After all, apparently, she was the sister-in-law I'd barely known about and never met. "Like I said, I'm Lina. Sam is my husband, and he's at war right now as are the rest of the men in Lunaka."

"*What*?" All of the color left Kelsi's face as her arms dropped to her sides. I could almost see her trying to pick up the pieces of what she thought was reality from within her mind. "How is this possible? Why aren't you out looking for him? He could be killed for who he is!"

Her words shook me visibly. I could only swallow numbly and try to get my voice to work. "Trust me when I say that it happened on accident and that I have people looking for him and trying to get him out at this very moment. Don't dare think anything different."

She held her chin high once more. "I see. I hope that you are right. However, I was unaware that my brother had married. I have not seen him for many years since I married my own husband, so I apologize."

Stifling the urge to twiddle my thumbs due to the awkwardness, I took Kylar back from Cayce and stepped closer to the door. I tried not to look up at Kelsi too much as I asked, "Would you like to come inside? It is very cold out here, and I prefer to keep my son out of it as much as possible."

Wrong words, Lina. At that, Kelsi's eyes locked onto Kylar in near horror. She said nothing, after all there was no denying Kylar's resemblance to his father. I opened the door and led her inside, lighting the candles stuck to our table to scare away the dark.

Kelsi moved like her feet were made of lead, carefully scanning the small room for every small detail, taking all our squalor in. I tried to ignore her as I began a fire and put Kylar in his makeshift crib close by, which was really a leftover produce crate from the mercantile.

After a quick look at the situation, Cayce gave me a knowing look and went back outside. She may be here to help me with the Rounans, but she didn't need to be involved in the Greene family drama.

I sat at the table and offered Kelsi a chair. "So, if you haven't seen Sam in ages, why did you seek him out today? Maybe I can still help you."

Kelsi took the chair, but her expression seemed lost now, all the energy vanished. She sighed, "To be honest, I just came to talk to Samton. I live in another compound to the east beyond Stellan with my husband and daughter. While my husband wasn't drafted, we live much closer to town than you do here. From the talk, it seems like the world is falling apart. I wanted to… I wanted to see Samton…before things became so crazy that they ban travel in Lunaka."

As the tea kettle began to squeal, I noticed the fatigue in Kelsi and wondered how long it had taken her to get here. We lived so far from Lun that the only news I ever heard was from Rachel, which always focused on the war itself. I realized slowly that I knew nothing of the status of Lunaka, anything beyond our compound for that matter, and the questions were suddenly brimming forth in my mind.

As I poured two cups, I struggled to decide which to ask first. My voice was hesitant as I spoke, "I'm afraid we don't know much here. What is happening in Stellan?"

"What's happening everywhere. Soläna, Canis, Stellan, Lun…" Kelsi shrugged and accepted her warm cup of tea from me gratefully. "People are at the end of their ropes. After the Darkness receded, everyone found their infants and grandparents dead. Now, less than a year later, everyone is finding their husbands, fathers, brothers, sons stolen from them. There're riots in the streets every night in the capital."

I couldn't stop the shudder running through me. I still considered Soläna my home. It was hard to imagine riots in the streets when normally everyone would be hanging decorations for the Spring Festival. Just last year, Sam and I had been there together. I'd thought before how devastating it would have been had I lost Kylar in the darkness, but I couldn't even entertain the idea now that Sam was gone. I could only shake my head. "I can't imagine."

Kelsi looked at me and smiled slightly, lopsided just like her brother's. "Some people are beginning to wonder if soon there will only be women left. There's a lot of hatred for King Adam right now."

"Oh, people started hating him ever since they figured out their ruse with Prince Xavier and Princess Mira." I smirked. It was inevitable in my opinion.

Sam's sister gave me a confused look. "What do you mean?"

"Remember? King Adam and Queen Jasmine told everyone that they were dead, but they weren't? I remember right after I defeated Duunzer everyone was really mad about it."

"Oh, yes…" Kelsi trailed off. Her brow furrowed at her tea. She looked up at me quickly, one eye squinted shut, "What do you mean *you* defeated Duunzer?"

Well, I guess I wasn't that recognizable. It was hard to keep the smile off of my face. "You don't recognize me?"

Kelsi's eyes widened considerably. "You're… You're the Allyen?"

I nodded, thrilled that for once I was getting some amusement out of this.

"Huh." Kelsi leaned back in her chair with a calculated expression. "I guess that must be why my brother was crazy enough to marry a Gornish woman."

My smile was wiped off my face.

She leaned down, her eyes glossing over every trait of my slumbering baby. "Is he…?

A slow burning hatred buried itself into my heart. Why was the Gornish-Rounan status of my son such a concern? Why couldn't people just be happy that we had a healthy child? "He's a Rounan, if that's what you're so concerned about."

Kelsi gave me a charming smile, nothing more than a mask. "Good. I'd hate for my nephew to be nothing less than the future Kidek." She stood from the table promptly and began to strap her amber cloak back on.

My mind spun. Archimage Dathian wanted my son to be Gornish to become an Allyen. Kelsi wanted my son to be Rounan so he could become Kidek. Why couldn't he just be Kylar Greene?

"Well, Lina dear, I really must be off. Better to get home before King Adam closes all the roads, but I think I will stay the night here since it's getting late. Do tell me when you've found Samton, I really am in need of a chat with him."

As Kelsi Roan exited the building, Rachel walked in with

her cloak trailing her, quickly downing her own cup of tea. "It seems that every day you humans become more rigidly stratified."

I groaned, "I hate to say it, but if this is why Rhydin hates Rounans, I don't quite blame him!"

"Enough to hang them?"

"Rachel!"

"I know, I'm joking, Lina, for Nerahdis's sake."

My eyes fell to where Kylar rested in his pathetic hay-filled produce box. "Sam never told Kelsi about me. Or Kylar."

Rachel took a deep breath, her eyes shimmering as she looked at me with compassion. "I'm sure it's not like that, Lina. Maybe he sent her a letter and she never received it. You have to admit that Lunaka isn't exactly the winner of the best infrastructure award this year. Or any year for that matter, but this year in particular with the-..."

"The war, I know. And Duunzer. And all the people it killed, and the draft." I settled my face into my hands. "Don't remind me. What I truly need is a 'closed' sign."

Rachel barely had time to open her mouth for a rebuttal when a light flew across my senses. I recognized the presences immediately. Seriousness and the smell of rock. The memory of play and the smell of the fresh, Lunakan wind.

Luke and James.

I jumped out of my chair so fast that it fell over, yanking open the rickety door before the Owens boys even had a chance to knock. Their nearly identical eyes widened in shock, although Luke's flashed a deep brown color like syrup, revealing his one Ranguvariian genetic inheritance.

Excitement bubbled up inside of me until I saw the looks on their faces. The shock didn't melt into victory or joy or relief. None of those things. The shock fell into disappointment. To anxiety. To the feeling of failure.

"S-Sam?" I could only whisper, their faces holding my heart captive.

Rachel's hand landed on my shoulder from behind, which pulled me back from the threshold in order to allow the two young men to come inside.

Luke ran a hand through his hair, exuding exasperation and stress. "We were following them so closely. Sam and the prince. Especially since we can't sense Sam since he's a Rounan. Then suddenly, Xavier's presence disappeared! We flew for miles but couldn't sense him anywhere!"

"When did this happen? Do you think they were discovered?" Rachel asked before I could take as much as a breath.

"Last night," James sighed, seeming more levelheaded at the moment. "We're speculating that they entered the mountains. That's why we can't sense Xavier, and therefore Sam, anymore. Just in case, we did try looking for bodies-..."

Rachel shot him a death glare, her pale hands hovering around my ears. Her voice was low and firm. "I thought the plan was to rescue them *before* they got to the mountains! We've known Sam's regiment has been heading for Caden's Plain for the last couple of weeks. That was the whole point because now we can't track them! Why are you two just now telling me this if they disappeared twenty-four hours ago?"

Luke threw his hands up as he was assailed by his elder sister. "We tried okay! Sam knew we were there and knew the plan we had in place. We were supposed to meet up with them, but they never came. For all we know, they still got away and took a different escape route. Or, they're dead. We spent the whole day trying to gather more information before coming to you."

More than a shudder ran through me. An indescribable feeling of terror, loss, and jitters. Sam couldn't be dead. I would *know* if he was dead. My nightmare always took place somewhere grassy with the mountains well in the distance, not among them. He was alive.

I paced as I thought through all of these things, but as my mind raced a million miles per hour, I knew rapidly what I needed to do. The Owenses wouldn't like it, but the Allyen couldn't hide away at home anymore.

"I'm going," I said with finality, "And none of you are going to stop me this time."

"Lina-…" Rachel reached for me, her hand aiming to sooth and change my mind.

"No!" I yelled at my friend, possibly for the first time. "Things just keep getting worse, and my standing by doing *nothing* isn't helping anything! I'm the *Allyen*, remember? Not some useless, defenseless housewife who can't do anything! These Rounans hate me anyway." I took my scorned friend's hand, begging her now, "Let me be the Allyen and save my people. Let me go save my husband and Xavier. I've always been able to sense Sam because we have such a strong connection! With you or without you, I'm going."

"Is this a bad time?"

The four of us were startled, abruptly turning our heads to the door where both Evan and Cayce stood. Cayce's expression seemed guilty while my twin's reflected more…dare I say it, *concern*, than anything else. Our relationship was still rather complicated.

"No," I breathed. "Actually, you have good timing. Last night, Sam and Xavier…disappeared. I'm leaving to go find them, and I needed to ask Cayce to help me with a few things."

Evan measured my expression carefully, but Cayce was the one to respond, her voice genuinely confused. "With what?"

"I need you to go find Kelsi in the compound. I'm sure she hasn't left yet. She's going to get what she's always wanted," I grumbled as I began to sort through my meager possessions for things to take with me on my journey. "Just tell her she'd be better at being the Kidek than me. That'll make her feel good, and it's true. Don't tell anyone why I left. No need for mass panic."

Rachel remained silent, which shocked me. I was still expecting some sort of negative response to my decision to go because I could already feel it in the air every time my eyes met hers. She kept glancing back and forth from me to her brothers, but those two seemed resigned to my decision.

As I continued to pack, I was also very aware of Evan's eyes on my back, but several minutes went by before he finally spoke. His voice was hesitant, quiet, but sure. "I'm going with you."

I whirled around, anger filling me at the thought of my brother thinking he needed to help me because I wasn't as strong as him. My words were like acid. "I can handle myself. Your spouse is fine, so you can stay here."

"But yours is not," Evan conceded, real care showing in his eyes as they met mine fully for the first time. "Please let me come. Let me help my sister."

My heart stopped. He had finally recognized me as his sister. I stared at him for a solid ten seconds, considering it. Then, I gave the curtest of nods while the smallest of grins appeared on Evan's face.

Luke suddenly piped up as I continued to pack my bag. "You know, if Lina and Evan are both there, their magic will be more powerful. If Lina has been able to sense Sam in the past, Evan's combined power could let us try sensing him even in the mountains!"

At that, Rachel's shoulders drooped. There was no denying the exasperation in her voice. "Fine! I give in! But you're not going without me and my brothers. We're not going to have *both* Allyens on the loose without some sort of Ranguvariian protection."

She continued to look angry until I wrapped her in my short arms. "Thank you, Rachel."

Soon, it was all figured out. Evan and I would begin to head to Caden's Plain in attempt to sense Sam and Xavier in the mountains, and if not, we would scout out their regiment when it emerged from the magic-less boundary.

Cayce would move in with Mira, Cornflower, and Cassandra so that she wouldn't be left alone and could protect them. She would also make sure our livestock were taken care of. Kelsi would get her snotty way and be temporary Kidek in Sam and I's absence. I was sure the Rounans would be thrilled to have one of their kind in charge, I thought facetiously.

As I turned to stuff my Allyen journal into my bag from the mantel, my eyes finally fell to the ground. Kylar still lay asleep in his produce box, his tiny pink lips open and his deep brown hair sticking in various directions. There was no way.

My heart felt like it would break as I lifted my season-and-a-half-old son into my arms, holding him close. I wished I could wake him to see his eyes once more, but I knew better than anyone to never wake a sleeping baby.

I breathed in deeply the scent of him, then kissed the top of his fuzzy head and held him out to Cayce. Her bright blue eyes became confused, but she took Kylar from me. Letting go of him nearly shattered me, but war was no place for an infant. I didn't know where I would be tomorrow, or even a week from now.

Rachel seemed to read my mind as she watched me slowly take my fingers from my baby's blankets. She dug through her pack and brought forth several feather charm necklaces, all of them brilliant purples, oranges, and greens. I remembered then how she and her brothers had given us a wind chime made of those feathers in order to shield the entire compound. I hadn't worn one of those feathers since I'd lost mine right before Duunzer attacked.

Rachel very carefully handed me a purple one, Evan a green one, and gave Cayce the rest to take to the Royals in case their own wind chime wasn't enough for so many magical people in one house. Rachel held back one orange one, which she lightly tied to Kylar's blankets. Now, he would be completely invisible to Rhydin. Even though Kylar was a Rounan, and you could only sense Rounans by looking at them, the feather would now hide him even if Rhydin or one of his people happened to see him. Rhydin would never know that I had to leave him behind.

I started mumbling again, barely coherent, "He really likes to sleep, so never wake him, and he eats every few hours and he has this one stuffed goat, oh where is-...?

"I'll take good care of him, Lina," Cayce promised. "He'll be fine. He won't know what to do with so many people to dote on him all the time."

I nodded, trying desperately not to cry, and hugged her over my slumbering child, thanking her.

Rachel touched my arm gingerly. "We need to meet up with Evan's Ranguvariians a couple of miles from here. For more protection. Then we can head out."

Evan and I agreed, and as we gathered our cloaks and

headed for the shabby wooden door, I hoped that this journey would not end in failure. With each step, my heart thundered, begging me to turn around and scoop up my child. But now, Sam needed me more. I would find him and bring him home if it was the last thing I did.

The air was damp as we headed outside, the sun beginning to plummet toward the western horizon where Mineraltir lay. It touched the magic-less mountains with its golden fingers, and the dying breeze ruffled my cloak once more before Rachel took my hand and squeezed it. The Owenses' wings appeared as they activated their flying spell. Then white.

CHAPTER SEVEN

THE DAY BEFORE

S moke clogged the skies. Nearly all of the fires had been put out by now. The sun was rising, yet its light struggled to break through the dreary fog of yesterday's battle.

The bank of Spenser's Lake was painted crimson, which stretched into the water to pollute the crystalline blue. Bodies were strewn everywhere, clad in Lunakan navy vests as well as intricate layers of emerald, Mineraltin cloth. They dotted the landscape like wildflowers, cropping up every so often in larger or smaller bunches.

The muscles in Sam's arms were aching, but he kept at his work. By now, his shovel had become an extension of his arm like a long, sturdy, flattened hand. Most of the other men in Sam's regiment didn't bother with the burying of the fallen, but a few straggled around to help.

Yesterday's battle had been ugly. Sam's regiment was heading to the mountains to cross into Caden's Plain, the patch of grassland in the middle of the Three Kingdoms, when a troop of Mineraltins appeared out of nowhere.

The only possible way they survived was because while Mineraltins were extremely offensive, they wielded such heavy weapons like axes and maces that they were slow and heavy. Their armor was minimal, due to their many weapons, while King Adam ensured Lunaka's soldiers to wear their weight in armor and chainmail. The army had always received the majority of his attention as king.

However, Sam wasn't minding which uniforms the bodies wore. He worked well away from the others, and every time he reached a new body, he rolled up the sleeve on the man's right arm. Perhaps every tenth arm he checked bore the geometric mark of a Rounan. The diamond shape on top of a square with a long point stretching toward the elbow.

Anger arose inside of Sam at the sight of every one. This war was not only destroying the land and the people of Nerahdis, but the Rounan people as well. It had to stop.

Within a couple of hours, Sam and the few other soldiers finished their task, using their shovels to pound the dirt and sand down firmly on top of the Lunakan soldiers. As for the Mineraltins, they were left where they had fallen. Sam hated this, especially for the ones who were Rounans. They were his people and his responsibility too. But, if he was suspected of caring for the enemy, he might find himself executed for betrayal.

Sam thought this rule was nothing more than a verbal threat until last week when a teenager was caught trying to bury a young Mineraltin soldier maybe a quarter mile from the Lunakan grave. He was killed within the hour. King Adam's generals had no mercy.

As Sam walked, he thought of Lina. He hated that he

hadn't been able to say goodbye to her. He thought of her all the time, especially when he thought he would die marching for miles on end or during close calls in the battles he'd seen. Death had stared him in the face more than once during his forced service so far.

Sam knew that the Ranguvariians following their regiment had hatched a plan to get him out, but he wondered what would happen when he returned home. His sword was stained with other men's blood and so was his mind. What would Lina think when she found out he had killed people? Men whose faces haunted him every time he closed his eyes?

The regiment came into view. All of the thick, canvas tents had been pulled down and packed away into the wagons, and the soldiers were beginning to line up in preparation to depart. Sam deposited his shovel in the nearest wagon and bobbed his way through the marching lines, looking for a tall soldier with his helmet on.

Today was the day. Sam had avoided this man like the plague ever since he showed up nearly a season ago in order to avoid suspicion, but Sam knew that they needed to be together on the day the Ranguvariians would rescue them.

It took a couple minutes to find him, considering their regiment consisted of about seventy men, but finally, Sam spotted a soldier whose body language resonated more with a leisurely stride than a militaristic march. He fell into line beside him, his feet easily falling into the rhythm by now.

"Done playing around?" The tall soldier snickered, his blue eyes sliding to look at him. The first words they'd exchanged during the whole season.

"It's the right thing to do. I'd want you to do it for me," Sam grumbled.

"Oh, don't worry. No one will even get close to you with

me around."

Sam broke formation to look the man in the eye. This Mineraltin prince was really somethin'. Sam had met him once or twice at his wedding and shortly before Kylar was born, but he really hadn't talked to Xavier much. Why Xavier ran away from the other Royals to come after him, Sam would never know. But, he knew Xavier was Lina's friend, so he tried to put up with him the best he could.

Xavier had shown up a few days after Sam was drafted, keeping a helmet on at all times to hide his bright red hair. Now, the Ranguvariians had to somehow get them both away without notice. It seemed to Sam that Xavier had only complicated things rather than helping. However, there was a plan in place for that night Sam truly believed would work.

The regiment planned to camp at the base of the mountains before journeying through them, crossing Caden's Plain, and attacking Mineraltir on the other side. A rather new settlement called Tranini to be exact. That meant a lot of young families, if the men were even there.

These were the newest orders from the head general, and Sam felt the same dread he always did when orders came down for an imminent attack. Why? He always asked himself. If Rhydin was behind this war, what was his motive? It was like Duunzer was here all over again, except there was no sign of Rhydin anywhere.

After a snip from his commanding officer, Sam moved his head back to look at the head in front of him, back in formation. It was several more hours before it even occurred to Sam that the mountains were remotely getting bigger.

As the morning evolved into a warm, spring afternoon, Sam began to sweat under his layers of chainmail, armor, and leather. It was like working out in the sun with his plow, except the horse was riding on top of him instead of pulling the plow for him. If this was what Middle Spring felt like in armor, Sam didn't even want to know about Middle Summer.

By the time the mountains were maybe a mile away, the sun had risen, reached its zenith, and begun to fall once more. The tip of the very tallest of the range, Caden's Peak, was beginning to turn red with the sunset when the marching began to slow.

Sam's brow furrowed in confusion. It wasn't time to slow down yet, they still had a decent amount of land to cover. The soldiers all began to murmur, and Xavier's eye met Sam's.

As the whispering grew louder, the regiment halted altogether. Different words made their way to Sam and Xavier, who were near the back of the confused mass.

"It happened again!"

"How did they kn-…?"

"It's the Liberator!"

"…evacuating."

Relief began to flood Sam's senses, and it was mere moments before Xavier turned to grin at him wildly. The Liberator had done it again!

Months ago, Sam had told Lina about how he'd heard stories of a random person going to the villages to warn them of the imminent attack so they could leave. A do-gooder no one knew, but who had a history of helping all of the Three Kingdoms whenever he or she could.

Sam couldn't stop the smile from coming to his face. Now, his regiment would not have to travel to Mineraltir! The town was empty! He would not have to defend himself today, much less possibly have to kill any innocents.

It was a toss-up how much of the regiment felt the same happiness Sam and Xavier did. Maybe a third of the men were grumbling with scowls on their faces. These were what was left of King Adam's volunteers at the beginning of the war. It was easy to see who had volunteered and who had been drafted. The soldiers of the draft couldn't help but cheer.

A black-haired soldier in front of Xavier turned to them ecstatically, his young face dramatized by the gap between his front teeth. "Can you believe it? What kind of person would help all of Nerahdis?"

Xavier laughed and rubbed his nose with his thumb. "I don't care. Whoever this guy or gal is, we like 'em!"

Once the soldiers heard a lot of angry shouting, they rapidly straightened back into their perfect lines and silence. Xavier stifled a giggle, trying and failing to maintain his composure.

They continued trekking as the sun continued to descend. Sam wondered why for a brief moment, then figured that the generals didn't want them sitting around doing nothing. The last mile or two before the base of Caden's Peak went fast, and Sam felt thrilled at the thought of finally stopping for the night. His legs were tight and sore while the rest of him ached to strip off all the armor and dive into the nearest river to soak. However, Sam's exhausted thoughts of how amazing cool water would feel came screeching to a halt as he realized that the regiment wasn't stopping.

What was happening? They should have stopped by now. The safe distance from the mountains' rocky slopes came and went, yet the soldiers continued to march. Other confused glances were exchanged by the men in front of him, but Sam's thoughts began to whirl a million miles per hour, trying not to panic.

They were supposed to set up camp outside of the mountains, that was where the Ranguvariians would help them escape. If they traveled into the mountains, no magic would work. Not only would the Ranguvariians be unable to help, but Sam and Xavier wouldn't have the power they needed to get away!

An announcement began to float back amongst the men, and while Sam only got bits and pieces of it, it generally went something like this: Due to Tranini being compromised, the general decided to march on through the mountains for a direct assault on Kaiya, the Auklian capital. The general wasn't going to give the Liberator any time to react. They would be marching through the entire night.

Sam and Xavier eyed each other. Now what?

As soon as he stepped foot onto the mountain's rock, Sam felt his magic stripped from him. Suddenly, the mere soreness in his legs transformed into pain that seared with each step. Xavier, too, began to breathe deeper and harder, and his red brow furrowed as he pulled his helmet down over his eyes.

Sam hadn't made many trips outside of Lunaka as part of his Kidek duties. Most Rounans came to him aside from the rare circumstance. Sam had forgotten what it felt like to be…well, normal. Bereft of the magic he wasn't accustomed to being without.

What would happen now? All the Ranguvariians would know was that Xavier had disappeared off the face of Nerahdis since no one could sense Sam in the first place, except for maybe Lina because of their bond.

An unknown amount of time went by as Sam mulled this around in his head and struggled to put each foot in front of the other. At some point, he came to the conclusion that he had no interest whatsoever in marching, swords blazing, into the heart of Auklia. That was a death mission, and Sam had every intention of seeing his wife and son again.

It wasn't more than a few hours before many of the men around them were groaning from exertion. Night had fallen, covering the mountains in a blackness kept at bay by only a few torches toward the front and one at the back of the mass.

The falling temperatures made Sam suddenly thankful for his armor that he had wanted nothing more than to pitch earlier that afternoon. Spring was so testy as far as warm afternoons and freezing nights. He tried to stay focused the best he could in the cold as his legs began to not feel anything at all. However, when the rocky path slowly turned into snow, it felt like their situation couldn't possibly get any worse.

In his misery, Sam turned his thoughts to home. At home, the prairie grass would be growing tall and green. He should be getting ready to burn it away from their fields to keep the soil from being overrun, almost like how the soldiers kept back the Mineraltins or Auklians. He should be calculating how much seed they would buy and where he should plant it all. Not planting bodies like he was now.

He should be home with his wife, when their first anniversary was several weeks ago, not half a kingdom away. Home with his son, who was surely growing as fast as the prairie grass as he approached being two seasons old in Late Spring. Sam hopelessly wished that he had never left the Rounan compound that fateful day when he was drafted.

As the soldiers crunched along in the snow, the regimental lines began to fade away. The icy trail narrowed to where only a few men could walk by each other at a time, and those with more energy began to push forward to the front of the mass. Likewise, those who were absolutely exhausted began to fall behind to create a separate group at the pack's rear. As Sam analyzed the sleepy, pain-filled people that occasionally fell behind him to walk at a slower pace, an idea occurred to him.

Sam began to shorten his steps, let his neck droop, and his arms fall forward. He let himself huff and puff without shame. Xavier didn't notice any difference until Sam slowly fell back, separating from the pack of young soldiers with energy to spare. The prince followed suit, his clever, rat-like grin flashing barely as he realized what was happening.

Another hour went by as the two men tried to make their falling behind look as inconspicuous as possible. Soon enough, they were walking side by side with the last man with the torch, lighting the back of the regiment's way. If they waited for just the right moment, they could beat it like a bat out of daylight and have a pretty good shot at getting away.

Xavier was becoming restless, sauntering about from side to side. Sam didn't dare open his mouth to tell him to be patient. The man with the torch could likely see less than anybody else at the moment with the drastic blackness all around them. If they were patient, it would work.

Sam looked ahead at the narrowing mountain path. They were getting pretty high up, the snow becoming deeper and deeper as it came up to their mid-shins now. But Sam was waiting for something specific. It was another thirty minutes before he found what he was looking for. A large rock sat right next to the path that the soldiers followed. The soldiers could only walk two by two now, one by one in some places, so once the line of Lunakan men reached the rock, it was large enough to hide them from view.

If they only waited a few moments more, most of the men would be beyond the rock and there'd be hardly any possible witnesses to the desertion about to take place. Sam swallowed hard, trying to ready his numbing legs to be as agile as possible in all this snow. Once they began, there was no stopping. Otherwise, it would awaken the soldier with the torch who could barely keep his eyes open as he stumbled ever forward.

When all but five soldiers had turned past the big rock, each one disappearing from view as they did, Sam and Xavier slowed even further. The man with the torch passed them without even realizing it, going beyond the rock as the two deserters stopped in their tracks. Soon, they were enveloped in complete darkness as the torch meandered farther and farther away.

A huge smile broke across Sam's face. He shoved a hand over his mouth to keep from making a noise. He couldn't see Xavier beside him, but he could feel the smugness radiating off of him. They were free! It wasn't until the torch disappeared altogether that the two dared to even move.

Sam heard the noise of snow being kicked. "Look at that! We didn't need those pointy-eared gremlins' help after all! It's a wonder more soldiers don't desert if it's that easy."

Groaning, Sam fell into a heap at the base of the rock, his legs burning now that they finally didn't have to bear his weight. "It wasn't that easy. Any number of things could have gone wrong!"

"Well, they didn't. Lucky us." Sam could hear the smile in Xavier's voice. "Now, if only I had my magic, I could light a way down this cursed mountain for us."

"We better just stay here until the sun comes up," Sam grumbled. "No use falling off the mountain in the dark. I can't even see my hand in front of my face!"

"You have a point." Xavier slouched to the ground, making what felt like an inordinate amount of noise as he contoured the snow into something comfortable.

A few seconds of silence went by as Sam bundled his cloak around his stiff armor, trying to get warm. It became obvious rapidly that Xavier was one of those people who couldn't handle quiet.

"So. I haven't gotten to really talk to you until now. You okay and stuff?"

Trying not to come across as irked, Sam responded, "Yeah. Much better now that I can go home."

"Good. Glad I could help."

Sam was grateful that Xavier had no way of viewing the expression that crossed his face.

"Well, this seems like as good of a time as any. I've gotta tell ya something and you're probably not going to like it."

Sam was so caught off guard that his impatience and frustration melted away. What could Xavier possibly need to tell him? However, once Xavier began, nothing could have prepared him for the information he was about to impart.

Xavier told Sam everything. Not one detail was spared from the meeting that Lina went to last season, leaving him home alone until he made his trip to Lun that he never returned from. Sam's mind struggled to comprehend everything Xavier told him.

There was such a thing as an Archimage. It was a position above the Three Kings, and apparently, his name was Dathian and he was a jerk according to Xavier. This man had a dream that there wouldn't be any Allyens after Lina and her twin brother.

Sam really got lost here, his knowledge of magic only so good beyond his Rounan heritage, but he was told this was devastating. If this happened, Lina would lose her magic because it wouldn't be regenerated with the birth of a new Allyen.

Sam's heart sank into the pit of his stomach when he realized the significance of this. Rhydin would win. Without the Allyens, the Royals and even the Rounans combined wouldn't be powerful enough to stop Rhydin. If they would even talk to each other. This could not happen.

Sam groped for Xavier's shoulder in the dark until he found it. "Why? How could this happen? Why won't there be another Allyen after Lina and her brother?"

He could hear a sigh. "That's the worst part, Sam, and I hate to be the one to tell you. But, it's because you're a Rounan. Your magic won't allow any other magic to be born of it. All of your kids'll always be Rounans. Her brother Evan married one, too. There's no way."

It was like someone slapped Sam across the face. It was his fault. He was a Rounan, he had married the Allyen, and now all of her children would be Rounans, too. The Allyen magic wouldn't be regenerated and Rhydin would win. How could he have known? What could he do now?

Sam began to think heartbreaking thoughts. Lina would never agree to a divorce. He needed to get up and catch up with the regiment. He'd let the next enemy he came face to face with kill him if it meant Lina could find someone else, have an Allyen child, and defeat Rhy-...

"But."

"B-But?" Sam stammered, broken out of his thoughts abruptly.

"The Archimage and the head honcho of the Ranguvariians think they found another way," Xavier said slowly, "They said they could possibly transfer the Allyen magic to a newborn with the capability for Gornish magic. A Royal newborn."

Sam's head spun. How was this even possible? It didn't align with any notion of magic he ever knew. Although, he didn't understand Gornish magic that well anyway. His mind stumbled to new thoughts. What Royal in Nerahdis would give up their newborn? Sam thought of Kylar and shivered. He wasn't sure he could.

Xavier reached along Sam's arm to touch his shoulder now, still unable to see anything. "Look, it's really confusing and complicated, but it'll be okay. We need to fix what happened, but it'll be worth it. You *need* to stay with Lina. That's why I came after you. Nobody else cared. Besides, I think I may have a solution."

"What do you mean? How could you possibly solve this?" Sam's frustration with himself seeped into his words. How could he have been so stupid to marry the Allyen? He wished he could see Xavier's expression to measure his thoughts.

The Mineraltin prince took a deep breath. "Mira's with child. She thinks I don't know. I'd have to be blind not to know."

Sam's heart thundered to a stop. "And you're willing to give your child up?"

The hand grew tighter on Sam's shoulder.

"Honestly, I wouldn't say willing," Xavier paused, and cleared his throat, "But as a future king, I must be, and I wish I was more so. Being for the greater good and all. But, there's no point in making a big deal out of a firstborn if there's no kingdom left for the child to inherit. And I know Lina would raise it like her own. If my child is taken, I want her to take it. You both to take it. Not Evan. Not a stranger. It will be worth it if it results in Rhydin's destruction."

Sam shook his head slightly, struggling hard to get his thoughts straight. He had just gotten used to the idea of having one child, Kylar, and now he was doing the impossible task of imagining having another so soon that was not his own. He hesitated before speaking. "You should decide this with Mira.

Not me. But I would protect that child as if it was Kylar."

He felt Xavier move, but no words came.

A few moments of silence stretched on, and it became promptly uncomfortable. Sam grasped at the first question that popped into his head. He asked, confusedly, the question that had been on his mind since the first day Xavier showed up, "So, why did you come after me? If everybody else didn't care, why did you come?"

"Oh. Well, I think it's stupid that they're mad at you just because you're a Rounan," Xavier responded as if the prior conversation had never taken place. "In my head, you're just as important as Lina. The Royals and the Allyens may be the ones to defeat Rhydin, but it's your marriage to Lina that's going to get rid of all this stupid strife between the Gornish and the Rounans. Can't have the kingdoms tearing each other apart even after Rhydin's gone."

Sam couldn't help but feel awed. He had never thought of it that way before. He had just accepted that Lina was more important to the cause than he was, and he was happy to be able to help her whenever he could, like in the battle with Duunzer.

He absolutely *hated* it that she had moved all the way to the middle of nowhere to be with him and his people were so ugly to her because she was Gornish. He'd never had a chance to say anything before he was drafted, always hoping that it would sort itself out.

Sam vowed right then and there that when he returned to the compound, he would put it right. He would gather them all together and fix it. Lina's job was to defeat Rhydin. His would be to defeat the hatred and discrimination that kept Gornish from Rounan. Sam felt invigorated with his new sense of duty.

A sudden thought occurred to him. "Xavier, how did you persuade the Royals and the Archimage to let you come after me?"

"Uh, well. I kind of just left."

"Without telling *anyone*?"

"Well, I did leave a note, but... Nope. Has never worked for me in the past."

Sam sighed loudly and said something he thought he'd never say. "You know, Xavier, I promise I appreciate it, but you *really* need to work on your communication skills if you're going to be king. You should have at least told Mira!"

"Well, you can't change the past."

Sam rolled his eyes. After a couple minutes, he was about to say something else when he detected a low snoring sound. Sam chuckled to himself quietly and shrugged down into a little hole by his rock to get more comfortable.

He couldn't believe everything he had learned in such a short time, and as he mulled everything over in his head to make sure he understood it all, Lina came to his thoughts as she always did right before sleep. She had gone through all of this by herself. How had she responded when she figured out it was because she had married a Rounan that the magic wouldn't regenerate?

Sam had only considered her being upset for his disappearance. Now, they were in a whole new playing field. He needed to get back to her soon. They needed to talk about all of this so they could be on the same page again. Everything felt wrong with the world when they weren't. Plus, this whole idea of Xavier and Mira giving up their newborn? It was hard to wrap his mind around.

Sam slept lightly on and off through the rest of the night hours. The rock against his back was hard, the snow beneath him was cold, and the thoughts in his mind would be unsettled until he saw Lina again. They were high enough in the mountains that Sam had a front row seat for the sunrise. It began as only a faint glow to the east where Sam knew the island of Caark to be but soon spread its rainbow of colors upward and outward.

He watched as the light slowly extended across the entire Kingdom of Lunaka. It crossed the canyon where Soläna lay, the town of his and Lina's youth. It ambled over Spenser's Lake, the large body of freshwater named after Lunaka's first king. Sam felt his skin prickle as the light brought a little warmth back into him.

Slowly, Sam began to realize that the mountainside wasn't completely silent anymore. The quietest of noises were reaching his ears from far, far away. Sam delivered a prompt elbow into Xavier's ribs, whom he could now see in the breaking dawn.

"Wha-...?"

"Shh!" Sam hissed, still listening.

The noises were becoming louder and louder. Ice slid down Sam's spine as he recognized the sounds of clashing swords and men's yells, eerily familiar now after all of the battles he had fought. Sam began to wonder if the regiment they left only hours ago had run into an enemy troop.

The clangs grew in intensity, echoing off of each of the snowy mountainsides in succession, building and building and building upon one another. Sam could suddenly feel the noise in his feet. He stood quickly with Xavier looking all around for this battle. Their ears rang with the now deafening sounds, and the mountain began to vibrate with the furious cacophony of what seemed now to be the whole of all three armies.

Crack!

Sam looked up in horror to the source of the new blast, not from the battle below but from nature itself. The mountain had shed its snowy skin, and the excess was tumbling down and down over itself right toward them. It consumed everything left and right. Trees were uprooted, rocks of various sizes flung about or pulled along for the ride, leaving the bare, decimated face of Caden's Peak behind its fury.

With a rush of adrenaline, Sam pushed toward the ground with one of his hands, willing his magic to help him with a gigantic leap away. Nothing happened. They were still in the mountains. Magic was useless.

Sam and Xavier began to sprint wildly down the mountain away from the rumbling avalanche, the narrow path ahead of them beginning to disappear as smaller bits of snow caught up with them and sped right by. The thunderous growl of the falling snow pushed out every thought in Sam's head as he suddenly found himself in a shadow. He looked up one last time to see the crest of an icy wave looming over him before his feet were picked up off the ground.

Xavier tried to reach for him, but Sam only saw Lina in his terror. Her tiny form extending out for help, her brown hair flung about by the intense wind of the displaced snow. Sam flung himself toward her, his fingers passing just through hers.

As he was pulled away, Lina turned back into Xavier being washed far away. Before he lost consciousness, Sam found himself swept up by the tumultuous snow, hammered by ice and all the debris it carried with it.

CHAPTER EIGHT

When Sam regained consciousness, the sun had moved a few hours' worth further west. His vision took forever to clear, definitely a byproduct of his splitting headache.

When he tried to move, not only did every muscle moan in pain, but he rapidly discovered that he couldn't. Most of his body was sandwiched in layers of snow that felt more like stone. His arms were pinned to his sides, and he could feel other debris poking him in various places. Panic arose as he wildly wiggled back and forth. Nothing would budge.

Sam looked around, scanning the desolate white landscape that did nothing but reflect the sun with its crystalline flakes as if it hadn't been a deathly disaster mere hours ago. His eyes landed on a few things that weren't reflecting sunlight: uprooted trees, large rocks, and other unrecognizable items.

When he looked up, he discovered that he was underneath several feet of snow and debris. Sam thanked his lucky stars that somehow his head had managed to remain unburied. He started scanning the landscape once more, desperately hoping that Xavier wasn't miles beneath him, and suddenly spotted a dash of red from underneath one of the boulders he had already looked over once. It was Xavier!

As far as what Sam could see from several feet away, he was pinned more than Sam was. While most of Xavier's body was covered in feet of snow and debris like Sam, the massive rock that had nearly hidden him completely was resting directly on top of his arm. Xavier's face was so white that it blended right in with the snow. Sam marveled at how narrowly Xavier had avoided the boulder being on top of his head or that he could reach air at all. They could have died.

"Xavier!" Sam called, his voice hoarse from his tight predicament. "*Xavier!*"

No response.

Sam tried very hard not to panic. But it was no use. What was he going to do? He was the only one conscious, and he had no magic to lift all this snow off!

He took stock of all his limbs. He could move his feet ever so lightly, but that didn't help with his arms pinned to him like chicken wings. If he could just get his arms free, he could probably pull himself loose. He rocked himself back and forth within his solid, snow coffin, hoping it would be enough to shift *something*.

Time went by. Sam didn't know how much anymore as he never took the time to check the sun. Every fiber of his body went into wiggling around in his little hole. Every minute he remained in his icy tomb was another minute closer to death of cold. Or, losing his feet to frostbite. Neither of which was particularly appealing.

Sam's mind flooded with images, trying to keep him awake. His parents when they were still alive. When he first met Lina. The triumphant look on her face when she defeated

Duunzer, and the hard hug she'd given him when he asked her to be his wife. The birth of their son.

For the first time, Sam wished the Liberator hadn't interfered with the army's plans. Then, maybe he would be safe and warm at home with his family. But, Sam wasn't dying here. There was no way he was going to allow himself to die here, or Xavier for that matter. So, he kept up the wiggling and rocking for an untold amount of time. Xavier never moved once, and it drove Sam faster to get out and help him.

As the sun rose higher, Sam noticed that the snow was beginning to melt ever so slightly, and it soon helped him to accomplish one or two inches of clearance on either side of his shoulders. It was eroded away by his constant moving and shifting, crunching the snow tighter and tighter to allow more space. In a sudden flash of hope, Sam reached with his free feet to find something to push on, and sure enough, he found the tiniest of footholds.

The sun rose slowly as Sam continued to work his way out of what might have been his snowy grave. He pushed on his foothold until he couldn't feel it anymore, but his elbows weren't quite clear of the snowy, debris-filled coffin. Sam tried to collapse his arms and his muscles, anything at all to make them thinner, and he reached forward with all of the strength he had left.

In a gush of melting snow and a scrape of skin, Sam found his arms free. It was only seconds before he pushed himself out of his hole. His entire body began to ache as blood was allowed back into various places that had been without for far too long. Yet, even that pain couldn't deny him the sweet sense of freedom.

Sam got his breath back for the first time in forever, and he began to feel hopeful that he would see Lina tonight. Sam carefully picked his way across the loose, dangerous snow toward the red-haired prince. His heart fell when he got a better look at him.

The Mineraltin man was still in the exact same position, his right arm and most of the right side of his chest underneath the gargantuan rock that had been pried loose by the avalanche. Xavier's face was pale, his eyes squeezed shut in pain and a few beads of sweat lingering on his brow. He wasn't completely unconscious, otherwise his face would be relaxed, Sam thought to himself.

As Sam limped on sore legs around the huge boulder, his breath caught at the sight of Xavier's hand sticking out from the other side. It was a sickening shade of purple. Sam couldn't even imagine what his crushed arm might look like. If something wasn't done soon, it could be too far gone to save. Sam leapt into action, beginning to push on the boulder.

Xavier let out a deafening bellow, and the rock didn't budge. He abruptly looked up at Sam with blue daggers. "What? You couldn't just let me die in peace?"

Sam groaned, "I'm trying to save you! Lina would murder me if I let you die. Not to mention Princess Mira!"

The pale man rolled his eyes. "I assure you, death is far less painful."

Sam readied himself to give the boulder another go, if only it would shut the redhead up.

A bugle sounded.

He froze, his blood turning to ice. That sound had become a noise of his nightmares. Always announcing bloodshed.

Sam promptly put his back to the rock, trying to hide and see what was going on at the same time. There was nothing to the east where Lunaka lay. Dread filled Sam as he dared looking to the west.

There was a green blot coming toward them, carefully skirting around the mountain's face on the treacherous snow. Sam's heart thundered in his chest. He could make out emerald green banners now, held by soldiers in thick, brown and green canvas uniforms. They were coming straight toward them.

Mineraltins.

Sam's breath hitched as he put his entire body into it this time. Xavier saw them, too. Sam bit down into his lip so hard that blood began to seep from it. Yet, the rock remained.

"You need to go," Xavier choked out, his eyes never leaving the approaching green.

"I'm not leaving you!" Sam hissed, remembering how Xavier was wanted dead or alive by Queen Jasmine of Mineraltir, his step-mother. "I'm going to get you-…"

"No, you're not! Once they recognize me, it's all over." The prince rested his cheek on the icy ground. "Now, quit being a goody-two-shoes, and *git*! You're more important than I am, remember?"

Sam was torn. He couldn't leave Xavier to this fate! Jasmine would likely kill him! As the Mineraltin troop approached, he found himself panicking. If they figured out he was a Rounan, much less the Kidek, he would be doomed, too.

All Sam could think of was Lina and Kylar. Did he run to protect them or stay to protect Xavier? Then again, what help would it be if Sam was captured, too? If he ran for it, he could bring back help if it wasn't too late.

In a split second, Sam made a decision he would regret for the rest of his life.

He ran.

LATER THAT NIGHT

After Rachel, Luke, and James transported Evan and I to the southwestern part of the kingdom, no words were spoken. The mountains were a million times bigger than they had just been, going from a vague border on the horizon to fierce, rocky walls whose peaks I could no longer see.

This was as far as the Owenses could get us since while they could still use magic, they couldn't transport through the magic-less boundary. The sun's light was fading fast, so speechlessly, the five of us moved into the mountains.

Even though I had experienced it before, I couldn't quite prepare myself for the feeling of losing my magic. It was like quicksand sucking at my ankles, ropes reaching up to grab hold of my wrists, all pulling me down under the weight of my own body. It seemed like I felt it more this time compared to the last time when arriving at the Archimage Palace.

Now, I had been depending on my magic for nearly two years rather than just a few seasons like the first time I crossed the mountains into Mineraltir with Luke. That was when we were trying to figure out if Xavier was on our side or not, before Duunzer. Now, we entered to find him once more, and just as important, Sam. Dead or alive.

I noticed Evan's expression of fatigue out of the corner of my eye. His eyes grew dark with circles underneath them, his shoulders slumping as his violin dipped a couple of inches. He never went anywhere without it, I gathered.

I wanted to reach out to him. To help him. But, I held myself back, unsure of how he would accept it. This brother of mine was still a stranger, a stranger who hated me because of Keera's death. Yet, he was here with me to search for my husband, so that was a start.

Rachel and her brothers halted before us, none of them showing any sort of signs of exhaustion. Rachel cleared her throat. "Here comes the hard part. Between you two and the three of us, we need to open up a channel of magic in order to find Xavier and Sam."

"How?" Evan huffed, "I can barely keep my head up in these mountains without my magic, how do you expect us to be able to sense someone?"

There was a twinkle in Rachel's eye as she spoke, turning to me. "Lina, it's time for you to discover what you've always wanted to know."

I felt myself perk up. I always had questions, to which was she referring?

"We're going to put the Allyen locket back together for the first time in over twenty years," the tall red-haired woman said, her joy evident as each word registered to my ears. Ever since we became friends, even before I discovered that I was an Allyen, she had watched me try and fail to open my mysterious heirloom of a locket.

My excitement rose as I immediately pulled my locket out of my tunic. It still hung from the strong, silver chain that Sam had given me at the Winter Ball before we were married, and its metal was always warm, whether it was against my flesh or not. I cupped it in my hands as I impatiently waited for further instruction, trying not to appear like a child on their birthday.

Evan's expression was blank, but there was no denying the slim presence of curiosity upon it. He reached up to his neck to pull on a thick, leather cord, which in turn produced a small disc from his tunic.

It was like thin glass although far more durable because it didn't look fragile at all. It was about the same size as my locket, but as thin as a hefty piece of parchment. The same circular swirl design that decorated my locket was imprinted upon the transparent disc, only without the amber jewels.

My eyes grew wide as a cat's. I never once imagined that the other half of my locket would look like that after learning of its existence a couple years ago. In order to keep Evan and I safe from Rhydin and his Followers, I read in Grandma's journal that we were separated along with the two halves of the locket so that our presences would be weaker.

Plus, it made the locket harder for Rhydin to obtain and reunite seeing as I grew up in Lunaka and Evan in Auklia, both of us surrounded by Ranguvariian soldiers sworn to protect us. The locket had not been put together since the day we were born.

Suddenly, the lime green mark on Rachel's pale cheek sparkled in the failing light. A grin flickered to her lips as her eyes turned upward. Above us were two shining orbs that became incrementally larger as they approached, like stars that had left the heavens in order to visit Nerahdis for a while.

As they grew closer, I recognized the familiar shape and colors of the Ranguvariian flying spell; wings of purple, orange, and green shards. Only moments later, two massive bodies hit the earth, crouching forward as their boots crunched into the hard rock of the mountains. I felt the blood drain from my face as the two beings straightened after their landing, revealing heights of well over six feet. More like seven.

Ragged breaths scraped by my lips as my eyes absorbed the two creatures. Leathery skin, high cheekbones, large, pointed ears like James's. Pupils narrowed to slits among pools of color that changed from a dark indigo to a light pink just as Luke's eyes changed color with his mood. They wore clothes like none I'd ever seen before; thick, coarse cloth with multiple layers, often with a red stripe around the border as well as a black, angular pattern.

Just as I was beginning to absorb the fact that these two creatures were full-blooded Ranguvariians just like Clariion Arii, one of them spoke. A voice that reminded me of a teenage boy in puberty resounded, "Hello, people! Nice to be together again."

James chuckled as the thinner, younger Ranguvariian talked, then added, "It's good to see you too, Bartholomiiu!"

I noticed Evan grin out of the corner of my eye, and I felt confused until I remembered that these two were his usual protectors. The other Ranguvariian, who was taller with legs like two tree trunks and dressed mostly in yellow, did not speak but moved to Rachel.

I recognized her giddy smile on her face, and when the two took hands, the Ranguvariian's eyes seeped into a deep magenta. The green pinwheel shape on Rachel's cheek was also printed on the Ranguvariian's hand.

A smile cracked my face as I remembered Rachel's lesson on *matrii*, the mark that every Ranguvariian male was born with on his hand, which was then copied to his wife's cheek the day they were married. This was Rachel's husband.

Rachel turned to the group and said, "Lina, this is Jaspen. He is my husband, as you humans call it."

After speaking, she turned to Jaspen expectantly, but his suntanned face remained content and stoic. She elbowed him slightly, to which he responded in a deep, guttural voice, "Meet you nice, Linaria."

"You'll have to forgive him, his Nerahdian isn't the greatest." Rachel giggled, "But he'll never get better if he doesn't practice!" She shot him a look, but a skeptical expression remained on Jaspen's face.

Evan chuckled a bit, "He couldn't speak a lick of it when he became my guardian. The fact that he can speak it at all is a feat, but he gets better all the time."

A smirk graced Jaspen's round face, his eyes becoming as pink as a rose. "*Dey, pmar alten miiucalou chet nten?*"

Evan and I's faces fell, the beautiful, lilting words falling on deaf ears.

"I say, 'yes, but this understand, can you?'" Jaspen beamed as he touched his long brown hair. "Cannot understand Ranguvariian, you. Then better learner, I."

Bartholomiiu gave out a gigantic laugh, clapping his hands and slapping his knee. "Good one, Jaspen!"

"Alright, alright, don't make fun of the humans anymore," Luke chimed in, although James and Bartholomiiu were still off in their little corner cackling their heads off. "Let's get this show on the road, we're going to have to search in pitch black if we're not fast!"

"You still haven't told me how this will be possible!" Evan whined as the Ranguvariians began to move around.

"Our magic is viable in the mountains. We're the only beings in Nerahdis whose magic is aside from Rhydin," Luke said as he oriented himself to create a circle with the others, "The problem is that without magic, Xavier doesn't have a presence. That's why we can't find him or Sam. Lina has a connection to Sam that is more powerful than magic, so we just have to hope that the combined power of the locket will be enough to amplify that connection."

Evan turned to me, a look of disbelief etched onto his worn face.

When I looked back to the five Ranguvariians, they had all

gathered around us now. They each in turn began to hum and activated their flying spell, their brilliant, multi-colored wings springing from their backs. The shining shards folded forward, creating a protective barrier around Evan and I.

Rachel spoke up, "We are going to surround you with our magic to see if we can help negate the mountains' influence. Go ahead and combine the locket halves."

As the two of us began to take our respective halves off, Luke raised his voice sharply, "No, leave them on! It only works if you're wearing them. You two have the magic, the locket doesn't."

Anxiety squeezed my heart as Evan groaned. He took my locket with as much length of chain as was available, inspected the ridges that I had clawed at for years trying in vain to open it, then took his transparent disc in hand.

Easily, he aligned the thin circle with the middle of the ridges, sliding it inside perfectly. All this time, I had been trying to open something that was not designed to open. Only put together.

The locket began to radiate heat, suspended in mid-air on its chain and cord from our two necks. Its light pulsed brightly, whole once more. Exhilarated, I turned my head to share this moment with Rachel. But, at the sight of her strained face and those of her brothers, husband, and friend, I realized that we needed to hurry.

Sam entered my mind. I imagined what his presence had always been to me in the past. It smelled like Lunakan soil, that earthy smell that cannot be described beyond dirt freshly tilled to be made ready for seeds. His presence washed security and warmth over me, just like normal. I wanted to cry the feeling was so powerful and so missed.

Soon, my imagination fell back, and I realized that I really *was* sensing Sam's presence. But, it was farther away than I'd ever been able to sense him before. Oh, so far away.

A golden beam shot forth from the large amber jewel in the center of the Allyen locket, traipsing over the rocks, the Ranguvariian circle, and up the mountain path out of view. As it stretched further and further, I could physically feel the sapping of my energy. Using magic in the mountains was coming with a price.

Seconds later, I was scooped up into a rock-hard arm before being launched into the sky. Evan was across from me in the other arm as the locket remained united, but there was no mistaking the absolute terror in his eyes. He may have seen a real Ranguvariian before me, but it appeared that I got the first flight back before the battle with Duunzer.

Jaspen flew as fast as he could in the direction of the light trail, the two of us clutched tightly to him as the wind roared around us. As the minutes ticked on, my eyes grew heavier and heavier. The spell was taking everything I had to maintain even for just a few moments. When I glanced at Evan, his brow was furrowed in concentration as he struggled to keep it going.

To my dismay, even with all our effort, the path began to fade. With the sun's disappearance beyond the horizon, we were able to follow it even after it became nothing more than a trace. The world was completely dark, the mountains only standing shadows, but the light kept leading us on. Sam was at the end of that light, I told myself as my limbs went numb. Sam would be there. I would see him again.

As the light truly vanished, Jaspen took us back down to the mountain, the others landing behind us. In an effort to keep moving where we thought the trail went, we were quiet, hoping to stumble across them at any moment.

Evan and I had to be braced between our Ranguvariian protectors now, absolutely nothing left but our fierce resolve. I tried not to become pessimistic since we were unable to see how far the light still had to go to find Sam before it disappeared. Surely, he was just around the next boulder. Or the next one.

The Owenses found a lantern in one of their sacks and lit it. An hour went by. Two. My confidence dwindled with the tick of the clock. It didn't work. It led us the wrong way. Or, it was miles further and the trail didn't last long enough. I wasn't strong enough for it to last long enough.

I asked Rachel if we could do it again, but there was no way. We had used far too much magic. A magic that was now in even more danger of running out unless we found a child who could regenerate it.

My eyes had been darting all over everything the lantern's light touched but soon became focused on the ground. The hard earth slowly turned into crunchy snow. Numbly, I put one foot in front of the other until I couldn't feel them at all. Rachel hunched forward wordlessly so I could crawl onto her back since I was a good two feet shorter than she was.

While he didn't breathe a word, Evan remained glued to my side. Regardless of our differences and our arguments, there was no mistaking the twin bond between us.

Later in the night, or it could have been morning for all I knew, we came across an area that appeared to have been wiped out by an avalanche. Our group stopped, and at someone's suggestion, we decided to stick around, make camp, and do some searching for a while.

As Rachel let me down and started a small campfire, I tried not to panic at the amount of fatigue I felt. No vestige of strength was left in my body, to the point where my limbs were useless to me and I collapsed to the ground. Evan sat opposite from me, keeping his distance but still close. He was so weary that his eyes could hardly stay open, his arms limp at his sides.

My thoughts turned to dismay. What if Sam *was* here, but he was buried in the debris? I couldn't bear that thought. What if he had gotten captured? What if he was still miles away where we could never catch up with him? My mind couldn't even begin to think of returning home without him.

Just moving my tongue to wet my lips was agonizing. My voice was hoarse. "Thank you."

Evan's head twitched, unable to turn any farther toward me. "We haven't found him yet."

"I know. But you put yourself through this torture to help me. So, thank you," I mumbled as my eyes closed, which kept me from seeing the lightening of Evan's expression.

Even as my body screamed in exhaustion, I opened my eyes once more to stare at the fire, trying to banish the negative thoughts in my mind. I probably stared at it for a little less than an hour. Another vague light was rising to the east.

As that light became stronger, my eyes noticed something different about one of the piles of rocks between me and the campfire. With the very last of my strength, I slowly moved my aching arm out towards it. My unfeeling fingers trembled over the gravel, like wooden blocks trying to do needlework.

I was sure my eyes were deceiving me when I knocked two stones of the way and a swatch of torn, navy fabric caught the light of the dawn. My exhausted mind thought nothing of it until my fingers touched it, pulling it further out from underneath the snowy gravel. Dirty, golden stars appeared, as well as the deep purple border that was nearly nonexistent, it was so torn. My breath hitched in my throat.

"What is it?" Evan moaned. He keeled over to lay in the snow.

I struggled to wet my mouth enough to speak, and a tear traced its way down my cheek. I barely whispered before I lost consciousness against my will, "Sam's bandana."

CHAPTER NINE

———⟨⟩———

I t was quiet. Too quiet.

The air in Auklia was different than in Lunaka. It was heavy and very humid. Sometimes, Frederick had discovered, it felt as if one were swimming instead of walking. It also always smelled of fish, which made him grateful that Lunaka did not have a fish industry. However, this was not on his mind as he slowly realized that the humid, fish-reeking air was now silent.

He and King Daniel had traveled to the Auklian frontline northwest of Kaiya, the capital, to rouse the troops. Morale was low because no end to the war was in sight, but more important, the people were losing their confidence in their ruler.

Vicious rumors were still circulating about Daniel's incompetence in leading due to the fact that the people believed he wasn't being proactive. He wasn't offensively attacking the other kingdoms or investigating them to discover who was to blame for Duunzer.

The citizens of Auklia were livid, still grieving over their lost grandparents and infants. To make things worse, Queen Lily was not speaking to Daniel, endlessly mourning the loss of their own child. Frederick was still needed in Auklia more than ever. Daniel was his ally against Rhydin, and even though King Adam, Frederick's father, had labeled his son as a traitor for helping Auklia, Frederick knew that he could not sacrifice his friendship with Daniel.

The only positive rumors going around were more stories about this "Liberator" that Frederick was becoming more familiar with. More and more often, all three armies were finding their targets abandoned, rendering them useless. All thanks to the efforts of the Liberator to warn the villages before the attacks came. He was being praised as a hero of all of Nerahdis. Frederick wasn't sure what to think of that, but that wasn't what felt off this morning.

The last few days, the oppressive air had been filled with the sounds of soldiers chatting, weapons being sharpened, and armor being repaired in order to be always ready for the next round of attack. They were the first line of defense against any outsiders. Frederick wished the people could see that Daniel was at least protecting them from invaders, even if they never stepped foot off Auklian soil. But now, Frederick's sweaty skin crawled in the noiseless void.

He leaped off his cot, nearly tripping in the mosquito netting in the process since he always forgot it was there. Grabbing his tunic, the Lunakan prince dashed to the front of the tent.

Outside, King Daniel stood motionless in his nightshirt decorated with the Auklian crest, a gold and blue design with swirling waves. The salty air was still, and the sand was cool underneath Frederick's bare feet. The sun was up, yet the world was silent.

Out beyond their encampment on the very edge of the horizon was light. Two separate lights, and not the light of any sun or star. Both were coming down the mountains in places miles apart.

Frederick's heart fell as the lights grew close enough to be recognized as flickering torches. What perplexed him, however, was the fact that there were two. Normally, it was just one. A small army from Mineraltir or a brigade from Lunaka. Why were there two? Were they going to attack in rounds, or each attack a side of the massive Auklian army?

A young sentry with hair the color of a frog and dressed in the light yellow of a low-rank soldier scurried across the camp and up to Daniel. His voice tremored with panic as he said, "Your Majesty, what are your orders? They're coming!"

Daniel's mouth pressed into a firm line. He was such a pacifist that it even drove Frederick slightly mad. He spoke hesitantly, "Who is approaching? Lunaka or Mineraltir?"

The boy gulped, his red eyes wide with fear. "B-Both, Your Majesty. Our scouts say that it is both *full* armies, Y-Your Majesty."

Frederick's heart dropped. Daniel's hand rushed through his ocean blue hair. This was unheard of. Not only for this war, but in all of Nerahdian history. There had never been a time where all three kingdoms' entire armies engaged with each other like this.

Frederick actually wished for a moment that the Liberator would show himself. He stepped forward, his hand on Daniel's shoulder. He kept his voice firm as he said, "Daniel, I know you prefer to be defensive, but-..."

Daniel whirled to face him, his orange eyes like fire. "Frederick, I understand you are here to help, but I cannot sacrifice my values! We remain here, and if they attack then so be it. I will protect my people, but I will *not* make this war worse than it already is by going out there!"

"I understand that. But this war may become even worse if you are overthrown," Frederick hardly whispered the last word, keeping it from the ears of the page boy. "Your people *need* to see some backbone from you for Nerahdis's sake! Otherwise, even if you keep them safe, they won't recognize it if you stay inside this frontline."

The blue-haired king's shoulders sagged, the weight of his entire kingdom upon them.

"They are traveling through Caden's Plain at this very moment. Let us move to meet them and keep the battle off Auklian soil for once?" The prince pleaded now.

Daniel disappeared back into the massive, crimson tent where the two Royals resided while on the frontline. Frederick thought that all was lost until a few moments later when Daniel reappeared. Now, he was clothed in his full war regalia. Blood-red, silk robes with golden armor strapped on top. Male Auklians only wore warm colors, and this color spectrum transferred to their military as well.

The young sentry in front of them was in buttercup yellow, as low as one could get. Commanding officers were typically a shade of orange, generals wore red, but the darkest red of them all was reserved for only the king. Daniel had not donned this attire for the entire war so far, and Frederick's heart shuddered at the sight of him wearing it now. It reminded him that he was out of place as a foreigner.

Daniel cleared his throat and motioned to the page boy. "Tell the men to ready themselves for battle. We move out to Caden's Plain immediately."

Awe filled the boy's expression as he saluted his king in

the Auklian way, holding his gaze as he crossed his arms over his chest. Then, he ran off throughout the encampment, shouting at the top of his young lungs the orders from the king.

The men went from staring at the approaching enemies in stone cold silence to a ruckus of preparation, dressing in their respective colors and armor, sharpening their weapons until the very last minute.

When the Auklians moved out, Frederick remained behind. He gave advice to Daniel, but he didn't fight his battles. Regardless of the fact that he had been called a traitor by his father, Frederick could not turn his blade against his kingdom.

Yet, he couldn't have known that Daniel and his army were walking into a bloodbath. He couldn't have known that Mineraltir and Lunaka also didn't know that all three armies would clash on this day until they arrived at Caden's Plain. He couldn't possibly have known that the orchestrating figure behind the whole war was manipulating them all like pieces on a chess board.

That figure was currently watching the battle unfold with a smug smirk on his face, waiting for what he had foreseen to occur.

They were gone.

Fearing for our wellbeing, the Ranguvariians never woke Evan or I after we passed out from using too much magic while they searched. When I awoke, the sun already fully risen, I almost could not contain my anger. Seeing the bandana still in my hand released a whirlwind of emotions through me. Terror, anxiety, anger, and depression, each in turn. How could they dare not waking us when my husband could be buried under feet of snow and rock or worse!

Yet, within the hour, we found where they had been after the avalanche. Even without magic, it was easy to tell. The sun revealed everything. Scraps of fabric littered the ground, as if part of their uniforms had been shredded in the slide.

The more obvious sign was the gigantic rock that sat amongst the shreds. It was toppled over, but it was stained with splashes of blood. The crimson soiled the white face of the massive stone, and I gulped at the thought of whatever fate Sam or Xavier met here.

A hand touched my shoulder, which stilled its quaking. I expected to see Rachel, but instead I saw the stoic face of my brother when I glanced to my left. This was the first time he'd ever given me any sort of familial touch, I realized, and I forced myself not to shy away from it.

As the Ranguvariians sniffed around the crime scene, Rachel moved to stand with me. She spoke with long pauses between her words. "If they were dead, their bodies would be here. This blood is evidence of that. But, it doesn't tell us much else."

"Then it's time to do the spell again," I said firmly.

"Lina, the magic-..."

"I don't *care* about the magic!" I whirled to face her, breathing erratically. "If you came all this way to find Jaspen's blood spattered on this stupid rock, what would you do?"

Rachel looked at me grimly, her red hair rustling in the wind. She turned to meet Jaspen's eyes from where he stood several feet away studying the blood on the rock, then she sighed. "I would find him. But I wouldn't jeopardize my people in the process. That's what leaders do. That's what my grandfather would do, and what I would do as his heir."

I stopped raging for a minute to stare at Rachel in a new

light. I'd never known she was the next Clariion, the next leader of the Ranguvariians.

However, I was not feeling even remotely selfless at the moment. My fingers were becoming jittery as my thoughts tumbled over themselves imagining the hundreds of dangerous situations Sam could be in at this very moment. Not to mention my springtime nightmare that was gaining on us with each day, waiting to become reality. I shook my head forcefully, beginning to speak, "But-...!"

"Wait!" Luke hushed me, his pale hand extended in my direction. His serious eyes turned a deep mud color in angst as they skimmed across the surface of the rock several times as if he were reading something.

"What is it?" I gasped, desperate for any sort of sign that he somehow knew Sam was okay. Evan held me back from shaking Luke with all the ferocity my five-foot frame could generate.

After what felt like an eternity, Luke finally glanced upward, a hint of a smile on his face. "I can sense Xavier. He's out of the mountains now."

"*Where?*" I screamed. It echoed off of the still snowy sides of the mountains. If Xavier was out, Sam had to be, too.

"What about Sam?" My brother, the ever level one, piped up.

Rachel's brow furrowed now as she concentrated, reaching out with her perfectly usable Ranguvariian magic. "I can feel Xavier too. But since Sam is a Rounan, I can't sense him. He could be with Xavier."

Unable to wait any longer, I pounced on Luke, gripping his collar with both hands with my feet on their tippy toes. "Where. Is. *Sam?*"

Luke slowly gripped my wrists and pulled me off of him.

His voice was hesitant as he eyed me carefully and said, "From what I can sense from here, it seems like Xavier came out down by Caden's Plain."

"Then let's go! They're so close, we need to catch up to them before something happens again!" I pleaded with a warbling voice.

I noticed that all of the male Ranguvariians present looked to Rachel before responding, and she gave a firm nod. How long had she been in control and I'd never noticed?

Rachel spoke, her voice full of authority, "We still can't use transportation magic, so let's fly. Caden's Plain is more out in the open than I would prefer to have both our Allyens be, so stay near the mountains."

Luke, James, Jaspen, and Bartholomiiu all murmured affirmation, and without much ado, Evan and I were picked up once more. Evan squeezed his eyes shut as he clung to Bartholomiiu this time, and I began to wonder if he was afraid of heights.

The Ranguvariians performed their flying spell, and the colorful shard feathers grew from their backs to form the magnificent, magical wings. Several of them were the same color as the purple feather around my own neck which kept Rhydin from sensing me, just as he couldn't sense Ranguvariians.

I tucked Sam's torn bandana into my tunic for safe keeping, and my thoughts trailed off once we jumped into the sky, the cold wind nipping at my cheeks. We raced down along the mountain slopes, and I impatiently awaited the moment that I would be able to sense Sam for myself. To sense him and then to see him and never let him go ever again.

New growth was bursting forth along the mountainside, becoming fully established now that it was toward the end of

Middle Spring. Wildflowers picked their way up the rocky foothills. As we approached Caden's Plain, which sat in the very heart of Nerahdis, more of the Three Kingdoms became visible. The lush, green trees of Mineraltir, the flowing sands and marshes of Auklia, and the mountain barricade of Lunaka all met together in this one place.

It dazzled my eyes to recognize such vastly different climates all conjoin into a simple field of grass. The fact that three such distinct and separate environments could coexist and blend together at this open plain fascinated me, but the peoples of the Three Kingdoms obviously proved to be unable to do the same.

Dark smudges lined the massive field as we grew closer. What were they? I squinted, trying to see what these tiny moving dots were.

Nobody lived in Caden's Plain. There were no towns or villages. It was kind of like an unspoken rule seeing as nobody reigned over it either. It wasn't divided between the Three Kingdoms like the rest of Nerahdis was three hundred years ago. The plain hadn't had a ruler since Emperor Caden, hence the name.

I shuddered a second. Rhydin had been emperor after Emperor Caden, and the whole world had forgotten. I couldn't let myself slip so easily.

"Oh, no!" Rachel gave a breathy gasp as she suddenly swerved underneath me, clutching me tighter. "Land! Land now, it's a battle!"

My heart dropped as our altitude did. Rapidly. I heard Evan cringe and let out a small squeal as we descended, and I tried my hardest not to panic at the feeling of falling. The wind ripped through my hair and my clothes, and my body felt weightless as my stomach flipflopped. I gripped Rachel's shoulders so hard I might have left a bruise if it weren't for her rock-hard Ranguvariian skin.

As the patchwork green and brown foothills reached up to meet us, I got a better look at the smudges in Caden's Plain. My breath was taken away as I slowly recognized the armies and colors of each individual kingdom.

To the west, a blob of brown and green with light armor and massive weapons that towered over their heads. To the southeast, a smudge of yellows, oranges, and reds with hundreds of flaming arrows flying forth every minute. And to the northeast, a group of navy-vested, heavily-armored men with the sharpest swords Lunaka could offer.

All three armies were here. The *entire* armies of each kingdom. They were only yards from meeting each other in the middle. This was truly a full, Nerahdian war. It would go down in history as the War of the Three Kingdoms. Not even the person going around to sabotage the battles could stop this one.

The second my feet touched the non-mountain ground, it was like a burst of lightning entered my system. My fatigue was wiped away, and the extra weight that it felt like I'd been carrying around was instantly lifted from my shoulders. I felt like I could stand straight again. It had been so long since I'd felt my magic.

Yet, it didn't feel complete. Like there was some part of it missing. I realized with a shock that Rachel was right. The Allyen magic wasn't replenishing itself anymore, so what Evan and I had used to find Sam and Xavier was simply gone. The magic's days were numbered, as were our chances against Rhydin. Unless, we found a child who could become the new Allyen.

Evan practically kissed the dirt he was so happy to be back

on solid land again, not to mention his regained energy. Definitely afraid of heights, I thought as I studied my brother.

Just as the thought crossed my mind to ask where they had sensed Xavier, I recalled my returned magic. I reached for Sam myself, hoping that our relationship would be strong enough for me to sense him from so far away.

My magical radar was immediately overloaded. There were a *lot* of mages here on Caden's Plain right now. Auklian Royals, Mineraltin Royals, Lunakan Royals, descendants of the noble families with historical ties to the Royals. Not to mention dozens of other Rounans that had somehow kept their identities a secret from their commanding officers, and those were just the ones in my line of sight at the moment.

I tried to tune into Sam's presence, his magical presence far more familiar to me than anyone else's. Just as a smile cracked my stressed face, having found the signature of Lunakan soil and security that I had been searching for, a much more powerful presence overshadowed it.

Dark, ancient, and cruel. Heat dropped into my stomach. It was Rhydin. It was the first time I felt him since I fought Duunzer nearly a year and a half ago.

The same dawning of dreadful recognition graced the others' faces. Rachel and Jaspen exchanged a look while Evan's expression darkened considerably with hatred. Luke, James, and Bartholomiiu nodded at each other as they checked the straps on their various leather guards shielding their arms, legs, hands, and shoulders. Readying for battle.

I remembered how it was like poisonous gas for Ranguvariians to be around Rhydin's magic. I remembered Rachel coughing and gasping for breath as she flew me to the castle to defeat Duunzer over a year ago because Rhydin's magic was draining hers. I remembered that, just like last time, our Ranguvariian protectors could only help us so much.

Evan's eyes met mine. Sam's presence and Rhydin's presence were in the same direction. This was on us now, and I found myself wondering if we were ready to be a team.

"I don't sense Xavier anymore!" James exclaimed, his freckled face becoming worried.

"Go to where you sensed him last," Rachel said calmly as she eyed me. She knew that I wasn't going to wait any longer.

The six of us took off toward the center of Caden's Plain as James headed in a different direction. I was in the lead as the only person who could sense my Rounan husband from so far away. The Ranguvariians angled themselves into a driving flank to shield us from as much as they could for as long as they could.

As we traipsed through the long grass, the battle became a haze around me. Soldiers were everywhere. Fog eclipsed them, affecting how much we could see to mere snapshots.

An Auklian wearing intricate layers of yellow silk robes shooting fiery arrows onto a Lunakan troop. An emerald-clad Mineraltin slowly stomping ever forward with his massive battle ax swiping at anything that dared move. A navy-vested Lunakan stabbing a Mineraltin through with a deadly broadsword. Blood was everywhere, and it tainted my vision red. The heart of Nerahdis itself was bleeding.

The roar of soldiers' yelling and screaming in bravery and pain was deafening. All because of Rhydin and his dark dragon. All because the kingdoms had pointed fingers at each other as to whose fault it was, when it was none of their faults in the first place.

How could the two of us possibly stop this corrupt warfare when the people didn't even fully understand what they were fighting about? Didn't even have a clue who Rhydin was? I wished the histories had never been wiped.

As we continued our path to the center of Caden's Plain, my mind began to realize something bit by bit. The thick grasses of the field had been beaten down by the footsteps of hundreds of soldiers. The fog continued to cut in and out. The mountains stared down at us in silent disapproval. I had never visited Caden's Plain before, yet...

Horror washed over me. It was my nightmare. The one I had witnessed on and off ever since Kylar was born. The bloody battlefield, Rhydin stealing my locket, and Sam lying dead in my lap.

Adrenaline replaced my horror, and my ears rang as a Mineraltin felled an Auklian to my left. There was no way Rachel would ever hear my words over the cacophony of metal and screams around us, so I quickened my jog to a sprint. Rachel's blue eyes blinked in confusion as I passed her, but she sped up too. We had to reach Sam before Rhydin did.

A cluster of rugged rocks marked the center of Caden's Plain, still several yards away. I was spurred on faster at the sight of the man I both feared and despised the most in all of Nerahdis.

Rhydin was solitary as he stood calmly on top of the tallest rock. The wind brushed past his midnight hair and long, billowing cloak emblazoned with his golden flame insignia. It seemed from where I was that he was just watching. Watching the various peoples of Nerahdis reduce each other into nothing but meat.

I looked around for Sam in despair, my hand finding my sash automatically and transforming it into my trusty sword. The clashes of swords, axes, and shields resounded everywhere, making my head vibrate.

I tried to sense him again, but he was too close to know.

He was *right* here, yet I couldn't see him! I started screaming his name out of sheer desperation, hoping by some miracle he would hear me. "*Sam!*"

When I whirled around to check Rhydin's position again, I realized with a jolt that he was staring right at me with his timeless, amethyst eyes. A smirk curled his pale lips, and my *Alyen nou Clarii* readied their weapons. People in black appeared out of nowhere, sparks of purple illuminating randomly. Soon, we were outnumbered by half.

Heat raced through my veins. Rhydin planned this. He *knew* that we would be searching for Sam and that we would end up in this battle. He could have even known about my nightmares. After all, he could see far more of the future than I ever could. It was a trap to lure us into the center of Caden's Plain for the real fight. Not kingdom against kingdom. Allyen against sorcerer. Light against darkness.

I gripped my sword tighter, involuntarily gulping as I tried to prepare myself. The last time I saw Rhydin, he had been atop Duunzer, a giant, dark dragon. The dragon had been the real opponent. Now, it was just us. No Einanhi, magically-created dragons like Duunzer. No big bell towers. Just people.

Evan stepped forward, flanking me closely, but it was then that my eyes alighted on a Lunakan soldier off to the side fighting for his life. It was the height and red in his hair that gave him away. Sam.

"Sam!" I shouted in vain, lost in the roar of war. Before even thinking, I sprinted for him. Bartholomiiu spun on his heel, reacting faster than any of the other Ranguvariians.

"Lina, *stop!*" Rachel yelled, sweat beading on her brow as Rhydin grew closer. She, Luke, and Jaspen were already engaged with all of the Followers who had appeared to overtake us.

I didn't hear her. I had tunnel vision on my husband. I didn't see any of the soldiers around us. I didn't hear Bartholomiiu's rapid paces from behind to keep up with me. I didn't hear Evan's or Rachel's cries to stop or come back. However, I did feel it when I was abruptly shoved forward into the tall, bloodied grass.

Turning, I panicked. There stood Rhydin where I had just been. He had leapt atop another of the boulders in the center of the plain, giving him the height necessary to grip the seven-foot Bartholomiiu by the throat. The thin Ranguvariian began to choke. The touch of Rhydin's skin against his own was searing his neck.

"Stop!" I yelled as I charged the fastest attack spell I could and flung it at Rhydin.

I swallowed hard as, to my shock, the spell that should have at least gotten Rhydin to drop Bartholomiiu simply fizzled into Rhydin's sleeve. The sorcerer looked at it as if it had tickled. Nothing more.

The blood drained from my face as I watched Bartholomiiu kick, scream, and wheeze. He was dying right in front of me, and my magic wasn't remotely strong enough now. I was half the Allyen I had been when I'd vanquished Duunzer after using so much magic to find Sam in the mountains. Bartholomiiu's body began to go limp, scarlet blood leaking from his lips. Instinct kicked in. I could *not* let him to die.

I jumped up and threw myself between the two, pushing Bartholomiiu out of Rhydin's grasp. The Ranguvariian fell to the ground like a sack of potatoes, not moving.

Before I could go after him, my jaw was crushed within an iron grasp as I found myself nose to nose with the most terrifying sorcerer in all of Nerahdis.

"Hello again, Linaria," Rhydin chuckled, his pale lips

parting to reveal teeth the same shade as his skin. His nostrils flared as he breathed in deeply, as if he were sniffing me. "It seems your magic is failing."

I struggled in his grip, restraining the urge to spit in his face. Did he know that our magic was fading? I promptly decided to lie just in case. I said through gritted teeth, "You wish."

Rhydin's amethyst eyes were intrigued, but he wasn't buying it. "You know what has to happen here, Linaria. You have seen it just as I have." His glance flickered downward. "After all, no need for a magic amplifier if there is no magic to be amplified."

As he reached for my neck, I saw rapid movement out of the corner of my eye. Jaspen snuck up from behind and proceeded to swipe his sword at the ancient sorcerer.

While Rhydin could not sense Ranguvariians, his instincts were far better in tune. He raised a shield of magic at the last second, which, while keeping him from being harmed, caused him to stagger and drop me.

I felt a break at the back of my neck, and Rhydin's hand closed on something as he moved away.

"No!" I yelled, lunging for the dark sorcerer.

Jaspen moved toward him too, but Rhydin swept his hand to the side, catching Jaspen across the face. The stoic Ranguvariian bellowed as Rhydin's fingers traced scorching marks from his temple, across his nose, to his opposite jawline.

As Jaspen fell to the ground, Rhydin looked with interest at his pale hand, amazed at this newfound power he had over the creatures he hated. Jaspen was incoherent on the ground as he struggled to get back up on his feet while I could only assume that Rachel and Luke were caught battling other

Followers.

Rhydin shook his fist in the air at me, which contained my locket. A rare wide smile spread across his evil face. "Thank you, Linaria, for this fine gift! I shall remember it always when I am emperor once again and visit your *grave*!"

I stood, not thinking, and tried a more powerful attack spell. Suddenly, other spells came from another direction, and Rhydin furiously blocked them all like we were throwing balls at him. I glanced to see Evan running towards us, trying to help me, but when I looked back, Rhydin had turned toward my forgotten husband off in his own battle. His hand glowed purple.

I propelled myself toward Rhydin, trying to stop him. With an unfeeling expression on his face, he threw his hand and a purple blast toward Sam. I saw it hit, but my eyes clouded with fury before I could see my husband crumple to the ground.

Screaming in anger, hate, fear, heartache, all of the above really, I mustered everything I had to take out Rhydin once and for all. So many years later, I wonder what I thought I could accomplish by doing this with reduced magic, but I could do nothing else in my grief.

There was another flash of purple lightning, and my world went dark.

CHAPTER TEN

E verything hurt. Opening my eyes sent waves of pain through my head. The smell of blood was still in my nose, and it made me wretch. In my few glimpses of the world, I could see the ceiling of a tent above me. I wished I was dead. Death would be far less painful than this.

A lilting tune came to my ears. It was airy yet accented with guttural sounds. I kept my eyes shut, afraid of the throbbing that would come with the light. But, as the song went on, a fraction of my agony vanished.

Very carefully, I opened my eyes the slimmest of slits. Rachel was kneeling next to me as I was laid out on the ground, her pale hands outstretched over my body as she continued her melody. Evan said once that Ranguvariian magic required song a lot of the time.

What happened to me?

I wracked my brain for my last memory, struggling to recall it. My name was Lina Greene. I was the Allyen. I was married to Sam and had a baby boy named Kylar...

Sam.

A fresh wave of pain rolled through me as grief gripped me tight. My head throbbed anew as tears leaked forth and sobs broke through my gritted teeth. Rhydin shot Sam. He was dead.

Rachel's song instantly stopped as she scooted toward my head, clutching my hand. "Lina!" Her voice was clouded with worry as she whispered, "What's wrong? What hurts? I'm so glad you're finally awake!"

I moved my head a fraction of an inch toward her, tears muddling my vision. I choked, "Sam... My locket... Bartholomiiu... We've lost, Rachel."

My red-haired friend's brow furrowed. The *matrii* or pinwheel mark on her freckled cheek glowed for a moment as she muttered something in Ranguvariian. Only moments later, Jaspen entered my tent of misery.

My breath caught at the sight of his face. Three long, jagged lines stretched from his temple to his jaw on the opposite side, growing thicker as they crossed the bridge of his nose. It was if he had gotten into a fight with a wild animal. They were deep and had turned a pearly white color as they healed, which stood out in stark contrast to his leathery brown skin. Rhydin did that. Just by touching him skin on skin.

The pressure of crying built up in my face again, threatening to let loose as I mumbled, "I am so sorry, Jaspen."

Jaspen's cat-like eyes melted into a cool blue color. "Linaria okay, I. Understand, I."

I stuttered, afraid to hear the answer, "Is Bartholomiiu dead?"

"No." Jaspen shook his head, beads in his hair rustling. "Is alive, Bartholomiiu. Very very hurt."

A thin wave of relief washed over me. At least I wasn't

responsible for two murders today. I let my head fall back onto the blanket underneath me, beginning to wonder what in Nerahdis I would do now. Failing magic, no locket, dead husband. How could Evan and I possibly save Nerahdis now? How could I possibly go on without Sam? He was my heart.

Grief swallowed me whole, tearing its way through my heart along all the old fault lines that had been ripped open when Rosetta, Keera, and Grandma were killed by Rhydin's Followers. The fractures for Sam stretched far deeper.

I glanced at Jaspen's scars once again, the reminder of my stupidity in going after Sam without help. Confusion seeped into my mind as I studied their white color and puckered edges. I asked quietly, "Rachel, how long has it been since the battle?"

Rachel grimaced. "Nearly a month."

My eyes widened so much they almost popped out of my head. "I've been unconscious for a month? What season is it?"

"Almost Early Summer." Rachel looked at me with sad eyes and cringed. "I'm sorry, but it's a miracle you're alive at all. Rhydin struck you in the head, but Evan deflected it just enough to not be fatal. My magic is limited against Rhydin's, so it's taken ages to heal you. It was touch and go for a long time. Even now, I don't think you're ready to move yet. You may not be able to transport for weeks."

I groaned, feeling the stabbing pain in my head again. I leaned forward again as I said, "Rachel, I want to go home. My husband is…is dead. My locket is gone. I want to be with my son."

Rachel quirked her eyebrow, and Jaspen revealed an expression of surprise. They glanced at each other briefly before Rachel rummaged for something behind her. Her confusion was evident in her voice as she spoke, "Lina, Sam isn't dead. And your locket is right here."

She lifted the metal chain, the silver orb of my locket still hanging firmly from it, safe and sound.

My breathing quickened rapidly as I whimpered, "What do you mean he's not dead! I saw him shot with my own two eyes! And Rhydin took my necklace, I felt it break, and he had it in his hand!"

"It wasn't a direct shot. I saw him go down, but he was up and gone after a couple minutes," Rachel said matter-of-factly. "I can't sense him so I don't know for sure, but I think it's safe to say he's alive. We think Rhydin may have simply aimed for Sam to mess with you and make you come at him. Right now, we think Sam is in Auklia because they're the only kingdom that takes prisoners. We're hoping Xavier is there too, but we can't sense him very well either. James never found him, but we can sense enough of him to know he's alive too."

Sam was alive. That thought echoed itself over and over and over until it began to seep into my bones as truth. Sam was alive. Every gnarl of pain in my muscles seemed to untangle themselves.

Sam was alive. Therefore, I was alive.

I drew upon my magic to try and sense him for myself, but I found two hands in my face.

"Stop!" Rachel yelled, raising her voice considerably, "Don't use magic! Evan told me how it's dwindling now. You need to save it for when you really need it."

But I do really need it, I thought to myself. But Rachel's stink eye remained on me long and hard until I relaxed once more.

"Anyway, Rhydin got your feather. Not your locket. I guess it pays to be wearing two necklaces at the same time."

Rachel grinned and handed me my locket.

The cool metal warmed up upon reaching my hand, but not quite up to its normal temperature. Even the locket was reflecting the draining Allyen magic now. It was hard for me to believe that it was here in my hand.

After half a year of the same nightmare, which should have been the future, I couldn't believe it was this wrong. My dream of Duunzer's arrival had nearly been spot on, yet the one of Sam's death, Rhydin's taking my locket, and my own death had turned out to be completely wrong. I began to wonder if my magic had been slowing down before we'd even known that it wasn't regenerating itself. Or, the future wasn't as easy to predict as I had thought.

While I was absorbed in my thoughts, Rachel reached down to squeeze my hand. She smiled lightly as she said, "I'm glad you're awake, Lina. Now try to rest until we can finish healing you."

"How much longer?" I looked up at her, my eyes pleading. "I want to go to Auklia as soon as possible."

"I understand. We're hoping for a few more days until we can travel without magic." Rachel nodded as she pushed my shoulders back down to the ground. "We don't want to risk transportation magic for a while yet, so you'll just have to be patient. I'm sure Sam and Xavier are in Auklia since they're alive. None of the other kingdoms would have spared them."

I nodded, trying to allow this to soothe me. But, there was no denying my heightening anxiety. Sam was alive, that was one thing. However, until I saw him with my own two eyes, my worries would never cease. There was safety in death. Nothing could have hurt him anymore. Life was what was truly dangerous. Where anything could go wrong at any time.

As Rachel ducked out of the tent to talk to Jaspen, my

thoughts cycled back to Kylar. If it was truly Early Summer, then it had been a whole month since I left my son back at the Rounan compound. How big was he now? How much had he grown? Had he started to eat people food? Did he still smell the same? Did he even remember me?

My heart trembled inside my chest as my arms ached for my baby. I vowed once more that I would return to Kylar as soon as I found Sam. I was not coming home without his father. Surely, Kelsi was handling the Kidek duties far better than I had, and the Royals would keep Kylar safe.

I suddenly found myself wondering about Mira and how her pregnancy was going, and Cassandra and if she had ever gotten well again after being so sick. I made a note to myself to ask Rachel later if we had heard any updates from the Royal cottage.

The hours stretched on. I slept on and off in spite of my worry, and between each bout of sleep, the pain in my head became infinitesimally better. This encouraged me to get as much rest as I could because it was my condition that was holding us back from heading to Auklia this moment.

I couldn't help but think that everything would be better once we got to Auklia and found Sam and Xavier. Therefore, I was a much better patient than I typically was. A lot of the time, my only company was Sam's bandana, which I thankfully found still stowed safely in my tunic, as well as the lilting sound of Evan's violin outside.

The next morning, the clanking of metal roused me from my slumber. Heavy rays of sunshine came through the flap of the tent, searing my eyes and my temples. At the sound of my groan, the person who came in promptly backed away, saying, "Oh, I'm sorry... I just wanted to see how you were doing, but I'll come back later."

"Wait," I said as I shielded my eyes from the light. "Evan?"

The metallic clangs stopped as Evan froze in the doorway. He dropped the flap, which covered the tent in blessed darkness. In a minute, my eyes adjusted, so I could see Evan still standing awkwardly in the very opposite corner from me.

He was wearing a salvaged set of chainmail now, likely from the battle and the source of the metallic noises. He looked like he was standing on pins and needles, and I found myself wondering why. This was the first time I'd seen him since the battle, and he saved my life. I remembered.

"Come here," I whispered in my pain and motioned to him.

My brother took several very short steps closer to me, making it seem like he had moved more than the six inches he actually had. His brown eyes measured me carefully, a bit larger than normal as if he was afraid his mere presence would hurt me.

I pulled myself forward into a sitting position and patted the dirt next to me. "You know, Evan, this is my first opportunity to thank you for saving my life, and you're doing a pretty good job of staying as far away from me as physically possible. What's the deal?"

"Sorry, I just…wanted to make sure you were okay," Evan mumbled, fingering the edge of his jingling chainmail.

"That's nice," I said awkwardly, then I cleared my throat and looked him in the eye. "Thank you, though. For saving me. If it hadn't been for you, I'd be dead right now."

Evan chuckled. Shock mounted inside me as I witnessed what seemed like the first ever smile to grace his round face. His hands found his hips as he said, "Yes, well, you owe me one now." The gleeful expression fell from his face almost instantaneously as he whispered morosely, "Actually, we're even. I never did apologize for blaming you for Keera's death. I should know better than anyone that it's impossible to prevent Rhydin from killing someone he wants dead."

A lump rose in my throat, and I gripped my knees harder. My voice wavered as I spoke, "Trust me, I tried to protect her. I tried to save her."

"I know," Evan said softly as he approached my blanket and sat next to me. "I'm sure our grandmother did too. At least we don't have to worry about them anymore. And I'm sorry about your sister. Rachel told me how you never even had a body to bury."

I sniffed and dug my fingers into my blanket, locking my teeth shut to keep myself from crying. I had cried far too much in the last twenty-four hours. It was embarrassing.

It was true though. Rosetta's body had simply dissolved into sand like nothing I'd ever seen. I had carried her doll and Keera's hair ribbon around in my pocket for a month after they died. Lunakan custom was actually to keep a candle burning for a month, but I couldn't do that where we hid in the forest. But someday, I would avenge Grandma, Rosetta, and Keera. Someday, we would defeat Rhydin. And that was all that mattered.

Evan and I talked for what seemed like hours. Previously, I had never conversed with him for more than five minutes because of the rut between us, but it soon melted away as if it had never been there, just how wagon wheel tracks smoothed out in the rain. The sounds of the camp outside of my dim tent hushed in the distance.

He told me about his childhood in Auklia, growing up there with our aunt and uncle, our father's younger brother. They had lived in the country outside of Rondeau, a small village in the far eastern region of the kingdom.

Uncle Jed wanted Evan to become a rice farmer just like him, but Evan wanted to be a violinist. Our aunt was the one to gift him his violin. Uncle Jed tried every day to change Evan's mind, but he didn't succeed before he was killed by Rhydin's Followers.

That was when the Ranguvariians found him, seeing as his magic had awakened during that attack. Keera told me that Evan had been around thirteen at the time. So much younger than I had been when I entered this new world of being an Allyen, only a couple years ago at nineteen.

I shared with him what little he didn't already know. My parents had died in the Epidemic when I was around seventeen, and while Rosetta was sick with it too, she survived. I had always helped on the farm, being the oldest, so taking it on was difficult but not foreign. It was far more difficult to convince the Royal advisor of agriculture that a lowly woman could do it, and therefore, King Adam indirectly. Thankfully, he was too desperate for a crop to argue.

Evan grew very quiet as I talked about my parents and how much I missed them, but when I stopped, he was full of questions about them. However, those questions differed drastically between the ones he asked about our father and the ones he asked about our mother.

He asked about a myriad of topics including Mama's looks, her interests and personality, and if she had ever made any sort of mention of him. About Papa, he only asked a couple of questions about his name, where he was from, and how he treated our mother.

This piqued my curiosity. It surprised me that he hadn't known our father's name, but then again, if he had been sent away as a newborn, I didn't know how much our aunt and uncle cared to tell him. As Evan rambled on, like a child that was suddenly allowed to talk even though he had been so silent for so long, my thoughts wandered.

Evan had acquired so much more of a magical education from his Ranguvariians than I had. After all, he had known about the whole Allyen thing for six years longer than me. I showed him Grandma's journal during our conversation, and it delighted me that he was able to see her handwriting too. Whenever I showed the book to Rachel or her brothers, or even Sam, it had only shown my own.

However, this only reminded me of the fact that there was supposed to be an Allyen every generation. We were going through so much trouble right now because another Allyen wouldn't be born after us to regenerate the magic, yet it was like the Allyen between Grandma and us was missing. If that Allyen didn't exist, then the magic would have died out long before our birth. Therefore, there *had* to be an Allyen between us.

But who was it? Evan and Keera, while she was alive, had made it very clear that my aunt and uncle possessed no magic. Neither of my parents had either, or at least none that they had led on to have. I couldn't help but think that my father would have used his magic to help out on the farm once in a while if he had possessed it. Maybe, he had wanted to keep it a secret until I knew...then never had the chance.

"Evan," I interrupted him as he droned on and on about the meticulous inner workings of his violin, "Do you know anything about the Allyen lineage?"

He hushed almost immediately, his golden-speckled, Allyen eyes watching me. "What do you mean?"

I shrugged, trying to make this seem less serious than it apparently was. I kept my voice light and airy, like I had no idea what I was talking about. "Well, there's supposed to be an Allyen in every generation in order to keep the magic alive. I was just curious who the Allyen between us and Grandma was. Do you know?"

All of the color drained from Evan's face. His hands knotted in his chainmail, and I tried not to stare. It seemed that the gears in his head were racing a million miles per hour.

It was several moments before Evan was able to speak. I tried to play it off that I was busy rereading my grandmother's writing in the journal, but in all honesty, my curiosity was killing me more with every second that passed.

Evan's thin lips opened and closed a few times before he decided on the words he was going to say. His voice was firm. "I do know about the Allyen before us. I had planned on telling you once I met you."

My brow furrowed. "And?"

A breath escaped, but Evan shook his head worriedly. "Not right now. It's not a good time. You're not healed enough yet."

"Evan," I sighed, reaching out to touch his arm. "You can tell me anything. You're my brother. I trust you."

His eyes widened, and his hand turned into a fist. He looked down, his brown hair hiding his eyes. He whimpered, "I can't tell you yet. I'm not ready to tell you. Not until I know how."

Evan stood abruptly, but I caught him by the sleeve, my eyes pleading with him to tell me. It was obvious how much this information was paining him, and it hurt me to see it.

"Please keep your trust in me. I *will* tell you once you're stronger, and I know how to say it," Evan murmured, not meeting my eyes.

He rushed out of my tent. A blink of light then darkness once more.

Why couldn't he tell me? I couldn't help but think that the answer must not be as simple as I'd thought. Perhaps, my parents were hiding far more than I'd ever dreamed.

My fingers began to fidget in my impatience, wondering and wondering and wondering how the information of who the Allyen before us was could be so painful. Evan's music began again, faster and frenzied. He seemed to play whenever he was deep in thought, I mused.

I mulled over and over these thoughts until Rachel entered my tent hours later for another round of healing. My chaotic mind was distracted when she mentioned that if I did well enough overnight we would set out for Kaiya, the Auklian capital, in the morning. Not with magic, but it was something.

I went to sleep that night with happy thoughts, dreaming of seeing Sam safe and sound in Auklia in only a couple of weeks. However, my dream melted into a nightmare as Rhydin's Followers chased me into the night.

CHAPTER ELEVEN

T he darkness was close and dank. The walls were made of roughly-sculpted bricks stained crimson after centuries of torture. Water dripped periodically, in ones and twos and sometimes threes, echoing upon the emptiness. The emptiness of the room and the emptiness of the people inside.

No light reached the bottom of the dungeon aside from one small torch down the hall. The magical handcuffs binding Xavier's hands to the opposite walls ensured that he would be unable to create his own fire.

The former prince had long lost the feeling in his fingers, palms, wrists, arms, and even his back as he hung from his chains. Especially his right arm, which had been hastily bound back together after being crushed by the stone in the avalanche. His bare feet dangled, barely grazing the hideous, brick floor below. Xavier's head drooped forward, hanging on simply by his neck. He wondered when she would finally end him.

Xavier had no idea how long he'd been here. Without any

light, besides the one eternal, flickering fire that mocked him day in and day out, Xavier had no way of tracking the days. To him, it felt like it'd been an eternity since he had been with Sam up on that mountaintop. He often thought about whether Sam survived or not.

He wondered if Mira knew he was captured, or how she was doing in her condition. Long ago, Xavier realized grimly that he did not know when his own child was due. He never had the chance to even tell his own wife that he knew about her pregnancy or ask why she felt the need to keep it from him. There was no doubt in his mind that the child was his, but it bothered him nonetheless.

A screech that could wake the dead bounced along the hollow walls, but Xavier did not stir. He was used to this routine by now. No matter how numb his body had become, he always felt this. The muscles in his arms and back tightened, awaking the soreness within them that groaned from ill-use. Loud clacking noises came from the hallway, tossing their sounds in strange directions.

They stopped in front of his cell, but Xavier did not look up. He knew who it was. It could only be one person. No one else wore those cacophonous heels. With a bang of metal, Xavier knew the key was inserted and turned while the whine of the rusty bars swung slowly along their track. Xavier continued to stare at his toes, dirty and clammy as they brushed the filth on the floor.

"Hello, garbage," cooed the woman standing before him, "How did you sleep last night?"

Xavier finally raised his head, his lips pressed into a thin line. He could barely see through his long red hair. It had grown significantly during his time in the dungeon, and he had no way of pulling it out of his face.

However, there was no mistaking the woman in front of him. Covered head to toe in every gold accessory known to mankind. The crown of the Mineraltin king on her midnight head. The heart-shaped face that was bent on his destruction.

Jasmine. His step-mother.

He glared at her, his eyes icy-blue. His voice dripped with hatred as he said, "Wonderfully. Here for another go, are we? Rhydin would be disappointed if he knew that you weren't strong enough to kill me."

"Oh, don't worry," Jasmine chuckled darkly as she tossed a plump hand through her onyx curls streaked with gray, "I promised Master that I would deliver your head to him...eventually. But I don't think I've gotten my use out of you yet."

Xavier's fingers fidgeted, and he wished he could pull his chains right out of the wall. He had tried hundreds of times. He spat in impatience, "What did I ever do to you? You got everything you ever wanted by marrying my father and ostracizing me! Wealth, a title, my father, the crown!"

"You did *everything* to me!" Jasmine screeched. She stalked forward and grabbed a handful of Xavier's loose red hair, yanking it backward to force his chin into the air. "You were *born!*"

Pain sliced across Xavier's chest as Jasmine uncoiled her angry whip. He couldn't help but smirk at her. She had no magic. She was useless. He had mocked her a few times about how Rhydin hadn't trusted her to give her some of his magic like he had done with his other Followers, and the memories made him grin.

That smirk earned him another strike. Agony rippled across his face, but Xavier had felt all of this before. He looked up at her with uncaring eyes. "I will always have been born to the true queen of Mineraltir. Nothing you can do can ever change that! The people want *me* on that throne. Not you!"

"Oh, I can't?" Jasmine snarled, "Once you're dead, it won't matter if you were born first or not. Ren!"

Out from the shadows came Xavier's half-sister. The girl mirrored her mother in every way; the two could have been twins if it wasn't for the twenty-year age gap. She was covered in every shade of pink in what looked more like a ball gown than an executioner's dress. Xavier just shook his head at her. She would never handle being queen.

Ren cracked an evil grin identical to her mother's. "Tell him, Mother. About the Allyen."

Xavier's ears perked up. This was new. Normally, the two witches would come in, insult him for a few minutes, and then beat him to a pulp. In all the unknown amount of days he had spent in this dungeon, they had never revealed any sort of information about the outside world.

Cold began to seep into Xavier's heart. What had happened to the Allyen? Was it Lina or her brother? Had they come for him?

"Aww, look at him," Jasmine sneered and turned to her pink, foul daughter, "He's curious."

Xavier rolled his eyes. "Tell me or don't tell me. I don't care," he lied.

The queen's scarlet lips turned upward, her devilish eyes peering straight into Xavier's soul. "Here's a riddle for you. One is dead and the other doesn't have enough magic to do a thing about it. Regardless of who is who, Master Rhydin will soon be emperor of Nerahdis once more!"

Xavier growled as he launched himself as far forward as his chains would allow, "He'll never win! The Allyens *will* prevail!"

"Well, they haven't come for you, have they?" Jasmine cackled, brushing her hand across Xavier's shoulders. "They don't care about you. If they did, they would have come for you weeks ago!"

"You're *wrong!*" Xavier bellowed, straining against his chains as if willpower alone could break them. He gasped and pulled, but nothing would break them. They were reinforced magically to keep him from using his fire. "You and I both know that you're hiding my presence so that they can't find me!"

"Then it seems you require more convincing," the dark-haired queen whispered cruelly. She raised her whip once more, brandishing its barbed ends, and Xavier gritted his teeth for what he knew was coming.

The castle remained silent up above because Xavier refused to scream. He declined to give Jasmine and Ren any sort of enjoyment out of his torture. But, what they didn't understand was that they could not break him. You could not break something that was already broken, and Xavier had been a broken man for as long as he could remember.

As the lashes came one after another, Xavier squeezed his eyes shut and locked his teeth. He thought of Mira. The only good thing in his life. He thought of how badly he wished he was curled up in bed next to her right now How desperately he regretted being so stupid as to go after Sam by himself. How fiercely he hoped that Jasmine was wrong and someone somewhere was coming for him.

That somehow his stupid life was worth saving.

A storm was blowing in across Lunaka's great plains. The sky clouded over, growing darker with every passing second as the prairie grasses bowed down to the strengthening wind. Young Princess Cornflower could smell the rain on the horizon and found herself anxiously awaiting the flash of lightning that buzzed in the air.

She loved thunderstorms, but they'd taken on a whole new meaning for her ever since her siblings, Frederick and Mira, moved her from the castle. Back then, she would climb to the tallest tower to watch the storm move across the canyon where the town lay and through the vulnerable farms up above. Now, out in the open, Cornflower felt immersed in the storms as they came, like she was a part of something much bigger.

As thunder boomed and the angry clouds covered the far away mountains, a scream shrilled through the air. Cornflower panicked for a moment before she remembered that her sister had gone into labor. The thirteen-year-old found herself wondering if this was normal, never having been around a birth before, but assured herself that it probably was.

Cornflower still couldn't believe that Mira had hid her pregnancy from her for so long. And everybody else for that matter. They were sisters, and even with the seven-year age gap between them, Cornflower still found herself put off. She knew that her siblings still kept things from her thinking that she was too young for them. It bugged her to death.

The young princess began to walk back to the Royal cottage, hoping that the labor was nearly over. It had been a full day since it began, although Cornflower had no knowledge of these things. She did know that the baby was early. Mira kept saying when it started, "It's too early, it's too early." Cornflower wondered what that meant.

The screams grew louder as she approached. Cornflower

was promising herself that she would never have children when she rounded the corner and was taken aback by a figure standing atop the hill across from the cottage. She squinted at it, wondering if it was Cayce.

Cayce often walked back and forth between the cottage and the Rounan compound, and they had sent a message to her about Mira's baby. Who else would be out as such a storm threatened to break loose at any moment?

Abruptly, there was silence from within the cottage, and a smile spread across Cornflower's face when a tiny cry broke the air. She clutched her long, scarlet skirts and hurried inside out of the windy, darkening prairie.

It was even dimmer indoors, but Cornflower knew the way to her sister's room. She trotted across the fancy carpets and past the regal portraits on the walls and pushed open Mira's door without knocking in her excitement.

The room was even darker than the outdoors and loud as the coming storm picked up the shingles and banged them back down. Mira sat propped up on what seemed like a hundred pillows with a tiny bundle in her arms. Her long black hair was plastered across her pale forehead, and the flickering candlelight tap-danced across her glowing face.

Mira looked up at her with pure joy in her purple eyes and said weakly, "It's a boy, Cornie."

A smile cracked Cornflower's worried face. She was an aunt again! And Dominick, Frederick's son, would have a little friend to play with. She hurried over to her sister's side. The baby was even tinier than Dominick had been when he was born. Cornflower wondered if this was what Mira worried over since he was "early."

He was bright red and quite honestly did not look that appealing to Cornflower, but she knew enough about babies to know that Dominick had looked like a little old man when he was born too. The boy wailed and wailed, tiny red hairs peeping out of his blanketed head. For once, Cornflower actually wished Xavier was here. The boy practically mirrored him.

Cornflower stopped short as she reached to touch the baby's hand when she noticed Cayce sitting in the corner exhausted. Her sleeves were rolled up to the shoulders, her arms recently cleaned, and her curly, lavender hair in disarray. Cornflower's brow furrowed.

Cornflower hadn't seen Cayce arrive. If Cayce was already here, then who was the cloaked figure outside?

A certain feeling began to nag at the back of Cornflower's mind. She put up her hand to Mira's trying to pass the baby to her and said, "One minute. I'll be right back."

She stood, beckoned to Cayce, and the two of them strode from the room. Cayce kept eyeing Cornflower for some sort of explanation, but she said nothing until they reached the front window. The strange person was still out there, but he or she was walking closer and closer. Cornflower didn't have quite as much magic as her older siblings, so she was not very good at sensing presences from far away. She murmured to Cayce, "Who is that?"

Cayce's jaw went slack for only a moment, and then she jumped into action. Cornflower didn't need an explanation. Cayce's words were firm when she instructed her, "Go get Cassandra and lead her and Dominick to the cellar. I'll get Mira."

"Then what?" Cornflower's voice quivered.

Cayce's full lips pressed into a line. No answer.

Panic arose into Cornflower's heart as she tumbled down the hallway to Cassandra's room. Her brother's wife sat in a flowy nightgown on the side of her bed, cradling her young, blond son in her arms as she sang him to sleep. Her blue eyes were hazy when she looked up, the way they'd been ever since she'd taken ill. She was still very sick and refused medical help from Lun in order to preserve their hiding spot from King Adam.

Cornflower rushed over to her before she had a chance to speak with her crackling voice and grabbed her arms, helping her up. Then, she tucked her nephew into Cassandra's thin arms and hurriedly helped her sister-in-law back into the living room.

Cayce had Mira in a similar state, the latter moaning with pain as she clutched her newborn. She flung the rich, embroidered carpet to the side to reveal a heavy wooden door in the floor. They had just raised it with Cassandra and Dominick halfway down the stairs when the door of the cottage exploded open.

The force of it knocked them all down, and Cayce whirled around to block a purple blast aimed straight for them with her Rounan powers. Cornflower jumped up to steady Mira as the smoke cleared, revealing the same solitary, cloaked figure.

Cornflower had never seen Rhydin before, but she didn't think this was him. Her senses were so puzzled by this man now that he was so close. He simultaneously felt like Rhydin's magic and like someone else she knew at the same time. Cornflower couldn't put her finger on it, and she was too terrified to think on it any longer.

"Who are you?" Cayce yelled, her hands still raised, ready to block anything. Cornflower eyed the size of the angular, Rounan mark on her arm and wondered if it would be enough.

At this point, Cornflower was practically dragging Mira toward the cellar door, trying to get her out of danger, but only seconds passed before she was flung away from her sister. Her head crashed into a wall, and her world spun. A scream sounded as Cayce flew the opposite direction, no match for Rhydin's Follower.

As her vision cleared, Cornflower experienced the first truly horrific moment of her entire life. Mira had fallen down, but she was using every ounce of energy to try and propel the cloaked man backwards with her magic.

The cloak was decorated with Rhydin's golden flame seal, but when his hood tumbled back in Mira's weak bursts of wind, it revealed a tanned, unshaven, middle-aged face. Mira sobbed as she clutched her baby, and the man grew closer and closer. Then, there were two bursts of blinding purple light.

Silence ensued. Cornflower trembled in the corner, and she could once again hear the approaching thunder outside. Her head pounded like a stampede of a thousand horses. She realized that she had squeezed her eyes closed as tight as she could and opened them warily.

The strange, brown-haired man was gone. Cayce was out cold against the opposite wall, her lavender curls spiraled out from her head in a strange pattern. There was blood leaking from her nose. Cornflower could not see Mira from where she huddled. Cautiously, she placed her hands on the cool stone of the floor, inching forward on her knees as if she was crawling across ice.

Lightning burst outside when a sob broke the noiseless void. The sound of it made Cornflower want to hurry forward and back away at the same time. The thirteen-year-old gulped hard, feeling like her siblings had not adequately prepared her for this. She numbly made her way around the plush sofa that had been pushed back several inches by the man's spells.

Mira was lying on the floor, but she was alive. Her

nightgown was bloodied in a few places, and her skin was the same shade as its white cloth. Mira continued to weep as Cornflower bravely made her way past the open cellar door. She could see Cassandra and Dominick at the bottom, perfectly alright aside from Cassandra's being too weak to climb back up the stairs by herself.

"Mira," Cornflower mumbled, "Are you hurt?"

No response. Cornflower grabbed Mira's elbow and pulled her to face her. The baby was still in her arms, silent as could be.

"Is he…?" Cornflower's voice clouded with tears.

"N-No," Mira choked, rubbing her son's tiny red arms.

Cornflower stared at the boy harder and could see his fragile chest moving up and down. Confusion swamped her senses, along with her throbbing headache. Why was he so quiet? What had the man done to him? She was only able to voice the second partially, "What did he do?"

Mira shrugged her shoulders weakly. "I-I don't know. He fired right at him… I tried to block it. Cornie, why won't he cry?" Instead, Mira began to cry, "What did he do to my baby?"

The princess wilted, having no answer. It wasn't like the baby could open his mouth and tell them what had been done to him. But something had. Even though Cornflower's magical abilities were limited, she could feel a darkness that had been left within the child. It made her uncomfortable.

Pattering sounds came from above them, and Cornflower knew that the rain had finally arrived. The young princess shuddered as she realized whom Rhydin's Follower's presence reminded her of.

CHAPTER TWELVE

I t took us longer than I would have preferred to get to Auklia since Rachel refused to use transportation magic. It was over two weeks before we set foot in Kaiya, the capital in the northwestern region of the kingdom. I thanked my lucky stars that Auklia's capital wasn't Coliare or Caenara. It would have taken months to get there.

Our journey was rather uneventful. I was able to walk a bit further each day, but most of the time, I was relegated to being carried by either Rachel or Luke. Jaspen scouted ahead of us for several miles, always ensuring that we wouldn't run into any other travelers on the roads. Of course, with the war escalating, there really were never any travelers.

I wondered if Auklia had passed a travel ban similar to the one in Lunaka. Even the quaint huts we passed on either side of the road seemed completely abandoned. The doors and shutters were all bolted down. I wondered if the people never came back after they were maybe warned of a battle by that person helping all three kingdoms.

Bartholomiiu hadn't returned to us yet. After he was injured in the battle, James transported him home to be healed. His wounds were too great for our little group of Ranguvariians to heal him themselves. I thought about Bartholomiiu every day. I hadn't known him very well, but he had nearly gotten killed by protecting me. I couldn't help but think it was my fault. I kept thinking about what I could do for him or what I could give him when he came back.

Ever since our conversation, Evan remained as far away from me as he could. I stared at the back of his head sadly more often than not during our journey. It reminded me of how he acted after figuring out Keera, our little cousin, had been killed.

Except this time, it actually hurt because I'd gotten to know him a lot better by now. During our hours-long heart to heart, I'd begun to truly think of him as my brother. My last living sibling. His avoidance cut me as deep as the melancholy airs of his violin in the evenings.

When I wasn't staring at the back of Evan's head, I gaped at the beauty of Auklia as we entered its heart. The grassy fields of Caden's Plain melted away into dark sand, which steadily became lighter in color and deeper as it replaced the bloodied dirt of the battlefield. Eventually, the sapphire-blue horizon came to meet the sand and grass-mixed ground perfectly, no trees to disrupt it. Everyone else trekked on without caring about the scenery, but I couldn't help myself.

During the times I was allowed to walk, I would explore as far from the path as I could without hearing a reprimand. I'd run my hand through the briny sand that reflected in so many directions it was like it was littered with gems. I had never seen sand before, and it amazed me how much grittier it was than the clay-like dirt of Lunaka.

I picked the reeds that sprung up on the side of the road, bending their stems into strange shapes and weaving them into things like necklaces or crowns like a child would. I am slightly ashamed of myself, looking back on it now, but there is something about visiting a foreign kingdom that reduces you to the amazement of a child.

When we passed the first rice paddy maybe a week into our trip, the sand beneath our feet had become more yellow in color, as well as moist enough for me to grab a handful and mold it in my palms. We only saw one person in the paddy, of all the ones we had passed, walking along the sandy and weedy ridges between the water-filled fields with baskets. I wondered what he was doing and how it related to the kind of farming Sam and I did in Lunaka. I wished I could ask Evan.

As we got closer to Kaiya, where Auklia Castle was, the air began to swelter. It had been extra humid since we traveled inside the border a few miles, but now it was almost hard to breathe, the air seemed so thick. It began to smell too, like an entire ocean's worth of fish had been dumped nearby to spoil. I glanced at Evan a lot during this time, but he seemed to breathe just fine. He must be used to it from his years of living in Auklia, I thought to myself.

After we hiked yet another sandy, grassy dune with still no sight of Kaiya, my internal groaning became audible as I asked, "Rachel, how much farther is it?"

"Just a bit further," she muttered as she wiped sweat from her rosy brow.

The whole lot of us had been slowly taking off clothing that day. A cloak here, pant legs hiked up there, a few missing armor pieces all around. It felt like we were being boiled alive under the Auklian sun like a great red lobster.

I felt bad for Jaspen, who remained covered from head to

toe. Dark marks appeared at the bridge of his shoulders and down his spine where sweat worked all the way through his cloak. Just looking at him made me feel faint.

I heard the roar of the city before I saw it. It was a chorus of yelling, screeching, wagons, and horses. When we caught up with Jaspen, the noise was deafening, like it was just over the next dune. Instead, I saw him give a curt shake to his head, his white scars shimmering, and Rachel nodded. To my dismay, they began to route us around the city to the west rather than through it.

Within the next mile, a couple knolls separated enough to give me a glimpse of the city of Kaiya. There was a vast mixture of different types of buildings. Some looked like small shanties, woven out of reeds and propped up on pegs, while others were like tents or built of ancient stone looking as if it had been underwater for ages. Those were the large buildings, and each of their windows were made of beautifully-colored stained glass.

The streets were narrow, and while the permanent structures were spaced with much distance in between them, every square foot was taken up by smaller, rainbow-colored tents. Ropes were stretched between the two sides of the streets with laundry, flags, and other paraphernalia hanging from them. Although I only saw it for a few minutes, it seemed to me the city was very claustrophobic. I much preferred the open, deep blue ocean that gleamed from beyond.

The most telling thing was the hustle and bustle of people, far beyond the usual for a capital city. People were running about screaming, the noise we had heard for miles, cursing the war and slandering their young king. A tightness entered my chest as I heard their desperation for answers and watched them wreak havoc on anything they could get their hands on.

When Frederick left the cottage to help Daniel, I never imagined that it was this bad. Auklia was in absolute chaos.

"There's the castle!" Luke exclaimed, which brought my wandering eyes back around.

Thin spires rose out of the sand a few miles ahead of us, glinting brilliant colors back at us in the sunlight. It was oh so tall, its walls built of the same ancient stone as the buildings in town except for the very tippy tops of the gigantic towers, which looked like they were glass. Auklia Castle was definitely the tallest of all the castles I had ever seen.

With a shock, I realized I had officially seen them all. As I child I never would have dreamed that I'd see every castle in Nerahdis before I died, much less before I was twenty-five.

As we grew closer, I could pick out the longer, rainbow banners that hung from the walls and flew from the flagstaffs. Instead of gargoyles, the castle boasted large sea creatures that I didn't know the names of but were vaguely fish-like.

A particularly large, crimson tapestry hung from the front gate, depicting a tiny baby with words memorializing him as just "The Prince." Grief entered my heart as I wondered if Daniel and Queen Lily even had the chance to name their young son before he was taken from them by Duunzer's Darkness.

Upon approaching the gate, one of the guards shouted at us, "Halt! Come no further if you value your lives!"

Rachel spoke up, projecting her voice across the moat separating us from the castle guards and the front gate. "The Allyens have business with His Majesty, the King! Let us pass."

"If you truly have the Allyens with you, go ahead and cross! Then we can run them through like they deserve!" The other guard bellowed back across the moat.

Shock entered my system. What did he mean? I *saved* Nerahdis by destroying Duunzer. I didn't think I deserved to be killed for that!

I could see Rachel grit her teeth. Luke set his jaw, but Jaspen never turned. Without a word, the three of them marched toward the bridge that crossed the moat. Rachel led, her husband and her brother flanking her. Their strides were all in step. For the first time, Evan met my eyes with confusion. What were they doing?

The sun bore down on the three Ranguvariians. The guards yelled some more, and they walked over to the massive switch that operated the bridge. It slowly began to rise, but the three soldiers of the Allyens marched ever onward.

When they reached the chasm, they all three crouched in unison and then completed a gigantic jump like I'd never seen with the help of their magic, although their wings did not appear. They easily leaped across to the two guards' horror and promptly knocked them out in no time. They never even stood a chance.

The bridge was lowered once again so that Evan and I could cross. I felt the humidity seeping upward off of the water filling the moat, and it made me sweat more than I already was. I averted my eyes from the two unconscious guards, afraid to look at them. I'd seen far worse things in life, but for some reason I didn't want the reminder that my Ranguvariian protectors could be kind of scary sometimes.

The Ranguvariians pulled on the thundering, metal doors and ushered us inside where surprisingly cool air met us. It felt amazing. I pulled at my clothing to separate it from where it'd joined to my wet skin hours ago to feel the delicious cold, waving it back and forth for more. I grabbed my canteen and downed it, no longer having to worry about rationing water.

It wasn't until it was gone that I finally looked around the main hall. Great, silver beams held up the dome of glass above, and there were specially designed windows within it that I was sure had something to do with the air circulation and how it remained untainted by the heat outside. But, I hadn't marveled at its beauty long before the sound of arguing reached my ears.

"Frederick, I did what you advised! I led my people into that battle against my better judgment! Now, they are angry because of the great losses we sustained. I *refuse* to enter this war again!"

The five of us rounded the corner quietly. Daniel was sitting on his throne, which was also made of glass, his head flung forward and his fingers buried in his navy hair. Frederick was standing next to him with his arms crossed, but his shoulders slumped, fingering his signature white tunic.

Off to the side of the room was Queen Lily sitting on a plush sofa, her nimble fingers stitching away at what looked to be yet another tapestry of her dead infant. Her bright orange hair, the color of tiger lilies, hung in curtains, obscuring her face.

Frederick stammered, "Daniel, I-…"

Rachel cleared her throat.

The two Royals looked our way, but Queen Lily remained engrossed in her work. Frederick smiled in recognition – and, perhaps, relief – and strode over to us at once. Daniel removed his hands from his hair and slouched backwards against the back of his throne, his arms crossed stubbornly.

"It is so good to see you all," Frederick said as he met each of our eyes in turn, his expression glowing with happiness. "How is everything? How are Cassandra and Dominick? Why are you all here?"

Rachel was just beginning to open her mouth when I couldn't contain myself any longer and blurted, "Please tell me you know where Sam is. Or Xavier. Are they here?"

Instead of saying, "oh, yes, of course, we have them upstairs" or something like what I'd been dreaming for nearly the past three weeks in order to keep myself sane, Frederick's blue eyes widened in shock. Then, his golden brow furrowed as he said, "What do you mean? They're not back in Lunaka by now? I thought plans were in place to rescue-..."

"There were," Rachel said grimly. "But, it didn't work. Both of them went MIA in the last battle. Since they never found us, we decided they had been captured, and Auklia is the only kingdom that takes prisoners."

Frederick could only blink for a couple of seconds, trying to absorb everything we had just told him. He mumbled, "So..."

"So?" I asked desperately, my hands clenching into fists.

I nearly dropped to the ground to beg when Daniel spoke up. His orange eyes were hard as he said, "I doubt they are here. I cannot sense either of them."

"You wouldn't be able to sense Sam until you saw him. He's a Rounan," Luke said slowly, almost whispering the last word. I didn't like it. It made me feel like my husband wasn't good enough for Daniel and reminded me of the way Archimage Dathian thought him unimportant. Evan took a step closer to me.

Daniel's eyes wandered to the ceiling, almost unfeelingly. "Then, we will check each and every dungeon. For them both. Perhaps, something is keeping us from sensing Xavier as well."

I breathed a huge sigh of relief. I couldn't help but think that I would be reunited with Sam before the sun set. And that

I would see Xavier again, too. Unfortunately, I couldn't have been more wrong.

After conversing with Daniel and Frederick for several hours in the throne room, all the while with Queen Lily ostracizing herself from us, we headed our separate directions for some much-needed sleep on something other than the ground. Rachel and I were led upstairs by an elderly maid with a kind face, who was dressed in a simple, light-blue frock.

My anxiety heightened when another servant led Evan, Luke, and Jaspen in the opposite direction. It seemed like only bad things happened when our group split up. Maybe, if I hadn't split up from Sam to visit the Archimage Palace, he would never have been drafted. Of course, I'd never find out what would have actually happened. I tried to satisfy myself with the thought that Evan had two Ranguvariians to keep him safe.

Rachel watched wistfully as her husband was led away, and Jaspen poked his head over his shoulder just once. When their eyes connected, I felt such a sadness that I wondered how often they were forced to spend their time apart.

All my thoughts and worries were forgotten when the maid opened the door to the room where Rachel and I would stay while we were in Kaiya. The room itself was decorated with nothing but seashells of every type. The ridged, flat ones lined all of the walls and surfaces, while great, spiral cones of beautiful oranges and pinks topped the poles on the four-poster bed as well as the door frames.

One entire wall of the room was made of stained glass, mixing all the colors of the rainbow together into what seemed to be a much larger image only to be visible from the outdoors. When the smell of salt reached my nose, I hurried on my tip-toes through the gorgeous yet fragile room to the balcony on the other side, set within the stained-glass wall.

I had misjudged how many stairs we had climbed. We were so high up that the capital city below looked only like a tiny, rural town. You couldn't even see the streets from this height, only the mass of assorted buildings.

Beyond that were the rolling waves of the ocean. The deep, sapphire that moved kind of like the fields of golden wheat at home once it was tall. We were so high that I couldn't see details, only the vast expanse that shimmered in the sunset.

It was so much more than I ever imagined it to be, but it wasn't long before I was tossed among my worried thoughts for Sam, Xavier, Bartholomiiu, and Kylar all over again.

The roaring sound of the ocean became the backdrop of my dream once my tired eyes closed. The world turned completely white; no sky, no ground, nothing but me in a blank void.

Suddenly, I was rushing forward and I didn't know why, as often happens in dreams. Sprinting through a void, nothing to see, I could hardly even tell I was moving forward. But nothing quenched the fierce desire to find Sam that continuously propelled me forward. Everything was a blur, and it felt like an eternity went by of just me running across a blind world with no structure.

My thoughts never turned to any of my other friends. Just Sam.

Sam. Sam. Sam.

I had to find him before it was too late. Too late for what? I didn't know. This dream was the vaguest one I'd had since I became an Allyen.

"Lina!"

I stopped in my tracks so hard that I tumbled over myself, bouncing on the flat, nonexistent white ground. My bare knees scraped the ground, staining the pure white with dirty crimson. This caused me to look down at myself for the first time. I wasn't in my normal clothing, just a ragged, baggy tunic that came to just above my bleeding knees.

"Lina!"

My head spun around. It was Sam's voice. It was undeniably his. To my left, I could see something. A small blackness that stood out against the blank white of the world. I jumped to my feet and dashed towards it. I squinted at it, but it only seemed to become blurrier. My heaving breaths were the only noises in the void now. No more ocean noises. My ears rang.

"Sam!" I yelled so hard that my voice broke. My eyes began to fill with tears. Would I ever find him?

As I gained on that strange coloring in the sea of white, the blurriness began to subside. The blackness reorganized itself into long, vertical posts. Bars, my mind realized with a jolt. It wasn't until I had run for several more minutes that I could see what was beyond those bars.

I was now maybe fifty feet away. An arm was reaching through the bars as far as it physically could, and it was clear enough now that I could make out the angular mark of a Rounan on it.

It was Sam.

"Lina!" He shouted again as his face appeared behind the bars, and then his auburn head of hair in dire need of a haircut. His expression was pained in several ways. Frightened, worried, injured. All of the worst things. His eyes, which were normally so vibrant and so full of warmth, were oh so hollow. It was shattering. Everything beyond that never came into focus.

My heart jumped for joy yet lurched in worry. Why was

he behind bars? It didn't matter. He was here. Nothing would ever separate us again. Our hands were within feet of each other when the entire world was sucked into blackness, rocking back and forth.

I had to blink my eyes several times to refocus them. Above me was the same shell-decorated chandelier that I had stared at before going to sleep. It took me a minute to remember where I was. Auklia. Kaiya. Daniel's castle.

I jumped when Rachel's voice came lilting through the balcony door. "Lina, you are darn near impossible to sleep around, you know that?"

I groaned, having a lot of trouble waking my mind up. I rubbed my temples as I said, "What do you mean? What happened?"

"You were thrashing the whole night!" Rachel grumbled as she walked back into the room. There were shadows under her blue eyes, and her bright red hair was in disarray. She looked downright exhausted, like she hadn't been able to sleep a wink in the one place where she didn't have to be quite as adamant about keeping watch.

"I'm sorry, I didn't realize..." I trailed off as I swung my legs over the side of the bed. My mind was carried away by the sight of Sam behind those bars, and my heart ached so much that I rested my hand there for a minute. My other hand dug under my pillow to stroke Sam's bandana.

Rachel's brow furrowed her pale, freckled forehead. "Did you dream something?"

Tears filled my eyes. My gut reaction was that I didn't want to talk about it. But with Rachel, that wasn't an option so I didn't even try. I mumbled, "More like a nightmare."

My friend came to sit next to me, her eyes piercing through me. "Well, what happened in it? Do you think it was the future?"

"I don't know." I shrugged and hugged my knees. I could still feel the scrapes even though they were invisible on my skin. "It was unlike anything I've ever dreamed. The whole world was white, like it didn't exist. All I could see of Sam was his arm and his face. He was behind bars."

Rachel raised her hand to stroke her chin like old men do with long beards. She thought for a few moments and sighed, "I think I'm going to have to consult with my grandfather on that one. I'm sorry I don't have an answer for you, but I'm sure your weakening magic has something to do with it."

I nodded, trying my very best to swallow the lump that had risen in my throat. Sam's face was haunting me. He looked so lost, and I couldn't find him. It broke my heart.

While Rachel left the room to converse with Jaspen about what I'd told her, I threw myself into getting dressed. An entire Auklian noblewoman's wardrobe had been laid on the petite, shell-studded vanity. My Lunakan attire must have been too dangerous for the riotous capital city of Auklia. As I petted the smooth, indigo silk, I remembered the last time I had seen the same material, although it had been far less fancy of an outfit.

Keera had worn something similar to this when I first picked her up in Stellan and took her home. I didn't remember what color it was anymore, but Auklian women wore cool colors while the men wore warm ones. I missed my little cousin. I missed her so much.

My fist tightened on the fabric that played like water over my body as I pulled it on. I would never forgive Rhydin for what he and his people did. Murdering my grandmother. Killing my cousin. Destroying my sister. And, for what he planned on doing. Forcing Nerahdis to accept him as emperor, something we hadn't had for nearly three hundred years. More like as dictator.

We could never let that happen. Rounans and Ranguvariians would die in droves. Who knew what would happen to people of Gornish descent like myself. Then again, I already knew what my fate would be if Rhydin ever succeeded.

I shook my head to clear it of those thoughts. There was no way Evan or I would let that happen. We would die first. Once we found the newborn child who could become the next Allyen and we had our full magic back under our belts, we would end Rhydin's campaign once and for all. He wouldn't even know what hit him.

But first, Sam and Xavier. I needed to get Sam back, and we needed Xavier's blessing if his child was to be the next Allyen once it was born. I swallowed my discomfort at that thought. I needed to get used to it.

Queen Lily would never give us a child of hers. Dominick was too old, and there was no telling when Frederick would be able to return, making another child of his not even a possibility. I seriously doubted any random noble descended from Royals would willingly give us their child either.

Xavier and Mira's baby was our only chance. If anything happened to that baby, the Allyens would be doomed.

Chapter Thirteen

Nothing could prepare me for the realization of how many jails, dungeons, and prison camps, both permanent and temporary, were in Kaiya, Auklia.

While their numbers alone were staggering, the vast assortment of inmates within them was mindboggling. Aside from regular criminals in for murder and robbery and such, each institution was absolutely bursting at the seams with captured soldiers from both Mineraltir and Lunaka.

I realized then why Evan and I had been provided with Auklian clothing. Our Lunakan attire would have incited even more anger from the imprisoned foreigners. I hoped at least a hundred times that they wouldn't notice our brown hair under our hoods. Full-blooded Auklians never had brown hair.

It took us nearly two weeks to comb our way through the various places that held prisoners of war nearest the castle. Each day, we were shuttled to the next dungeon in the shuttered Royal carriage in an attempt to keep our eyes from seeing the true state of Auklia.

Upon entering the capital city for the first time, it was ten times worse than what we had seen from afar. The smell of a million fish was interlaced with the odors of waste and sewage. It smelled as if the entire city was rotting with decay.

We passed hundreds of people sitting or lying on the side of the road, dressed in rags that looked like they were molding, their caps outstretched even for the smallest copper piece. Those that were empty-handed hurled insults at the carriage as it raced down the narrow sandy roads. Curses at the crown mostly. Thankfully, nobody seemed to know that the Allyens were in town so far.

We rode through the noble district one day in order to visit a prison camp that had sprung up on the opposite side of its boundary, much to the dismay of the wealthy residents. It was like night and day between this district and its much larger, poorer counterpart.

The noble buildings were tall, glossy triangles reminiscent of the castle and its spires. They looked like they were hosed down daily with ocean water to keep them so clean, and there was no smell other than the brine of the massive body of water less than a quarter of a mile away.

The people here wore silks beyond my wildest dreams. The gentlemen and ladies alike wore long silk robes that reached their feet, cinched at their waists with beautifully crafted sashes adorned with gold coins and baubles that reminded me of marbles.

Of course, as always, the men wore reds, oranges, and yellows while the women displayed blues, greens, and purples. The immaculate, beaded train of one noblewoman's dress slowly made its way through each of those three colors and all the shades in between.

The spring-up prison camp was a far different story. The

Mineraltins and Lunakans kept at this one in particular were in appalling conditions, worse than the rest of the dungeons we had searched so far. The tents were spindly with no clean water. It was obvious by their soiled and rotting bandages that none of them had been tended to in weeks.

At the beginning of this process, I thought that Auklia was doing a great thing by taking prisoners, rather than just slaying anyone left behind. However, as we visited more and more of these encampments, where none of the soldiers were treated correctly, my opinion started to change. We saw three times as many prisoners each day than we saw actual citizens of Auklia. The Auklian people were vastly outnumbered, they had taken so many soldiers hostage. There were thousands of them.

I used to think it was great that they avoided bloodshed as much as possible, but the drain on the Auklian economy was palpable. The people were on rations. There wasn't enough food to go around with thousands of soldiers to provide for. Many of the people were so hungry that they refused to work for the crown. This explained the smell of rotting fish. They were left upon the shoreline, no one around to clean and process them.

It was no wonder Daniel needed Frederick's help. But to me, it didn't look he was doing a thing to fix his people's living conditions. I asked him once why he didn't just send the wounded soldiers home to their respective kingdoms. He responded that they would only attack again and that keeping them in custody was the only way to stop the attacks. I wondered if Daniel was delusional enough to think he had enough dungeons for the entire armies of Mineraltir and Lunaka combined.

As we rode along in the Royal carriage on the way back to

the castle after a long day of checking more jails, dungeons, and prison camps, I felt at a loss. Nearly two weeks and around half of the areas checked, but still no Sam or Xavier.

My hopes of finding them alive were draining rapidly. They had been missing for a season and a half. It had been practically half a year since I left for the Archimage Palace and last saw my husband. Nearly a season since I'd seen my son. I was beginning to feel like they were both a figment of my imagination.

Thump!

The abrupt noise sent a jolt through my system, and Evan moved closer to me. Something red was smeared on the large window of the carriage. That was followed by more red and some translucent yellow. The sounds of them colliding with the carriage almost sounded like a hailstorm at home. It didn't take me long to realize that they were rotten tomatoes and eggs.

Rachel and Luke, who were on the opposite felt-lined bench from us, moved quietly to ensure that the carriage doors were locked. The thumping noises were soon accompanied by yelling and shouting, but I tried to tune the hateful words out. I raised my legs to my seat and put my head between my knees, covering it with my arms as it continued ceaselessly.

I knew the people were upset with King Daniel and Queen Lily, but deep down, it felt far more personal. Their guards had wanted to kill me. And Evan, because we were the Allyens. We were the ones that defeated Duunzer, Rhydin's dragon that brought all of their misery upon them. Why couldn't they see that?

"Why are they complaining about us? I don't understand."

I peeked up at Evan from my knees and focused on the words being hurled about outside. "Why don't you help us?"

"The Allyens are good for nothing!" "They're no help, hang them!" "The Liberator is actually helping us end this war!"

Rachel sighed, "There are some who don't understand why the Allyens aren't helping discover the culprit behind Duunzer."

"But we already know! It's Rhydin, but no one believes a three-hundred-year-old sorcerer exists!" My brother's voice rose. A tomato smacked the side of the carriage.

"I know, believe me." Rachel lifted her hands in defense. "But, there's a difference between the truth and what people are willing to believe. Unfortunately, it's Rhydin's move right now. We can't play until he reveals himself."

Luke crossed his arms over his armored chest and said, "Yeah, so in the meantime, we're going to take advantage of the time we have to find Xavier and Sam. If we needed to make a move now, we'd be in big trouble."

Evan's eyes found the floor of the carriage then met mine. They were sad. They were tired. Our magic was dwindling. A lot of the time, I couldn't sense the people around me anymore, and it made me feel blind. I had come to depend on that skill, even though I'd spent the majority of my life without it.

The part I hated most was that we had no idea how long it would be until it was truly gone. Until it would be too late, new Allyen child or not.

I raised my chin a little higher once we exited the city. "Who is the Liberator they were talking about?"

"I'm sure you've heard the stories. Some amazing person swoops in to tell the targeted towns that they're going to be attacked so they can pick up and leave. Doesn't matter what kingdom they live in," Evan said, possibly with a hint of sarcasm. "People are beginning to believe that he or she is the only one trying to actively end the war, so it's fueling all their hate of the Royals. And us now, I guess."

"I see," I mumbled. "Sam told me about that person a long time ago."

Evan peered at me sadly as the carriage came to a stop in front of the castle. A couple footmen stepped forward and opened the nasty door to the nasty carriage. Rachel and Luke both stood immediately, the carriage slightly too small for their almost Ranguvariian heights.

Evan paused for a minute before following them, gripping my shoulder tightly as he did. "Wait."

Rachel and Luke turned mid-step, both their hands outreached for the massive door into the castle.

Evan took a deep breath, readying himself. "I think it's time to use magic to find Sam and Xavier. Our hesitance to use it could be the very thing that kills them."

"No, definitely not, it's-…!" Rachel spun fully around, her hands on her hips, ready to give us a good lecture. But my brother never gave her the chance.

"We're not in the mountains. It won't take that much. Xavier has magic, we'll be able to sense him across the whole continent. Lina's bond with Sam will help us sense him. But spending each day searching a tiny handful of a hundred prisons isn't going to save them!" Evan spoke more firmly than I'd ever heard him speak before. His hand was still tight on my shoulder. "Please. All I'm asking for is a minute at most. Just to narrow down our search. Otherwise, we might as well call it off right now because we'll never find them if we have to search the whole continent."

Rachel set her jaw. Luke looked concerned, but it was more than obvious who was in charge of making the decisions around here. Rachel's *matrii* began to glow light green, and she whispered a few, musical words before stopping and listening for a moment. She was consulting with Jaspen, I thought to myself.

It was several more moments before she spoke hesitantly, "Fine. But I'm cutting you off at thirty seconds. Not a millisecond more."

Before she even finished speaking, Evan whirled around with a serious look in his eyes. Dead serious. He pulled my shoulder so that we were facing each other, and he eyed me carefully. He whispered, "Better do this now before she changes her mind. You focus on Sam, and I'll find Xavier, okay? Are you ready?"

I swallowed hard. Anxiety and hope billowed through me. If we used too much, the magic would be gone forever. Yet, I couldn't wait any longer to find my husband. I gave a curt nod and pulled out my locket while Evan located his disc. We stared at each other for a moment, lining up the two halves carefully, and plunged them together all at once.

A burst of white light exploded from the joined locket, but we didn't have any time to lose. I drew upon my magic, trying to suppress the sigh of relief at how good it felt to have it at my fingertips once more.

Rachel counted the seconds out loud. "One. Two. Three."

Rapidly, I thought of Sam's presence in my mind and focused on it, expanding my search with every second.

"Nine. Ten. Eleven."

I pushed out beyond the city of Kaiya. He wasn't here. I became immensely grateful that Evan had volunteered this, or we could have been searching for weeks more with no luck.

"Seventeen. Eighteen. Nineteen."

Nowhere in Auklia. I was going to have to open up my senses to all of Nerahdis. I could see it all in my head. The prairies of Lunaka, the forests of Mineraltir... Caden's Plain... The island republic of Caark.

"Twenty-Five. Twenty-Six. Twenty-Seven."

It was then that I sensed him. His presence was unmistakable. And oh, so far away. He was in the Great Desert. Southwest of Iondria, the only recognized settlement. I tried zeroing in closer.

"Thirty! Stop now!" Rachel shrieked.

Our magic shut off. I immediately felt cold without it even in the desolate Auklian heat and humidity. Evan and I were both breathing hard; I hadn't noticed until now. Zoning in on a presence in less than thirty seconds was a feat. My limbs felt heavy. I wondered how much magic we had left now, but I was too excited. I knew where Sam was!

"Well?" Rachel quirked her eyebrow, her arms crossed over her chest. "Where are they? Was it worth it?"

I couldn't stop from beaming. "Sam is southwest of Iondria in the Great Desert! I know it!"

Evan gasped between breaths. "Xavier was hard to locate. I can barely sense him. His presence is very weak. All I could tell was that he's somewhere in Mineraltir."

Rachel looked from one of us to the other and shook her head. "Why would Sam be in the Great Desert? There's nothing there except a teensy trading post. And if Xavier's in Mineraltir, there's only one place he could possibly be."

"But he was behind bars in my dream! He could be in danger!" I whined, taking a few steps closer to her.

"Well, if Xavier is in Mineraltir, it's a wonder Queen Jasmine hasn't killed him yet," Rachel murmured. "We need to save him first. He is in more danger."

"But-...!"

"Know Sam why in desert, I."

The four of us turned to the behemoth door to the castle. There stood Jaspen, still covered head to toe in his cloak in an effort to keep any of the servants from seeing him, but the tips of his ears made bulges on either side. He exuded heat, his leathery, scarred face streaked with sweat.

"Why?" Rachel questioned, looking frustrated that she didn't know all.

Jaspen turned to her and put a big hand on her shoulder. "Talk to Clariion today, I. Prison tower find there by searching others."

"But who would have a prison for soldiers of war all the way out there? No kingdom wants anything to do with the Great Desert, that's why it's unincorporated!" Rachel was almost shouting now.

"But need lie low who?" Jaspen nearly whispered as he looked down at his frazzled wife lovingly and took her hand.

It hit me almost like a brick. I breathed, "Rhydin. Rhydin's tower is in the Great Desert! Where nobody will stumble across it!"

"Of his places, one, at least. Are correct, you." Jaspen nodded at me a little breathlessly. The heat was getting to him after just moments of being outside all covered up.

My heart fell into my stomach. Rhydin didn't just shoot at Sam, he captured him! And he knew. He knew Sam was a Rounan. The *Kidek* no less! I nearly screamed, "We have to go after Sam right now! He could die any second!"

"So could Xavier," Luke grumbled, different emotions warring across his face that turned his eyes a rainbow of colors.

"Let's move this conversation inside," Rachel said quietly, eyeing the two footmen who were currently washing the splattered tomatoes and eggs off of the carriage.

If it wasn't for the intense fatigue I was beginning to feel after the use of magic, I would have been bouncing on my heels in worry and stress. The five of us disappeared through the gateway into the main hall of the castle, its beautiful, cooling air hitting us instantly.

Daniel and Frederick were both seated inside, which seemed to be the bulk of what they did with their daylight hours. Daniel sitting on his throne of glass while Frederick paced the floor spouting ideas for what Daniel could do to make his situation better. All. Day. Long. Honestly, if I was Frederick, I would have gone home months ago.

As soon as the door was shut, I launched my case. "Rachel, it's no secret that Rhydin hates Rounans. *He's* the one that started the hangings three hundred years ago, the one who's responsible for keeping the hatred of them alive. The only thing he could *possibly* have in mind for Sam at this point is death!"

"Lina, I understand what you're saying, but-..." Rachel tried to say before being interrupted.

Luke spoke firmly, "You also have to understand that Xavier, the future king of Mineraltir, is being held by the one person who hates him most. Who will torture him until he loses his mind!"

"That's just speculation!" I flung back at him, "We don't *know* Xavier is being held by Queen Jasmine! Evan said he's *somewhere* in Mineraltir, he could be anywhere in the entire kingdom! We know for sure that Sam is in Rhydin's prison tower!"

"Hey!" Frederick called from the opposite side of the room as he began to trek his way over. "What are you all arguing about?"

I groaned loudly, but Evan beat me to the punch. "We

discovered the locations of Sam and Xavier. Neither of them is in Auklia. Sam is being held in one of Rhydin's prison towers in the Great Desert, and Xavier is somewhere in Mineraltir."

Frederick grimaced. "If I know Xavier, the only reason he would ever set foot in Mineraltir right now is if he was captured."

"Which is why we need to rescue him immediately," Luke mumbled.

"While Sam is stuck with the world's biggest Rounan hater," I snarled.

"I see your dilemma," Frederick acquiesced, his hand absent-mindedly scratching the back of his tanned neck. "It sounds like you may need to split up."

Ever the compromiser, I thought to myself, but I jumped on this one. "Yes! Let's do that! We'll go get Sam, and you guys can go save Xavier! It's perfect, that way we don't have to choose!"

"Lina, we can't split up. Without James and Bartholomiiu, we don't have the numbers to keep you and Evan safe," Rachel responded, her blue eyes sad. "We're not trying to make you think we're having to choose between who is more important to our cause. I promise you that-…"

She stopped speaking when she recognized my body language. My arms were crossed firmly and defensively, my eyebrow quirked, and my eyes hard. My chin jutted out as I weighed my words, and I spoke out of my pain. "I don't believe you. You think Xavier is more important because he's Mineraltir's heir. That Sam isn't important."

"Lina," Rachel moaned, threading her freckled fingers through her tangled hair.

"Have solution, I," Jaspen said quietly, reminding me that

he was there.

Now that we were inside, Jaspen had pulled his heavy cloak off to reveal his thin, Ranguvariian garments underneath. A bright, yellow tunic with tribal designs on it and a thin red border, his sleeves etched with beautiful beads. His long, leathery arms were completely bare to help with the heat, aside from the occasional piece of armor, which was tight and hot-looking. He bent down from his seven-foot height to whisper in his wife's ear. After all, she was the official leader apparently.

Rachel nodded a few times and straightened her Auklian dress when Jaspen resumed his stoic position in the background. She sounded like a polished speaker when she opened her pink lips once more. "Our cause means nothing if we lose our Allyens. It is my decision, as the head of the *Alyen nou Clarii* and the future Clariion, that we shall return home to Lunaka. By now, Princess Mira will have given birth to her child. Especially with your usage of magic today, I feel that this is most important at this time. We do not know how much time we have left."

"And, no offense, but you two look terrible," Luke said quietly, his nostrils flaring slightly in judgment.

Evan and I looked at each other. Closely, this time. Evan's naturally round face was thinning, making his cheekbones more prominent while his cheeks were becoming hollow. His lips were thin and cracked. His hair had dulled in color, and his fingers seemed like nothing more than flesh and bone. The skin underneath his eyes was puffy and almost violet-colored.

I could only assume that I looked the same, being that we shared the magic and were twins. What would happen when the magic couldn't strengthen us anymore? I imagined what it felt like to step onto the mountains, multiplied it, and shuddered.

I shook that thought from my mind as soon as it formed. I couldn't let my anxiety get into the way of my finding Sam and taking him home to Kylar. That was the only way our family would be whole again, and I refused to accept any other outcome.

"No," I whimpered, as I met Rachel's eyes once more.

Rachel's expression changed from one of confidence and strength to one of confusion. "What do you mean no?"

"No!" My voice gained ferocity. "I refuse to return to Lunaka without Sam!"

"Lina, I didn't ask for your opinion," Rachel answered, her eyes hard. "We're going home to Lunaka to regenerate the Allyen magic with Mira's baby. And that's that!"

"What would you do if you hadn't seen Jaspen for half a year, huh?" I wailed, my hands scrunching into fists.

Before Rachel could respond, Evan reached forward and placed his hand on my shoulder. He was like the calm right before the storm. "I agree with my sister. We are not going to take Xavier's child without asking."

"He surrendered the ability to make that decision when he left without telling anyone! We can't wait any longer!" Rachel's temper flared in a worse way than I'd ever seen.

Evan shouted, his expression incensed, "You can't make a big deal about Xavier being the heir if you're willing to sacrifice his own heir!"

Before I knew it, the main hall of Auklia Castle turned into a gigantic yelling match. Evan backed me faithfully, not any more willing to steal a child without full permission than I was, while Rachel and Luke vehemently tried to order us home to Lunaka to regenerate our magic. Frederick watched from where he stood, his mediating skills overlooked, like a dog who had been beaten.

Daniel remained sitting on his throne, mulling over the state of his kingdom and the chaos that consumed it, both outside the castle walls and within. I wondered if he could even hear us in his stress.

Unbeknownst to me, because I was busy arguing against using Mira's baby without permission and for rescuing Sam as soon as possible, Jaspen quietly slipped away undetected.

Close to forty-five minutes went by before we had all kicked and screamed ourselves out. Rachel was pacing, silently but belligerently, while Luke sat on the floor, his eyes still possessing a lingering red color.

I rubbed my temples over and over, like it would help me uncover an all-powerful solution that would make everyone happy. But I didn't think one existed. Evan was stolid as he stood next to me. He had cooled down the fastest. I was still discovering my brother's little personality quirks.

Frederick took a deep breath after having stood and watched us the whole time, then he spoke, "I believe you all should perhaps seek some solace by yourselves. Get some sleep. Maybe, answers will come in the morning."

We all nodded numbly, but before we could go our separate ways, the small metal gate to the tower stairway flung open with a clang. Jaspen tripped through it, completely out of breath like he had run the full length of the castle, his eyes the same color as his golden-yellow tunic with fear. Within his long hand was a crumpled piece of paper.

He sank to his knees before he was halfway across the floor to us, and Rachel hiked up her long, purple skirts to meet him in the middle. They sat huddled on the floor for a few moments while we called to them, asking what was going on.

Rachel slowly stood, the paper within her grasp now, and

helped her tall husband to his feet. Her eyes darted from side to side as if she were reading something, the gears in her head spinning too fast for her mind to keep up.

Finally, Frederick moved toward her, compassion filling his voice. "Rachel, tell us what's happened."

"Th-The child," Rachel stammered, her hands reaching for her head to still herself. "M-Mira's child."

"What about it?" Frederick asked calmly, trying in vain to reassure her.

Rachel glanced upward with a gasp, forcing herself to say the words. Forcing herself to meet Frederick in the eye. "He's ruined!"

CHAPTER FOURTEEN

"What do you mean 'ruined?'" Evan asked calmly as the rest of us stared at Rachel in a mixture of terror and confusion.

"The… The princesses were attacked a few weeks ago," Rachel mumbled, her coherency failing. "They were attacked by one of Rhydin's Followers. The baby…"

After Rachel's words came to a stop, Jaspen stepped forward, now having caught his breath. "Attacked by Rhydin's magic, the boy. Now, is tainted, the boy."

"Attacked," I breathed, shaking my head. My heart went to Mira. I couldn't imagine.

"Tainted?" Frederick spoke up, his face creased with worry. "What about my family? My wife and my son? My sisters?"

"They're all fine," Rachel whispered, her eyes downcast, and nodded at Evan and I. "Cayce and Kylar are fine, too. Just the newborn was affected."

A few seconds passed before Luke took a deep breath,

readying himself to answer Frederick's first question. "The baby has been touched with such great, dark magic that a part of it will always be in him. It has left a mark on him that can never be erased. Therefore, light magic like the Allyen magic can never inhabit him."

Evan and I's gazes met, and I knew that we had come to the same conclusion. We needed a Royal newborn to regenerate the Allyen magic. Xavier and Mira's baby, who we had been depending on this whole time as our lifesaver, was no longer an option. He was tainted on the very day of his birth. My heart twisted at such a thought, envisioning the day that my son entered the world and how wonderful it had been.

Nevertheless, Daniel and Lily had lost their son in Duunzer's darkness and judging by the Auklian queen's constant, overwhelming grief, there wasn't another child coming along anytime soon. My eyes wandered to Frederick where he still stood apart from us, his mouth hidden with his hand. He had been away from Cassandra for even longer than I had been away from Sam.

There were no other Royals on our side who were old enough to bear a child or married for that matter. Arii had already said Dominick, Frederick and Cassandra's son, was too old.

We would never have enough magic to wait another nine months for a child to be born. There was no one to stop the end of the Allyen magic now. Rhydin had won.

I saw Evan gulp. A coldness descended on the glass throne room. I didn't want to be the one to ask the question everyone was thinking, but my anxiety would not let it lie. I whispered, "So, what do we do now?"

A few minutes passed in silence. Evan and Frederick's eyes were trained at the ground while both Luke and Jaspen's loyal gazes never wavered from my red-haired friend. The quiet extended long enough that even Daniel and Lily gravitated a little closer to us, both of them broken from their respective, stress-induced trances.

Abruptly, Rachel cleared her throat and began to straighten her disheveled skirts. Then, she adjusted her high collar until she looked picture perfect, folding her hands neatly in front of her like a princess. Her voice was cool as she proclaimed, "We lead those that depend on us for as long as we can. I will discuss further matters with my grandfather promptly."

With that, she walked away from us toward the double glass door that led to the staircases, leaving us all in her wake. Jaspen began to follow her, but I tugged on his long, yellow sleeve to stop him.

I looked up at him solemnly and whispered, "What is the boy's name? Is he okay other than...other than being touched by dark magic?"

Jaspen nodded silently. "Unsure, right now. Is Taisyn, boy's name."

"Taisyn," I murmured as I released Jaspen's sleeve. He jogged a couple steps to catch back up with his wife who had disappeared upstairs.

I felt sick. We should have never left Lunaka. This would have never happened if we had been there. Guilt swallowed me whole. It could have just as easily been Kylar, my own son. It was definitely time to go home.

But how could I go home without Sam?

I tapped Evan's shoulder and pulled him away from the group. Frederick had also left to go upstairs, likely to write a letter to his stressed family while Daniel and Lily melted back into their own problems.

Luke moved away to give Evan and I some privacy.

Looking into Evan's eyes, I noticed how fully he gave me his attention. We had grown a lot since our first meeting when he would barely give me the time of day.

"Evan, the Ranguvariians are right," I confessed quietly to keep Luke out of earshot, my fingers rubbing together awkwardly. "It's time to go back to Lunaka. If our time is truly at an end..." – I paused, the thought still made me gag a little bit – "Then, I don't know about you, but I'd like to spend whatever time we have left before Rhydin comes for us with my family. Not off in another kingdom trying to stop a war out of our control. But I-..."

"You can't go home without Sam," Evan finished my thoughts, his expression thoughtful.

Words couldn't make it past the lump developing in my throat, so I just shook my head.

My brother set his hand on my shoulder, gripping it firmly. "I understand that. I, too, think it's time to go home. Our time may be almost up, but I'm not going down without a fight."

"What do you mean?" I questioned, my voice rising in volume. Luke glanced our way for a second then looked away.

A mischievous grin I had never seen before spread across Evan's face. "I don't feel like giving Rhydin any sort of satisfaction that he's won. I'm going to ruin his plans as long as I can. Go get Sam. I'll go save Xavier. They deserve to be rescued before we're useless and no one else can get them. We'll show Rhydin that he can't have our people. Magic or no magic."

"B-But what about after Rhydin kills us?" My voice trembled.

"We'll send them to Caark, to the Great Desert, to the Ranguvariians, maybe even away from Nerahdis as a whole. You and I will make sure that even though we failed, our family won't have to pay the price," Evan muttered, his eyes downcast.

"But what about the rest of the people of Nerahdis? They'll be abandoned!" I nearly yelled, and Evan shushed me.

"They can't all fit in Caark." Evan shrugged, and when he saw the horrified look pass over my face, he added, "It's an unfortunate truth, Lina! And something we can no longer do anything about. Now, I am going to go talk to Luke about coming with me to get Xavier because the clock is ticking."

"You're going to tell him you're going? But they'll just stop you!" I argued, grabbing his elbow before he could walk away from me.

He turned back to me and grumbled, "Don't forget, Lina. They're our protectors, not our bosses. They're here to keep us safe, and Luke can still come along to keep me safe in Mineraltir. It's his choice really, although his transportation magic would be very beneficial. I'm going regardless."

As Evan walked away toward Luke, the ground rocked underneath me. I watched Luke's face turn from calm to frantic, his eyes flashing numerous colors, but Evan didn't stick around to give Luke an opportunity to say no. He immediately walked off, likely to go gather his things and ready himself for his trip to Mineraltir. Luke was instantly on his heels, and I wished I could be that confident. But, I wasn't willing to give up, so I knew whom I had to face.

I trekked up the glass staircase to one of the upper floors which housed the room Rachel and I had shared for the last several weeks while combing Auklia's prisons for two people who weren't even in the same kingdom. The seashell decorations had lost their novelty long ago, and while still beautiful, they now only reminded me of how far away I was from home.

Rachel was not in the room, likely still communicating with her grandfather, Arii, or perhaps Jaspen. I took advantage of this time to change out of the fancy Auklian duds loaned to me upon arrival and back into my simple, brown tunic and trousers.

When I held them up to my nose, I could still vaguely smell the earth of Lunaka, but most of what plagued my nose was the brine of the nearby ocean. I had never been so homesick in my entire life, nor had I ever been away from home for so long. I was turned around busily packing my few possessions and tying my usual red sash that hid my sword tightly around my waist when I heard the door open.

Rachel's blue eyes were wide in confusion when she took in the sight of me in my Lunakan clothes all packed up, but to my surprise, she suddenly revealed her brilliant white teeth in a rare, genuine smile. "I see you are taking my advice and readying yourself to go home. I'm glad you see it my way."

Although I was inwardly cringing, I braced myself. Evan was right. I was the one in charge around here, and she'd have to kill me to make me go home without Sam. I tried to make my voice sound authoritative. "Rachel, I'm not going to Lunaka. Not without Sam."

Rachel's red brow furrowed, her mouth opening and her finger rising to make a point, but I didn't let her have the chance.

"I'm not going back! I'm rescuing my husband. You can come if you want, but I'm still going," I said firmly, sticking my fists to my hips for extra effect. "If the impending loss of my magic is going to allow Rhydin to kill me anyway, then there's no point in being overprotective now."

My friend's shoulders slouched. Hurt traveled across her face before she walked forward and threw her arms around my head since she was so tall. My face was buried in her chest, so I could hardly hear her words. "Jaspen and I will take you with our magic. We wish we could protect you from everything, but we know we can't. But, if Rhydin is there, please do not blame us if we take you back to Lunaka without Sam."

I swallowed hard, but I didn't need any convincing to know it was a risk I would have to take. After all, one lone Allyen with failing magic had no chance of breaking into one of Rhydin's prison towers all by herself, much less getting across the continent in less than half a year. I could only give Rachel a nod in agreement, but once I did, she was a whirlwind.

She cycled around the room a few times gathering her things as she spoke in the fluid Ranguvariian language that was still like music to my ears. True to typical Ranguvariian style, a plan was instantly in place. We would transport to Iondria in the Great Desert well before dawn to ensure we made it to the tower before sunup. Both Rachel and Jaspen were confident that was the optimal time to stage our break in.

Before bed, I meandered out to the dark, empty hall and walked barefoot to the opposite wing of the castle where Evan, Luke, and Jaspen were. Auklia Castle echoed a lot in the night, I noticed. It must have been all the metal and glass supporting rather wide-open spaces. My light footsteps sounded like thunder whenever the castle slept. Sometimes, it reminded me of home and how the floorboards seemed to squeak so much louder while Kylar was sleeping.

There was a balcony at the end of the hallway where Evan's room was, and to my surprise, I saw his short frame standing at it before I ever reached his door. Wordlessly, I thundered the rest of the way down the hall to join him. His eyes were trained on the ocean as its cool air brushed the hair from them, but he looked surprised when he saw me.

Before he could vocalize the question on his lips, I answered, "Big things are happening in a few hours. I just wanted to see you before we split up and wish you well, brother."

Evan remained emotionless. "You're concerned we'll run out of magic before we see each other again. Aren't you?"

I sighed, "It's going to be close. You can't blame me for trying."

"We won't die when the magic runs out, Lina. Only when Rhydin easily takes us out," Evan whispered.

The roar of the ocean swallowed up our words for a few minutes. I gazed out at the city of Kaiya, one that I felt I was getting to know pretty well now. I picked out the brightest lights as the areas of town that still maintained their appearance while where I knew many of the prison camps were huddled was plunged into darkness.

How much longer could Daniel keep this all going? How much longer before the people revolted and placed a new ruler on the throne? Or, perhaps, could the Auklian economy even live with such an oversized strain on it? Would the Three Kingdoms of Nerahdis become only two?

Evan cleared his throat, which brought my attention back to him. He was swallowing several times, his eyes darting between me and the city below.

"What is it?" I asked as I folded my hands on the balcony ledge.

"I need to tell you something. Something I should have told you a long time ago," Evan said quietly, not able to meet me in the eye anymore.

I continued to look at him, but I tried not to hurry him. After all, he had promised me that he would tell me about the

Allyen between us and Grandma Saarah once I was stronger, and I felt as fine as one could be with weakening magic.

My twin took a deep breath and declared, "I know whom the Allyen before us is, but I don't know how to tell you this without destroying everything you think you know."

My eyes widened, and a small amount of fear gripped my heart. My voice quivered as I responded, "What do you mean?"

Evan's breathing began to quicken and grow erratic. He continued to stare out at the ocean, as if in hopes that I would simply disappear. As I stared at him in anxiety, I realized how truly terrified he was to reveal this information to me, and I wished I knew how to help him. I began to utter a few senseless words, but he interrupted me.

"No. I'm not ready to tell you," Evan conceded to his fear. "Just please trust me that I'll tell you once I can. Please don't hate me. Please just trust me. You'll understand why this is so hard as soon as you know."

Before I could say one more word, Evan threw himself from the balcony and bolted down the hall to his room. I stood in his wake in shock. Evan was always the calm one of our group. The one who didn't get worked up easily, and even if he did, he always managed to be the first to cool off.

What could be so terrible about the Allyen before us that could reduce him to such fear? Why did he think it would destroy everything I "thought" I knew?

I went to sleep that night with more uncertainty than the finalism I had hoped for. Regardless of whatever secret he was hiding from me, I was unable to get a real goodbye from my brother. I desperately hoped that our magic didn't run out to allow Rhydin to come for us before we were both home in Lunaka with our respective rescues. At one point, it may have been good enough, but not anymore. Evan occupied a special place in my heart now.

No sooner than I closed my eyes, I felt Rachel jiggling me awake. I fought the fierce to desire to pull my Auklian silk pillow back over my head, but it was a close one. My eyelids screamed for sleep, but nothing could quiet the remembrance that today I would see Sam. Today, I would see my husband for the first time in half a year.

My blood pumped faster, and I jumped out of bed. Rachel and I had slept in our clothes, so we grabbed our things and supplies, all readied the night before. It was still dark throughout the castle, no light trickling in from the various glass windows or from the dead chandeliers above our heads. Our feet echoed loudly, and more echoes came from the opposite wing. Luke and Evan were leaving at the same time for Mineraltir.

We all reached the throne room at the same time. I, for one, was washed over with relief that I would hopefully never have to step foot in this room again. Too many arguments here. Too much dysfunction.

Queen Lily was not to be seen, but Frederick and Daniel stood expectantly in the middle of the room. They seemed like polar opposites to me. Like the sun and the moons. Frederick was always working, always fighting. Trying for what was best for his people and never giving up even after his father disowned him. Daniel, on the other hand, seemed to have lost his fire. He tried to reflect what Frederick gave him, but to no avail, remaining in the shadows. I wondered how long it would be before the sun went down on his reign.

"I wish you success, Lina," Frederick said as he smiled sadly. "Thank you for always having faith in me, even before you knew who I was. I-... I will miss you very much."

His words tugged on my heart, reminding me of how we had met as children. I'd given him so much hope that he could be a good ruler, even though I didn't recognize him. Frederick put his hand forward, as if shaking hands was the way we'd say goodbye.

Wordlessly, I pushed his hand aside and threw my arms around his wiry neck. Frederick was no longer the Royal that I had feared my whole childhood. He was the one who told me I was an Allyen. He was my teacher. My friend.

I pulled away slowly and curtsied deeply. "Thank you, Frederick, for everything you have done for me. You will always be my king."

Frederick's gaze softened, and he looked away before anyone could see his emotions. Daniel gave me a sharp look from the corner of his eye, but I had no words for him. Perhaps, he wished I did.

My brother gave his attention very briefly to Daniel, after all, Daniel had once helped him with his training, and then walked to the center of the room. Luke took his place next to him as Rachel and Jaspen guided me in the same direction but with a substantial gap between us. Our respective Ranguvariians took hold of us in order to guide us to our destinations and double-checked that each of us still wore our feather charms to keep our presences invisible.

Even as the Ranguvariians began to hum their transportation spell, Evan's eyes remained trained on the marble floor. At the last minute, just as the Ranguvariians' colorful, shard wings wrapped around us to speed us away from each other, Evan looked up and met my gaze. He smiled sadly, but before I could give any sort of response, we were whisked hundreds of miles away from each other.

When I regained my orientation, my skin immediately

recognized the change in climate. I felt strangely lighter as I realized how much I'd gotten used to Auklia's insane humidity. It was sweltering and crushing all the time, and while my feet landed on sand once again, the air felt so much clearer. I couldn't help the deep breath that dove into my tired lungs. It was still dark outside, not even a faint glow to hint at the coming dawn, so I couldn't see anything.

"This way," Rachel said with a tug on my arm to let me know which way that was. "We are just outside Iondria, the trading post, so we need to get moving."

I stumbled along as I followed her, although it was really more like she was dragging me, leading me to wonder if Ranguvariians had some sort of night vision. The sand felt a lot deeper here rather than in Auklia, so my feet sunk with every step.

I lost all sense of time as they tugged me along in the dark. We crossed too many dunes to count. Part of me was slightly disappointed. I had never been to the Great Desert before, and I was missing all of it.

Finally, firelight appeared ahead. My eyes rejoiced to have something to look at. Rachel pulled me down behind the last dune between us and the fire, and Jaspen dropped to my other side. I continued to stare at the abandoned fire in front of us, but when I glanced to Rachel and Jaspen, they were both looking up. When I joined them, my heart fell.

The fire was several feet away from a massive tower that stretched tall into the night sky. You could only tell where it started and ended by the absence of stars, it blended in so well. Rhydin's prison tower easily dwarfed Auklia Castle in height alone. It made me feel like an ant. I turned back to Rachel and whispered, "Is Rhydin here? Can you sense him?"

"No," she breathed. "I can sense a few of his Followers

inside, but not him."

A flood of relief rushed through me. We had a chance to get inside! I wished with all of my might that I could have enough magic to sense Sam, but I knew without a doubt that there would not be enough. Our magic was almost gone.

Two guards dressed in black came around the corner and took their posts by the fire. Rachel and Jaspen suddenly weren't next to me anymore, so I watched the guards intently. They had no idea what was coming.

If I hadn't been staring nonstop, I probably would have missed their blows. The Ranguvariians were so speedy that the guards didn't even have time to look. They both keeled over on the ground, knocked out, within seconds. Joy surged through me that, perhaps, within minutes, I would be with Sam once more.

Rachel gestured to me, and I hustled over to the two of them as fast as my weakened state could muster. They both grimaced, and when I reached them, Jaspen gently pulled me up onto his back without a single word. I wasn't fast enough to not get caught apparently. The two Ranguvariians tip-toed around the tower to the dark side that wasn't illuminated by the fire.

"There aren't any windows," Rachel murmured as she studied the building. "There has to be some sort of vent for air somewhere, otherwise they'd all suffocate."

She and Jaspen stretched out their arms and began searching for a vent. Meanwhile, the clock was ticking in my mind, and with each tick, my fear heightened. Rachel summoned her wings and began to search higher up, but it felt like an eternity before she called back down to us that she had found one. There was a hushed, metallic clang, and she dropped to the ground next to us.

"Give me Lina, and stay here," Rachel ordered rapidly, "We'll meet at the rendezvous point once I give the signal."

As Jaspen handed me over, he caught Rachel's hand and gave her a peck on the lips. An unspoken conversation went through the air above my head, but I tried not to notice and to give them privacy.

Then, Rachel jumped into the air and guided me to the air vent, which was hardly big enough for a person. It was tall and thin, and only a little over eighteen inches in width. Jaspen would have never fit through it, and it was a miracle that Rachel and I could wedge ourselves into it. I had wondered why she had told him to stay behind.

The vent opened up into a long, thin chamber only the tiniest of bits wider than the opening. We shuffled forward, our arms outstretched in front of us due to the tightness of the vent. I thanked my lucky stars that I wasn't claustrophobic, otherwise this would be a huge problem.

Hundreds of questions cycled through my head. How would we find Sam if Rachel couldn't sense him, and I didn't have enough magic to? How did we know which way we were going? What kept us from bumping into one of Rhydin's Followers at every turn?

Rachel was behind me, seeing as she had to keep us airborne while I climbed in, but we didn't dare talk. Instead, as we moseyed along, she would tap on the heel of my boot every time our vent came to a crossroads. She would nudge it to the left or to the right, push it down or lift it up according to what direction we needed to go next.

I was dying to ask her how in Nerahdis she knew which way to go, but that question had to wait until we could talk freely without fear of discovery.

At long last, light began to filter into the vent-space in front of us. Rachel continued to nudge me forward, so I sped up toward the light. My arms and legs were beginning to cramp from having such restricted movement for so long.

Due to my awkward position, my fingers reached the wrought-iron grate before I could really get a good look at it or make sure no one was on the other side. I pushed with my fingers, but it didn't budge.

Dread slid down my throat. What if I was too weak to get the grate off? After a reassuring tap on my boot, I pushed harder with as much of my hands as I could. Nothing.

In shame, I turned my head over my shoulder and uttered as loud as I dared, "I can't…"

Without a sound, Rachel wiggled her arm up next to my legs. I rolled over to hug the side of the vent to give her room. A barely audible whistle resounded, and a bright green surge left Rachel's hand, flew past my face, and slammed the grate open.

I kicked myself forward and snatched the grate out of the air before it could thunder to the ground. Suddenly, I found myself hanging halfway out of the vent with only Rachel's hand in my sash keeping me from falling on my head.

Rachel lowered me carefully then pulled herself out of the vent. We were in a small, white-tiled staircase that led upward to a thick, wooden door. I fought the urge to ask questions and followed Rachel as she snuck up the stairs.

Once at the top, she pulled me to the side, hidden from the door, and knocked on the door loudly. My ears rang with the sound, and anxiety gripped me hard. Why was she being so noisy?

The door swiveled open heavily, masking us further, and none other than Eli strode through. My fear turned into anger as I recognized the former Auklian advisor that had lured me to Lunaka Castle the night my magic awakened nearly two years ago.

Eli looked around for the source of the knock, and when he glanced the opposite direction, Rachel lunged for him, lifted him high over her head like the fierce Ranguvariian warrior she was, and threw him down the stairs. He smashed into the stone wall at the bottom with a sickening crunch, and his massive glasses fell to the ground in pieces. His moan told me he was still alive.

Rachel flew through the door and promptly knocked out the other two Followers inside, one of which was Terran and a woman I didn't recognize. I cautiously followed her and pulled the door shut behind us.

Now that we were finally alone, my questions erupted. "Where are we? Where's Sam? How did-…?"

"Sam has to be the most important prisoner in this tower. After all, he is the Kidek. Once I sensed that most of Rhydin's Followers were in the same chamber, I knew it was probably a safe bet." Rachel grinned from ear to ear, her face bright with the sweat of victory.

She wandered around the room that seemed like some sort of antechamber to the door opposite the one we came in. When she pulled on it, it was locked, but it didn't take us long to find the keyring dangling from a hook on the wall. She asked breathlessly, "Are you ready to see Sam?"

I nodded like a child on their birthday and nearly ran across the room, even with my ever-draining energy. Rachel stuck a key into the lock, but the wrong door opened.

CHAPTER FIFTEEN

Rachel threw herself in front of me as the door we had previously entered opened once more. In the dim torchlight, all I could see at first was a dark, black cloak decorated with Rhydin's emblem. Panic raced through me. I felt blind without my magic to help me sense who this person was or what kind of powers they possessed!

My Ranguvariian protector let out a fierce war cry and lunged for the figure in black. An explosion of violet energy rocked the tower, and I found myself falling backward. Rachel blocked most of it, but when I regained my senses, a loud thud resounded as Rachel was thrown against the hard, brick wall.

Beads of sweat gathered on her forehead as she struggled to remain conscious, so I didn't have to be told that this person was using Rhydin's magic. Rachel wouldn't last long, and neither would I if I had to use magic. I jumped to my feet and spun to face the door that separated me from my husband.

"Stop!" A man's voice shouted from behind me, but with less anger than I would have imagined. "Please. Turn around so I can see you."

My breath stuck in my throat as I rotated ever so slowly, my hand still firmly latched to the iron key in the lock. Once I had turned, the man closed the door once again and drew his hood away from his face to let it fall against his shoulders.

This was a new Follower. Or, at least one I hadn't seen before considering he looked to be in his forties. He was short, and a little too thin. There were gaunt hallows in his cheeks and under his eyes. His brown hair was speckled with gray as well as a receding hairline, and his face was unshaven. The shape of his face triggered something in my memory, but I couldn't put my finger on what it was.

"Linaria... How you've grown," the man said as he took a couple steps nearer. "I was hoping I would see you again. It's been many more years than I imagined. How old are you, child?"

I took a few steps backward to counteract them. The back of my neck began to crawl with the Follower's strange questions. My voice quivered as I said, "Twenty-one. Who are you?"

"Lunaka's sake, has it really been twenty-one years? No matter, we will remedy that soon enough. I am so glad you have come to join me at last!" A strange, crooked smile stretched across the man's aging face, like he had not used those muscles for many years.

I threw my hands up as he tried to come closer. "Stop! Look, I don't who you are, but-..."

"They never told you. Did they?" The man's countenance suddenly changed, his awkward smile disappearing. His eyes took on a darkness that wasn't there previously.

Wait. His eyes. They were brown with speckles of gold in them. Like Evan's. Like mine.

The blood drained from my face. I stammered, "Y-You're an Allyen, aren't you?"

"Used to be, you mean," he growled, "Until my master bequeathed me a far more powerful magic to help him save Nerahdis!"

"*Save* Nerahdis? Rhydin wants to take over Nerahdis and destroy it!" I yelled in my confusion, "He only brought us death and devastation with Duunzer! I should know, I'm the one who had to stop it."

"Yes, *save* Nerahdis! Duunzer was the only way to be rid of all those scheming Royals who only abuse their power! Master would have vanquished the Darkness as soon as he ensured all the Royals met their rightful end," the man spat. "Then, Nerahdis could have had peace and harmony at long last. Rhydin *will* be the one to liberate Nerahdis! You have mistaken my master's motives, Daughter! Join me and help us achieve peace!"

"D-..." I choked, "Daughter? You are the one who is mistaken! Tell me who you are at once!"

The man chuckled, then he snarled, "My name is Robert Harvey. Son of Allyen Saarah. Fifteenth Allyen. Loyal Follower of Rhydin. Father of Evanarion and Linaria. Does that get who I am through your thick head?"

"No." I shook my head, my hands tightening into fists. "You're lying! My papa's name was Liam!"

"No," Robert growled. "That backstabber married my Elaine to hide her from me after I left to join Rhydin! He sent my son away to where I couldn't find him! They knew he was the one I wanted to train, but you'll have to do now. Anyway, they both got what they deserved when they died in Master's Epidemic. If only we'd gotten their little brat too! At least she's ours now."

Rosetta. My sister whom I'd taken care of for so long. Whom I'd mourned for months after Rhydin killed her.

I screamed, picked up the nearest chair, and flung it as hard as I could at Robert's head. With the distraction, Rachel abruptly leapt to her feet, and I found myself wondering how much she had heard. She conjured her brilliant green magic and blasted Robert out the door.

Once the door was barricaded, Rachel raggedly ran over to me and placed her hand on my shoulder. "Lina-..."

I spun away from her as if her hand had burned me and screamed, "You knew! *Didn't* you!"

"Lina, I-...!"

"*How could you not tell me?*" I roared.

A new, muffled voice resounded from beyond the locked door to which my hand still gripped the key. "Lina? Lina!"

"Sam," I breathed, then I muttered over my shoulder to Rachel, "This isn't over. You owe me some *serious* explanations!"

Rachel gripped my arm hard as I turned the key in the lock. "Evan told me that he wanted to be the one to tell you! I didn't mean to keep this from you for so long!"

Evan. All his attempts to tell me something important, and his inability to turn it into words. My heart shattered.

I threw the now unlocked door open. A foul stench reeking of dust, blood, and body odor assaulted my senses and distracted me from my tumultuous thoughts. The cell was tiny and made of large, black bricks, but all I saw was the familiar six-foot form that dangled from chains attached to his wrists.

His uniform was tattered and bloody from a wound to his head – the same wound I had seen him receive the day I thought he had been killed. He looked dreadfully thin and bony. My heart ached.

"Lina," Sam whimpered weakly, his hollow eyes staring down at me as if I was the only thing keeping him conscious. "The chains…"

A single second didn't pass before Rachel used her magic to slice them open. Sam slid down the wall into my arms, but I wasn't strong enough to keep him from sinking to the filthy floor. I swallowed my tears as I cradled his head and held him tightly. He was here. We were finally together again. My fingers burrowed deep into the tatters of his uniform, unwilling to ever let go of him again.

Rachel promptly knelt next to us, fished a Ranguvariian feather charm out of her pocket, and dangled it above Sam for a few moments as she hummed a strange tune. Sam's eyes opened a little wider after a minute, barely to be seen underneath his auburn hair that had grown out longer than I'd ever seen before.

A few of his minor cuts and bruises disappeared while the more major wounds scabbed over and diminished a bit in size. My eyes met Rachel's clear blue ones when she stopped humming, and she gave the smallest of nods.

"We need to get out of here. Robert may return with reinforcements any minute," Rachel muttered as she stood once more and helped Sam to his feet.

Sam and I both nodded. We didn't need to be told twice. The three of us funneled back out of the cell into the in-between room, but Sam broke away from my hand as Rachel and I headed toward the door that led to the staircase. He began turning over bins and cabinets and desks as fast as he could.

"Sam, what are you doing?" I asked hurriedly, feeling the clock ticking on our escape.

Suddenly, Sam unearthed a huge packet of papers from a

thick folder hidden on top of a cabinet, and a wild grin spread across his face. "I'll tell you later, let's go!"

He gripped my hand tightly and pulled me along after Rachel, who was continuing on down the stairs. She whispered loudly, "We can't go back through the air vent, Sam will never fit. We'll have to find another way out."

Panic lodged itself in my chest. This tower had no windows. Numerous vents, but those wouldn't work. Just one door. A lone Ranguvariian, a magic-less Allyen, and a wounded Kidek weren't going to make it out of here alive.

"Rachel, we're never going to make it! Just transport us out of here!" I spoke as quietly as possible, but my fear made it difficult.

Rachel's brow furrowed. "I can't! Transportation requires some sort of door or window, otherwise you can't do it inside a building! Don't worry, I still plan on getting you two home to your son with your magic intact if it's the last thing I do."

Sam's hand tightened on mine, and I could see questions and realization brimming forth in his eyes and on his lips. How much did he know? Did he have any idea how close Evan and I were to losing our magic forever, which would allow Rhydin to dispatch us easily? There was so much I needed to tell him before it was too late.

We continued to hurry down the stairs. I wished I remembered how far up we were and how much farther down we still had to go. My legs burned with the exercise, and I sorely missed the extra energy my magic used to give me.

Every once in a while, Rachel would stop us as one or two of Rhydin's Followers walked down a nearby hallway or turned the other direction. Each time I held my breath, willing them not to turn down our hallway or staircase. After all, I had thrown a chair at Robert. He had to be heading back to that room with tons of Rhydin's Followers to finish us off or force me to join him.

Rachel paused at a corner, but as we waited for whatever Follower to pass us by, I heard her mutter under her breath that the one approaching had no magical presence. As I began to wonder if Rhydin even had civilian supporters who couldn't use his magic, Rachel abruptly grabbed and silenced the person who came around the corner. The person was taller than me but kicked and screamed and squealed, which told me that this was a young woman.

Rachel held a dagger to her neck. The young woman's face was obscured by her heavy cloak. "Hush now, or you're done for. Now, you're going to help us escape and not make a peep, alright?"

The hooded head nodded rapidly as she stared up at the ceiling to keep the dagger away from her neck. Rachel kept a firm grip on her, but she removed the dagger and yanked the hood off the young woman's head.

My heart stopped. Was I seeing things because of my draining magic? Because here in front of me stood none other than Rosetta herself. She had grown in the last couple of years, but there was no mistaking her dirty blonde hair and hazel eyes.

Something snapped inside of me, and before I knew it, I had stepped forward and latched onto the girl's throat with my hand. I spoke lowly and harshly, "Why do you look like my dead sister? Is Robert messing with me? Reveal yourself immediately!"

"L-Lina!" The girl choked, her hands gripping mine. "S-Stop! It's me! I'm the real Rosetta!"

"*Liar!*" I knocked her head against the wall.

Tears streaked down her face as the false Rosetta

blubbered, "No, I'm not! Please let me go! You have to believe me. Mikael and Kino faked my death with one of those Einanhi things because Mikael wanted me with him!"

My brow furrowed as I considered the possibility of this. After all, while Keera had been stabbed to death, Rosetta's body had pretty much dissolved into sand shortly after I touched it. I only had enough knowledge of magic then to know it was drenched in Rhydin's magic, not whether it was real or not.

I loosened my grip ever so slightly as I said, "Tell me something only my real sister would know."

"I-I-I read all the time, and I'm in love with Mikael, and-..."

"Anybody knows that! Try harder!" I gritted my teeth.

"Y-You used to wake me up for school every morning by dumping a bucket of water over my head! Mama used to do it, and after she died, you did it too," Rosetta warbled, her hazel eyes filled with sadness.

I dropped her immediately, and she began to choke and cough. I stared at her. It could only be her. My baby sister. I threw my arms around her and sank to my knees, clutching her tightly. I sobbed, "I thought you were dead because of me! Why didn't you contact me?"

Rosetta pulled away and wiped the tears from my eyes, as if our roles were reversed. "I'm so sorry, Lina. They wouldn't let me do anything here, I was kept locked up for a whole year. Mikael got them to let me out just recently."

"Mikael," I breathed, remembering the boy Sam had taken in that had betrayed us all. He was the one who had let Rhydin into the house where Grandma, Rosetta, and Keera had sheltered. An intense hatred bubbled up within me. I asked her fiercely, "How could you stay here with him? After everything he's done?"

Rosetta looked down sadly and mumbled, "I love him, Lina. Even with all his faults, I can't stop loving him. I want to save him and get him away from here! He'll listen to me one day, I'm sure of it. After all, we're married now."

My heart sank. My sister was married to that traitor. I looked up at Sam, and a tense, hurt expression occupied his face. No one had felt more betrayed by Mikael than Sam, the guy who took him in when he was left an orphan by the Epidemic.

"Okay, this is all really great and all, but we have a prison to escape," Rachel interrupted, as her hand tightened like a shackle on Rosetta's wrist. "Rosetta, you have an opportunity to prove to us that you're different from your traitorous husband. Get us out of here!"

Rosetta nodded quickly. "I'll do whatever I can to get my sister out of here. There's a lift in the core of the tower that can take us right to the balcony on top. Follow me."

Silently, Rosetta threw her huge cloak over Sam and I, the most recognizable ones of our group. Rather than try to coordinate our walking, Sam took a couple of deep breaths and scooped me into his arms with much effort. The sparse healing he had received wasn't quite enough to return him to his full strength. He clung to me tightly, fiercely working to keep me off the floor.

I was reminded of when we traveled this way when Frederick and I had gone into hiding after my magic awakened. We all followed Rosetta closely, and it became very apparent that Rhydin's Followers were used to seeing her in the tower. No one questioned where she was going or who Rachel and her cloaked friend were.

It wasn't long before we reached this lift, which looked like it worked similarly to the pulley mechanisms back home in Soläna. Only minutes passed before the oppressive, musty air of the tower was replaced with the clear, pristine atmosphere. The sun had risen to shine its light on the sand dunes, which sparkled in its rays.

As Rachel called Jaspen to our location, Sam set me back on my feet to give Rosetta her cloak back. I turned to her and clasped her hands. "Rosetta, please come back with us! Don't stay here with these evil people!"

Rosetta shook her blonde head sadly. "Lina, you know I can't. I will not abandon my husband, just as you couldn't abandon yours."

I swallowed back tears. She had noticed the tiny ring on my finger. "Rosetta, I can't live knowing that you are stuck here with Rhydin's Followers. Y-You're an aunt, and you've never even met your nephew! I'm so sorry I never told you what was going on back then. I was trying to protect you, and I only put you in danger-..."

She held up her hand to stop me. When did she become so grown up?

Rosetta said rapidly, "You did what you thought was best. I understand that now. People are coming, I can hear footsteps. You need to go! I promise that I will save Mikael and bring him home with me! I will meet my nephew someday, I promise!"

By now, Jaspen had arrived and taken hold of Sam's arm to transport him away. Sam panicked slightly upon sight of him since he had never seen a full Ranguvariian before. Rachel moved toward me promptly, ready to do the same.

I spoke rapidly as Rachel pulled me toward her, "*Please* be careful, Rosetta! I love you, I can't lose you again!"

"You won't, I promise! Now go! Be the Allyen. Save us

all." My sister smiled sadly, and that was the last thing I saw before the world turned white.

Instead of prairie, I saw nothing but slate gray mountain faces. I felt confused for a moment until I remembered that while the Ranguvariian ability to transport was pretty amazing, they were unable to do it through the magic-less mountains.

That was why when Luke, Rachel, Mira, and I were fleeing the Darkness in Mineraltir, they had to stop and sprint the last jaunt to the mountains. Although, that time was even worse because they couldn't even use their flying spell because of the advancing Darkness, Rhydin's magic.

This time however, Rachel and Jaspen simply summoned their beautiful wings, scooped Sam and I up, and flew as fast as they could through the nearest mountain pass. With everything going through my mind, I didn't register much, so it felt like only seconds before the world blinked white once more.

The smell of prairie grass filled my nostrils, and it almost overwhelmed my senses. I didn't have to wait for my vision to clear to know that we were in Lunaka. Home.

When my eyes opened, I discovered that Rachel and Jaspen had transported us into the middle of a corn field beginning to dry out for harvest now that the summer was nearing its end.

I looked around frantically, the corn stalks too tall to see where Jaspen and Sam had landed. I called out in a bit of fear, "Sam? Where are you?"

"Follow me, Lina," Rachel said, her expression thoughtful. "They're not far off, I can sense Jaspen. We're just outside the Rounan compound. We'll meet up there."

I nodded hesitantly and swallowed my impatience. We

carefully walked down the rows of the corn as the world turned into a great, golden hallway. The dawning sunlight flashed across my face as I moved through the stalks, and I was reminded of when I used to do this as a child.

Papa used to play with me as he did his work, trying to find me in our little corn field. My heart began to ache. Was the man I treasured in my memory truly not my papa?

"Rachel?" I mumbled as we neared the edge of the field.

"Yes?"

"Are you sure Robert is my father?"

My red-haired friend quit walking and turned to face me, her eyes solemn. "I am afraid he is. I am so sorry, Lina. I would have told you a long time ago if I'd known Evan hadn't had the chance."

"Oh, he had a chance. Several of them, actually," I said bitterly.

Rachel rested her hand on my shoulder and squeezed. "Don't be too hard on him, Lina. Jaspen told me that it absolutely crushed Evan when he told him about Robert. He must have been terrified to do that to you."

I groaned, "It's better than not knowing! If he's my father and another Allyen, why isn't he weakening like we are?"

"His magic has been replaced with Rhydin's. Remember, Allyen magic is different than regular magic. It's closer to Rhydin's in the fact that it isn't your life support, only something that lives inside of you and strengthens you. Something that can be given to other people or taken away altogether." Rachel began to walk again, slower than before.

Then, she continued, "My grandfather was devastated when Robert abandoned us for the very enemy he was supposed to destroy. However, we were so thankful that he had at least rejuvenated the Allyen magic with you and Evan before he left. Protecting you two immediately became our top priority because with your father actively helping Rhydin search for you, you two were the most endangered Allyens than ever before."

"No," I mumbled, remembering one of the things Robert had said. "You left me in Soläna while Evan was sent to Auklia because Robert wanted Evan more than me. Right?"

Rachel's expression turned pained. "Ultimately, Rhydin needed both of you out of the way. But yes, we knew Robert wanted Evan in particular to train him to be evil along with him."

So many months ago, when this all began and I met Evan for the first time, he had been angry with me because I was the one our mother kept. I myself had questioned our mother's decision and how she could ever choose which one of us to keep with her.

Easy, I thought. I wasn't the one our father wanted. Evan was the desired Allyen child. That's why they sent him away for extra protection. I viciously began to think about how I could rub this as salt into Evan's wounds for not telling me about Robert.

Quit it, Lina! You're not the only victim here. Evan had no control over this situation either.

As we finally exited the corn field and the Lunakan landscape was once again spread out before us, I recognized Sam and Jaspen's frames waiting for us at the top of the next hill where the entrance to the Rounan compound was. There was a third frame with them I didn't recognize.

I began to think over in my mind all of the things I needed to catch Sam up on. My true father. My brother. My failing magic. The fact that all our children would only be Rounans, so we had tried to find a Royal newborn to save the Allyen magic. Plus, probably more that I couldn't even think of simply due to the fact that we had been separated for half a year.

It seemed that Sam had acquired a little more Ranguvariian healing in the time it took for our group to reconvene because as soon as he saw me, he ran forward. He gripped me tight and exuded happy thoughts. That he had missed me, and where was Kylar, and he couldn't wait to see his people, and, and, and.

Instead of returning his joy, I felt like a black stone in his arms, weighing everything down. I found myself wishing that I wasn't the Allyen. That Rhydin didn't exist. That we could be a normal, married couple who could raise their son in a quiet world. But that path was never an option for me.

I was just about to open my mouth to start telling Sam everything when Rachel eyed her own husband and a Ranguvariian I'd never seen before. She asked, "What is it?"

The third Ranguvariian simply looked from one to the other, evidently not knowing any Nerahdian, and disappeared into a blink of light.

Jaspen watched the other Ranguvariian go, and then he spoke warily, "Has update, Clariion Arii."

Rachel moved forward and whispered with him for a few moments rather than force him to butcher his speech further.

Suddenly, a packet of papers was waving in front of my face, and a giddy Sam thrust them into my hands. "Guess what?" He proclaimed happily.

The papers were soiled in a couple of places, but there was no denying that they were absolutely covered in people's names, addresses, and other information. I flipped through it for a few seconds before I found Sam's own name, as well as the name of his sister, Kelsi. It abruptly dawned on me. I spoke slowly, "This couldn't be?"

"My Rounan records that Mikael stole from me when my house was ransacked the day your family died," Sam said, sadness dampening his joy a bit. "Now, even if my people are never quite safe, Rhydin at least doesn't have all this extra information."

A smile cracked my weary face. "That's wonder-...!"

"We need to move. Now."

Sam and I jumped, and we both looked at Rachel and Jaspen. They strode toward us rapidly, and, once again, each of them took one of our arms. I cried out, "What? Why? Where are we going?"

Rachel's blue eyes penetrated mine as a relieved smile spread across her face. "A new Royal has just been born."

CHAPTER SIXTEEN

While my mind erupted with questions as to which Royal relative could have possibly just had a baby, Rachel and Jaspen immediately scooped Sam and I up once again.

Their colorful shard wings reappeared, but rather than the world turning white with transportation, the two creatures began to fly as fast as an arrow away from the Rounan compound. I found myself marveling at the fact that we were close enough to this Royal child that we could fly instead of transport. Where could we be going?

The wind buffeted our faces as its roar stopped Sam and I from speaking to each other. He glanced at me several times, and I couldn't figure out for the life of me whether he understood what was going on, was confused, or both.

I kept expecting the Ranguvariians to rotate around and head east toward the rising sun. Soläna, where the vast majority of the Royals and nobles live, made the most sense in my mind as the location of this pop-up child with the capability for magic.

When Rachel and Jaspen simply continued southwest, I wondered if there were some nobles descended from Royals hiding out in the city of Lun. It had to be Lun. If it was any further away, we would have had to use actual transportation magic. A whole new wave of confusion crested over me when the small Royal cottage came into sight.

It had been ages since I had been here. What was once covered in several inches of snow was now nestled among wildflowers and emerald prairie grasses. Why in Nerahdis were we here? Mira just had a baby, and one of Rhydin's Followers had shown up minutes later to keep us from ever turning him into the next Allyen.

Sure enough, Rachel and Jaspen swiftly landed in front of the cottage's ornate, wooden door. Before a second could pass, Rachel barged in without knocking while Jaspen promptly drew his weapon and stationed himself a few yards from the door.

"Lina, what's going on?" Sam asked quietly as he reached for my hand. "Why is Jaspen ready for a battle?"

I turned to him as I heard Rachel bellow my name from within. "How much do you know?"

Sam relayed to me everything that Xavier had told him before they were separated as we headed inside the fancy foyer. He knew that there was such a thing as the Archimage. That the Allyen magic was dying, and it was because Evan and I had both married Rounans. Once the magic was gone, it would be child's play for Rhydin to wipe Evan and I off Nerahdis's face and succeed with his dark plans.

But, there was a slim possibility that a Royal or noble newborn could become the next Allyen because of their malleable, latent magical qualities. Apparently, Xavier had known about Mira's pregnancy and had told Sam that he was willing to give us Taisyn if it meant defeating Rhydin. As Sam remembered the end of his time with Xavier, he suddenly became very quiet.

Something about my expression must have tipped Sam off because his brow furrowed. His voice was low, but he almost sounded paranoid. "What is it?"

I heard Rachel call for me once again, louder this time. I began to walk a little faster through the empty, lavish living room. I stuttered, "W-We can't use Taisyn. A Follower touched him with dark magic right after he was born. That's why Jaspen is standing guard."

Sam looked like I'd slapped him. Then, he cautiously said, "Lina, there's something I need to tell you-…"

"Lina, are you deaf? I need you *now*," Rachel yelled as she finally surfaced from one of the bedrooms down the hall and clamped a hand around my wrist like a shackle.

Rachel dragged me away from Sam to the same bedroom she had just exited, and my eyes suddenly became sponges to the plethora of people sandwiched inside. Along the blue-painted wall decorated with paintings of Lunaka sat Princess Cornflower with young Dominick in her lap, Mira, and Cayce, Evan's wife. A small, green bundle was in Mira's arms, but my sight was arrested by the toddler in Cayce's.

My heart broke in half at how much Kylar had grown in just a few months. He was so much bigger, and his little head bobbled around on his newly defined neck. In just another season, he would be a year old. He was looking around at everyone, and his eyes that mirrored Sam's halted on me, studying me.

I didn't give him time to recognize me or not. I ran to Cayce and plucked him up, trying not to cry as I breathed in his smell for the first time in ages. Behind me, Sam had come to the door, and he drew me back to him with his long arms. My family was whole again.

"Ahem."

I looked to the source of the noise and suddenly found myself blushing. Arii sat at the bedside of a woman who was so pale that it was hard to tell where her pale skin ended and her white sheets began. The chair did little to mask Arii's Ranguvariian height, and he looked out of place in the small, Royal room with his bright orange robes and pointed ears.

Rachel stood next to him loyally, but abruptly, I realized that it was not a strange, pale, haggard woman in the bed, but Frederick's wife, Cassandra.

Sam took Kylar from me as I rushed to her bedside. Her face was so thin and gaunt that I could hardly recognize her, and her midnight hair had lost its sheen. Her favorite rayna flower pin was sitting on her bedside table, dusty from ill-use. The illness had nearly claimed her.

I turned to Arii and noticed the terribly tiny form in his arms. Realization shocked its way through me. How was this possible? My breathing became erratic, my eyes searching from person to person to gain some shred of understanding.

"Lina." Cassandra opened her eyes and beckoned to me with a bony finger.

I returned to her and sat on the fluffy, white bed next to her. "Cassandra, what is going on here?"

"I don't have magic, Lina," Cassandra breathed, "This is the only way I can help you defeat Rhydin."

Arii suddenly pushed his little bundle into my arms. Thinking that he wanted me to hand it to Cassandra, I tried to show it to her, but she held up a hand.

"She's yours now. The next Allyen." Cassandra's eyes closed again. "I found out shortly before Frederick went to

Auklia, but as soon as I heard the Allyen magic was ending, I knew what I needed to do. After all, I won't be able to take care of her."

I clutched Cassandra's hand as my throat began to enlarge in size. "Cassandra, what about Frederick? Does he know?"

Cassandra turned her head a fraction of an inch and looked deep into my eyes. "Lina, this is all I want as I lay here at death's door. You will do this for me, won't you?"

My mind raced with memories of Kylar's birth and of when I saw Frederick last. My friend. My mentor. How could I do this to him?

"Do this, or my death will mean nothing. Or my death will only be the first of hundreds." Frederick's dark-haired wife squeezed my hand with all the strength she had left.

Finally, I stared down at the premature baby in my arms. She was red and micro-sized, almost like a doll. The little hair she had was as dark as her mother's. I could only just narrowly see Frederick's wiry frame. How could I take her when she wasn't mine? Yet, how could I not if Nerahdis had any hope of surviving Rhydin?

My eyes turned upward to the dirty, bloodied face of my husband as he stood in the midst of all the clean Royals holding our own child. He nodded.

I took a deep breath and motioned to Arii. "Do it."

Loud noises began to echo from the outdoors. As Arii turned to me like lightning, Rachel, Mira, and Cayce swept out of the room. I decided I didn't want to know how many of Rhydin's people Jaspen was currently facing in order to allow the Allyen magic to regenerate.

Arii reached for my locket and unfurled Evan's half from within his sleeve. There was no time to wonder at this. Arii combined the two with a burst of light and then wrapped one necklace around my neck and the other around the tiny baby's.

The old Ranguvariian looked flustered as he mumbled, "It's been two hundred and forty-eight years since I have done this."

I gulped. Arii placed each of his hands on our heads as Cassandra looked on. I couldn't tell if she was still seeing us or not. The Clariion began to hum to himself as his magic came forth and light flooded the room. As it continued, I slowly realized that I could sense it. It felt ancient and reminded me of the mountains and the trees.

The warm feeling continued to grow, and my cheeks flushed with heat. The child began to cry, and instinct kicked in as I tried to calm her as I had done with Kylar so many times. It didn't seem like very long until I felt super charged with energy. I felt like I could go run ten miles! The child's eyes opened as she squealed, and I saw her ocean blue eyes transform, acquiring the color of my own. Brown with golden specks.

Arii lifted his hand from my head and placed it with his other one on the child's. While she started to settle, her vague midnight hairs began to turn a familiar shade of auburn, the very color of Sam's hair. My eyes widened at the sight, desperately wondering why Arii felt the need to change her hair color after her eyes already reflected her Allyen status. Even the wiry cords along her neck and jaw that reminded me of Frederick melted away.

When Arii finished, breathless from the effort, he turned to me with eyes the color of sapphires. "The regeneration is a success. Likewise, now, no one will ever know that this child was not born to you and your husband."

As the child began to suck her thumb, I stammered, "What do you mean? Why is that important?"

"My dear, I simply believe that this could make it easier on everyone involved," Arii murmured. "Rhydin knows, unfortunately, or he would not have sent his Followers here today. But, it will make the situation safer for the child as she grows up and will protect the general populace's faith in the strength of the Allyens. It would frighten people to know how close we came to losing the magic forever. It is also my suggestion that, perhaps, Prince Frederick is not made aware of this event's transpiring. He has just lost his wife. He does not need to lose a child too."

I glanced downward. Cassandra's chest was no longer rising and falling. Even though I had barely known Cassandra, just as Frederick's wife and my old schoolmate, I found myself swallowing tears for Frederick's sake. The memory of war torn Auklia destined for economic ruin, its failing king, and its angry masses flashed in my mind.

I mumbled, "Arii, do you have a way of getting a message to Frederick faster than a letter?"

The three-hundred-and-twenty-seven-year-old nodded.

"Tell him to come home," I said, as I clutched his...*my* daughter closer. I stood from the bed and walked to rejoin my silent husband in the doorway.

"Allyen Linaria."

I met the Ranguvariian's eyes.

"The new Allyen child needs a name."

Glancing from Sam back to Cassandra's flower pin on the table, I didn't even hesitate. "Rayna."

Evan had wondered why Luke suddenly needed his half of the locket. They had barely gotten away from Mineraltir Castle when he anxiously asked for it and disappeared in a puff of colorful, Ranguvariian magic only to pop back up seconds later.

It all made sense when Evan's magic came flooding back to him within the hour. He had gone from sitting by the campfire maybe an hour after dawn feeling cold and numb to bouncing around like a hot ball of energy.

Evan was overjoyed to feel his magic rushing back to him, stronger than he ever remembered it. They would live to fight Rhydin another day! The problem of their magic running out had been solved. Now, they could focus on discovering Rhydin's involvement in the war and stop him before it was too late.

Xavier looked slightly relieved when Evan told him of the return of his magic, which was saying something. It had been a miracle they'd been able to bust Xavier out of Jasmine's dungeon, and the appalling conditions they had found him in still unsettled Evan.

Luke possessed quite the mental map of Mineraltir Castle because of his time there with Lina a couple years ago before the Darkness hit, so it wasn't difficult to find the dungeon. Jasmine had confined Xavier in a solitary cell to demoralize him further, and due to the length of his imprisonment and the strength of the magical handcuffs on his wrists, she had grown cocky and only kept one guard stationed at the door.

It was quite a bit easier to free Xavier from Jasmine's physical prison than Evan expected, but the man's state of mind was another story entirely. He had been locked up for two seasons and was mostly by himself except for the daily sessions of torture inflicted upon him by the queen, his stepmother.

Evan didn't blame him for being quiet, withdrawn, and

stern. The only two words he had said since his release were "thank you." But, when Evan's magic came roaring back that morning at the campfire, Xavier's face cracked the tiniest of grins.

"What is it?" Evan asked, thrilled that Xavier was showing even a remote amount of emotion.

"They did it, didn't they?" Xavier responded, his voice cracking from ill-use. "The Allyen magic is saved, and now we can save Nerahdis. I finally did one thing right."

Evan blinked at the Mineraltin prince and thought for a moment. "What do you mean?"

"I gave Sam permission to use my child before we were separated." Xavier beamed as Luke and James continued to work on healing his many wounds. James had come just before they broke into the dungeon, having rejoined them since leaving to take the injured Bartholomiiu home.

Xavier continued, "We're saved, and it's because Mira and I had a child at the right time. To think, I'm the father of the next Allyen! Hey, short stuff, do you know if it's a boy or a girl? I don't even know. How's Mira?"

Evan's mouth went dry. Xavier had shown just a glimmer of his old self again. How could Evan tell him? "Uh... Your child is a boy. They called him Taisyn. I think Mira is fine."

Luke eyed Evan cautiously. Evan didn't need him to say anything to know that he was urging him to tell Xavier the truth.

"I've often thought I never should have gone after Sam. It just made things worse. But if I hadn't, I couldn't have told him that he could turn my son into the next Allyen. Now, it was all worth it," Xavier mumbled as he looked deep into the fire.

Evan cringed. "Xavier..."

"What?"

"I don't know what child they turned into the next Allyen, but...but I'm rather sure it wasn't Taisyn." Evan grimaced.

Xavier's expression turned to a deadpan. "What do you mean they didn't use Taisyn? Why ever not? Who else could there have possibly been?"

"Well," Evan hesitated, his hand scratching the back of his neck nervously. "Something happened."

Xavier jumped to his feet and stormed into Evan's face. "Stop beating around the bush and tell me! Why didn't they use my son?"

Evan shuddered and spoke rapidly, "The day he was born, a Follower showed up and used magic on him. As far as I know, he's fine, but he's been tainted by dark magic and could never become an Allyen."

The prince dropped to his knees. His expression was like he'd seen a ghost. He remained there for several moments speechlessly, and Evan wondered if he should say anything else. He didn't know Xavier that well. They had only seen each other across the Archimage's table before Xavier disappeared to go find Sam.

After a few minutes went by, Evan looked back down at Xavier after glancing at Luke a few times. His ragged, bloody clothing hardly covered him. Nearly two seasons' worth of lash marks decorated every patch of skin Evan could see, some fresh and oozing while others had long ago scarred over. His right arm was mangled to the point where Evan seriously doubted he'd ever be able to use it the same way again. Xavier only had one shred of hope that something good had come out of the last season and a half, and Evan had just dashed it away.

"Take me home," Xavier barely uttered.

James remained stock still as Luke tried to approach him.

"We will once we have healed you a bit more. It will unsettle your wife to see you like-…"

"Take me home *now*," Xavier snarled before strapping his jaw shut for the remainder of their time together. His one good fist clenched over and over as Evan feared his fire magic would spring forth any second.

Luke nodded sadly, his eyes changing to a light shade of blue, almost the same color as his siblings'. He placed the lightest of hands on Xavier's shoulder just as James came to take Evan by the arm.

The world seeped slowly into blinding whiteness this time, and Evan wondered if Luke and James were trying to stall. Upon arriving at the mountains which separated them from Lunaka, Luke and James seamlessly picked up their passengers and flew them over the snowy range.

While icy crystals buffeted Evan's face and filled his skin with pain, it took only a few minutes for the Ranguvariians to fly them across the mountains. Then, everything turned white once more before Evan felt his feet settle in crunchy snow.

He opened his eyes, and there before him was the Royal cottage. It made Nerahdis feel small with how quickly the Ranguvariians could get them from one kingdom to another, Evan marveled. That trip would have taken him weeks, and Evan found himself grateful that he had asked Luke to help him save Xavier.

Evan stumbled into a jog when he noticed Xavier rush off to the cottage's front door. Flames erupted from Xavier's fingers when he found the door locked, and he began to bang on it so hard Evan cringed.

Jaspen came around the corner from the other side of the cottage, his expression bewildered and obviously wondering what was going on. Evan keenly noticed that it looked like

Jaspen had been fighting recently due to his disheveled appearance and breathlessness.

As someone from within finally opened the door to the fuming Mineraltin prince, Evan turned to Jaspen and asked, "What happened here? What child is the new Allyen?"

"Tried to stop us, Rhydin's Followers," Jaspen responded in his broken Nerahdian as he shifted a few of his colored tunics back into place. "Is former daughter of Prince Frederick and Lady Cassandra, the new Allyen."

"Former? What do you mean?" Evan questioned, feeling panic arise within him. "Where is my sister?"

As Jaspen methodically explained the day's events to Evan, that Frederick was unaware he had a second child, Cassandra had succumbed to her illness after childbirth, and Clariion Arii had suggested that Frederick not be told, the color vanished from Evan's face. Rayna's appearance had been magically altered to match Lina and Sam to further the secret from the world.

Evan felt shaken. This was exactly what he and Lina had tried to avoid by gaining Xavier and Mira's permission to use Taisyn. All of the Royals knew. There was no way Frederick could go his whole life without ever discovering that Rayna was born to him. Evan was filled with dread. Just as Jaspen began to talk to him about their next steps in going on the offensive against Rhydin, an explosion sounded from within the cottage.

He and Jaspen rushed indoors to find a scene in the living room. A fresh, black scorch mark had appeared in the middle of the fancy, plush rug that decorated the Royals' floor. It was a few feet from where Xavier knelt on the floor, his wife, Princess Mira, huddled beside him as she clutched their baby boy. Across the room, Princess Cornflower stood hesitantly in a corner, her nephew Dominick tight in her grasp.

Upon the sight of Cayce, his wife, Evan rapidly crossed the room and threw his arms around her. Over her shoulder, Evan saw his sister and her husband, who was just as filthy and bloodied as Xavier was.

Lina smiled the smallest smile she could manage at him, relieved he was alive, but Evan could tell there was something holding her back. Her eyes searched his in sorrow, and Evan wondered if it was because of the situation surrounding Rayna.

When Lina and Sam walked past him and Cayce to the center of the room without words, Evan knew it was something else. He and his sister had come so far over the last several months. What had happened to sever their new connection?

Lina handed her husband the baby she held so that he was now juggling a toddler in one arm and the newborn in the other. Evan didn't envy that, and while part of him wished he had been present for the decision as to which of the current Allyens would parent Rayna, he knew it would be better for Lina to do it. She was already a mother, and she was so close to Prince Frederick.

Sam took a few steps backward with their children as Lina placed a hand on Xavier's shoulder. Those two had a special connection as well that Evan would never quite understand. After a few moments went by, Lina straightened awkwardly and turned around, her eyes wide and horrified.

Evan's lips parted to ask the question, but Lina's husband beat him to the punch. "What's wrong?"

Lina stuttered, "T-Taisyn is blind."

CHAPTER SEVENTEEN

The prairie was dying. The summer heat was beginning to let up, and each evening felt just a mite cooler. The world had dried out and turned brown as the calendar grew closer to Early Autumn. A few weeks had passed since Rayna became the new Allyen, and, compared to the rest of the year, it seemed rather quiet.

For a couple of days, we all remained congregated at the Royal cottage, and the divides between us seemed palpable. Xavier cut himself off from everyone except Mira. He never left her side, even for the briefest of moments, and kept Taisyn close at hand. They often shut themselves into their bedroom, not to be seen for hours at a time, and I found myself wondering if they would be able to overcome this.

No one ever brought up Cassandra's death. The Ranguvariians took it upon themselves to bury her since Frederick wouldn't likely make it home in time. No one really talked at all since it happened. Cassandra was dead. Taisyn was blinded by the attack that left him tainted with dark magic. Rayna was our daughter now, and everyone had been told not to tell Frederick. Xavier was broken, and I... I didn't even know how to begin.

Cornflower became as silent as a statue after Cassandra's death, wordlessly going about her day caring for Dominick until Frederick returned from Auklia. One morning, she confided in me that the Follower who blinded Taisyn had the magical presence of an Allyen corrupted by Rhydin's dark magic. Cornflower was unsure whether to tell me or not since she was unsure of her abilities. But, I knew better, and it choked my heart all the more to learn the evil my father was capable of.

After a few days, Sam decided that we needed to return to the Rounan compound. He was anxious to check in on his people after so long, and I didn't blame him for that. Evan and Cayce came with us in order to give the Royals their space since they had acquired a house of their own in the compound before we left back in the spring.

Evan tried to talk to me a few times during our twenty-mile journey back, but I was nowhere near ready. I had already been furious that he hadn't told me about Robert. That he was our father, not the man that I had grown up calling "Papa." Now that I knew what Robert had done to Taisyn, I felt enraged.

My mind agonized over how it could be possible, but deep down, part of me knew it was true. How could he leave my mother? How could the Allyen abandon Nerahdis to serve Rhydin and be his instrument of evil? Rhydin apparently thought he was helping Nerahdis in some shape or form by taking it over in place of the Royals, according to Robert. I couldn't understand how they were so disillusioned as to think that they were doing good or that infecting a helpless newborn with dark magic could be okay. As far as I could see, the corrupt Royals were the ones on Rhydin's side.

When we arrived in the compound, I immediately began to see why Arii thought changing Rayna's appearance was a good idea. The Rounan people were overjoyed at the sight of Sam. They cheered and clapped and hugged him like he was the best thing that ever happened to them. A few of the women sent hurried, warm glances in my direction, and their smiles always widened a bit at the sight of Rayna in my arms.

We had been gone long enough that none of them even questioned that she hadn't been born to us. In fact, Sam was congratulated a few times. I wondered what would have happened if they had seen a child that didn't look anything like Sam but had my Allyen eyes. A child who wasn't a Rounan on top of that? I could only imagine the rumors. I began to be grateful for Arii's wisdom.

Over the following weeks, as Sam caught up with Kelsi, his sister, about life in general and other Rounan affairs, I found myself gravitating away from them both. It only took about five minutes to remind me that Kelsi was not someone I liked to be around, and I didn't want to be reminded that Sam had never told her that he married me. Eventually, we needed to have a chat about that.

But, he was busy getting caught up on his job, so I spent a lot of time outside, away from everyone except Kylar and Rayna. I tried to readjust to my once normal routine, but it felt foreign now. Everything had changed.

One day, I was sitting outside mending Sam's bandana since it was shredded in the avalanche as Kylar showed off his new crawling skills. I enjoyed watching him, but it made my heart ache at how many of his milestones I had missed. He hardly stayed in one place now.

Rayna was asleep on a blanket next to me, her tiny limbs flailed out around her. My heart still struggled with the concept that she was now mine, but it was better than it had been a week prior. I hoped that someday it would be hard to remember that she hadn't been born to me.

"Lina?"

When I turned, I felt the color drain from my face. Standing silently just a few feet away was Prince Frederick himself. My heart dropped into my stomach. I had heard he had returned to the cottage a while ago, but I hadn't been prepared for him to come seek me out. He had never come to the Rounan compound before. I couldn't help a quick glance down at Rayna. I wasn't ready to lie. What was I going to say?

I mumbled, "Hey…what are you doing here?"

Frederick nodded slowly, and immediately it seemed he was a decade older. Lines had appeared along his brow, and his golden hair had faded. He said quietly, "It took a week to attempt to give Daniel any last advice. The Ranguvariians brought me home as fast as they could. I would have come sooner, but I needed some time…"

I looked down, not knowing what to say. What could I say? How was I going to explain Rayna? My fingers twiddled as my mind raced.

"I never once thought this illness would take her." Frederick's brow furrowed, and his expression took on that of someone who had been grieving for weeks.

"None of us did," I whispered sadly as I hugged myself uncertainly.

A small cry brought my attention back around to the two infants as Kylar slid flat on his stomach unexpectedly. As he erupted into tears, Rayna awoke and stared at him drowsily, unsure of what was going on.

I turned and scooped up my son, somewhat glad that he hadn't outgrown needing me for this yet. It was almost like slow-motion when I saw Frederick glance from Kylar to Rayna, blink a few times in confusion, and turn to me. I knew the question before it even passed his lips.

"Is this the new Allyen?" he asked. "I heard you were able to find a newborn with Gornish magic in Lun. Who was she born to?"

"U-Um," I stuttered as I panicked. "She's... She was the daughter of a noble in Lun. Someone distantly related to your family, I think."

Frederick quirked an eyebrow, his gloom suddenly cast off. "Oh, really? Which one? Cousin Albert or Aunt Meg? How did you get them to let you have her?"

I exhaled deeply. There was no way. Arii was having delusions of grandeur if he thought we could keep this a secret from Frederick. The world was one thing, but Frederick was another entirely.

Secrets between people weren't worth it. They only caused pain and divided people from the ones they cared about. It was a wedge between Sam and I when I tried to keep my nightmares from him. It literally separated Mira and Xavier when he left without telling her. And now, I wondered if my relationship with Evan would ever be the same. I couldn't lose Frederick too.

"Frederick," I said as I placed my free hand on his shoulder. "No one in that cottage wants me to tell you what I'm about to tell you. But, out of respect for our friendship, I find it necessary to tell you something that is going to be very hard for you to hear and cannot be undone."

The Lunakan prince looked at me like I'd pulled the rug out from under him. He glanced from me to Rayna lying on her blanket and back again. "Go on."

My confidence began to falter. "You're right, that child is the new Allyen and she has saved us all. But, she didn't come from a distant relative in Lun."

As Frederick began to breathe a little deeper, I tightened my hold on his shoulder.

"Arii did what he thought was best, but I don't feel right keeping this from you when everyone else knows. It was Cassandra's dying wish that her child, *your* child, become the next Allyen in order to save Nerahdis." My throat began to clog as I tried to hold back tears. "I'm so sorry, Frederick. Arii changed her appearance to protect our family and so Nerahdis won't lose any more of its faith in the strength of the Allyens. Our magic was nearly gone, there was nothing else we could do-…"

He held up a hand, and it was silent around us for a moment except for Kylar's babbling. He was stone-faced as I desperately tried to read his expression. He peered around me to stare down at Rayna, and I couldn't help but feel like a child-stealer. His voice was garbled when he said, "Did Cassandra say why she never told me?"

I shook my head dumbly. Another secret. I took a stab at lightening the blow, having no real idea whether Cassandra had tried or not, and said, "You know mail has been iffy since the war began."

Regardless, Frederick's eyes closed as if he had been struck. "So, I am to lose both my wife and my daughter?"

"Frederick, I thought you would want me to tell you! This way you can try to be in her life!" I pleaded with him.

He shook his head like it was a twitch. "No. I understand why you did it, Lina. If you hadn't, Nerahdis would be lost. It will be less painful if we just continue to pretend that she truly is yours. After all, she looks the part. It could complicate things if the people of Nerahdis discover that she was born a princess. A Royal." Frederick's voice turned to stone as he looked toward the rest of the Rounan compound. The Rounans would hate her if they knew. He continued, "The part I don't understand is why you all kept this a secret from me for so long! For even a moment!"

"Frederick, I'm-...!"

He held up his hand once again. "I already have to deal with the fact that Daniel's ineptitude kept me from my wife during her final weeks and that Xavier blames my absence for his son's blindness. I know you had no choice. Just give me some time. Please."

Frederick scurried away empty-handed. His horse was just a few yards away tethered to the side of our barn that didn't face the compound.

I gripped Kylar tightly, wondering now if I had in fact made the right decision. There was no way I could have convinced Frederick that one of his relatives in Lun had given her to us. It would have come back eventually, and the situation would have been ten times worse.

I sighed and sunk to the ground. Kylar squirmed out of my arms to try and explore again, so I let him go. Instead, I turned to the newborn on the ground, picked her up carefully, and let her rest against my chest.

After how much Kylar had grown and how much of that I had missed, part of me was rather happy to have another newborn to care for. I only wished it was under better circumstances, and that I wouldn't have to miss any more of either of their lives.

I stared at the two children in front of me. Back in the spring, I had been frustrated that everyone wanted Kylar to fit one of two molds. Dathian wanted him to be Gornish to become an Allyen, while Kelsi was thrilled he was a Rounan so he could be Kidek. It made me feel like my son wasn't good enough.

Now, so much faster than I'd ever imagined, Sam and I were the parents of two. One would become Kidek, one was the new Allyen.

While this should have relieved me that no one would fight over my son anymore, I only drooped all the more. Neither of my children were quite a year old, barely nine months apart in age, and they were already being forced into roles they never asked for. Just like Sam and I. I sighed.

As I waited for Kelsi to leave our house, I also silently hoped that Frederick, Daniel, and Xavier wouldn't be too torn apart by what had transpired. Rhydin could only benefit our arguing. When I finally saw Kelsi leave, I gathered my two infants and their paraphernalia. It was lunchtime, and my stomach roared for sustenance.

Inside, Sam was seated at the wobbly table studying his records in depth, still updating them since he hadn't had access to them for two years. He was all cleaned up now, and the only reminder of our harrowing ordeal was a white, jagged scar running from his brow down to his jaw. Every time I saw him, I reminded myself of how differently things could have been if my recurring nightmares had truly played out.

I tossed his newly-mended bandana onto the table in front of him and set the children down in their little hay-filled produce boxes. Sam had picked up a bigger one for Kylar when we got home, so Rayna occupied Kylar's smaller one now.

I called to him when he didn't look up, "Are you all caught up now? What did Kelsi have to say?"

Sam finally sat back from his stack of papers and sighed heavily. "A lot has changed. The compound's population is staying about the same, but there are a lot of people coming and going. It's hard to keep track of, although Kelsi did her best."

"Why's that?" My brow furrowed as I stirred the stew on the fire. It had been going since morning, and it smelled heavenly.

Sam shrugged as he reached for his bandana and tied it back around his head. For the first time in ages, he looked like himself again. "Well, there's a lot of people coming to our compound from other Rounan settlements displaced by the war. With armies marching around everywhere, a lot of these secret places aren't secret anymore. Our compound is the largest one in Lunaka now."

"Then, why are people leaving?" I asked as I dished up food. I tried to pay attention to his words, but my mouth was watering so much it was almost impossible.

"That's what I'm worried about. People are afraid that our compound will be discovered as well, so they're leaving for even more remote areas of Nerahdis. A lot of them are even heading to Caark," Sam mumbled.

"Caark?" I scoffed. "The island off the coast of Lunaka and Auklia? Why would anyone go there? There's nothing there. Just a tiny fishing industry that everyone wonders how long it'll survive."

"No Royals," Sam said matter-of-factly as he shoveled stew into his mouth. "The fact nothing's there is exactly why it's so safe. It has no bearing on Nerahdis as a whole. I don't think Rhydin even cares about it since the Darkness never arrived there back with Duunzer."

After a few seconds of silence and several spoonfuls of

stew, I contemplated that information just as I tried to get a piece of meat out of my teeth. "So, if Caark is so apparently safe compared to the rest of Nerahdis, why do you seem upset that people are leaving our compound to go there?"

"For starters, if every Rounan goes to Caark, it's not exactly going to be safe anymore," Sam grumbled, "Secondly, my eyes have been opened to how seriously we probably need to prepare for when our compound is discovered."

"When? Not if?" My spoon froze.

Sam nodded sadly. "I just think we need a Plan B. That's all. Rhydin is still out there. Now that your magic is back, it wouldn't surprise me if he's planning out his next big move as we speak. It's foolish to think we can actually live here quietly for the rest of our lives. We're lucky to have the two years that we did."

A few moments of silence ensued. I knew that Sam was right, but I didn't like thinking about it. I wished I knew Rhydin's plan. It had to be imminent with how quiet things were. I decided to change the topic of conversation. "So. Sam, I need to talk to you about a couple things."

Sam set his spoon down and glanced at his paperwork once more. "I thought we were all caught up by now?"

"Not quite," I muttered and looked him in the eye. "Why didn't you tell Kelsi that you married me?"

Sam looked back up at me innocently. "Oh. It wasn't intentional, I promise. I guess I just hadn't figured out how to tell her and just kind of forgot. She's my sister, but we don't talk that often."

I sulked. "Does it embarrass you to tell people that you married a Gornish woman?"

"No, of course not!" Sam urged. He reached across the table and gripped my hand. "I have never once been embarrassed or regretted marrying you! Lina, I've loved you since we were kids. I'd never change that. You and our kids are the best things in my life. I'm sorry that I forgot."

I nodded quietly and squeezed his hand. If we were going to lose our home again then fine. But I couldn't lose Sam.

"Besides," Sam said as he returned to his stew, "I've decided to be more active about making Rounan-Gornish relations better. I think we could really change things around here. I'm sorry I didn't try sooner."

"That's great," I said numbly, seriously doubting it would actually happen, but I appreciated his effort. I braced myself to tell him about Robert. I hadn't done so yet. "There's one other thing I need to talk to you about."

"Wait, let me go first. I've already talked to Xavier about this, but I need to tell you something so that you know," Sam said hesitantly. He clenched his hands into fists on the table. "I did a lot of things while I was in the army. Things I'm not proud of."

"Sam, it's war, and you were protecting our kingdom-..."

"I know," he cut me off, "but I did something that I regret every day. When Xavier and I escaped from our regiment, you already know about the avalanche. I was able to free myself, but Xavier was wedged under this huge rock, a-and Mineraltins were coming... Xavier told me to run, and... I did. It's my fault he was captured and tortured, and he couldn't return to Mira before Taisyn's birth to protect them. It's all my fault."

I stared at him in shock for a few seconds. "What did Xavier say?"

"He doesn't see it that way," Sam mumbled ashamedly. "He doesn't blame me because if I had stayed, I would have been captured too. Apparently, he blames Frederick, which isn't great either."

I took a deep breath as I mulled over my answer. "We can't control everything, Sam. We can't see the future. I'm sorry it happened, but if Xavier has forgiven you then I think it's time to move on."

"What about you, though? All this talk of me being ashamed of you, but are you ashamed of me?" Sam responded quietly.

"Never." I smiled at him.

Just as Sam returned my smile, a knock pounded on our door. Sam began to rise from the table, but I beat him to it. I could sense who it was. The concerned face of Evan, my so-called brother, was behind our door.

The short man pleaded, "Please, Lina, I'd really like to talk to you!"

"And I really wouldn't!" I said loudly, but Evan stuck his boot in the door before I could slam it in his face. "Move your foot!"

"I'm not leaving until you tell me why you won't talk to me!" Evan answered resolutely. "Sam, I know you're in there! Make her open the door!"

I whirled to face Sam, but he cleared his throat and chuckled, "She's my wife, Evan. Not my daughter. I can't 'make' her do anything!"

"Please, Lina, I thought we were on the same side!" Evan called through the shoe-wide slit in the door.

"Then why didn't you tell me about Robert, huh? How could you leave me so clueless?" I yelled, my voice beginning to break.

Evan hesitated before he responded, "Lina, I... I'm so sorry. I didn't know how to tell you! It was going to ruin everything you thought you knew!"

"Who's Robert?" Sam whispered to me from across the room.

My tongue took its sweet time mulling around my teeth before I answered, "Our father. I was just about to tell you. He's one of Rhydin's Followers. The one who blinded Taisyn."

Sam's eyes widened in shock and confusion.

"I'm so sorry, Lina! It broke me when I found out, I was trying to spare you from that!"

"Instead, you didn't prepare me for when he would try to *recruit* me and hear him condemn the man I called 'Papa?'" I flung my fist into the door.

"You saw him?" Evan whimpered.

"Yes!" I shouted, "And guess what? I found out why you were the one sent to Auklia!"

"Why?"

"Because Robert wanted you. He wanted to take you and train you to be a Follower just like him," I said icily. "You were so angry with me because I was the one our mother kept. But she kept me because I wasn't the one our father wanted for himself to help '*liberate*' Nerahdis!" My voice transformed into something ugly as I quoted Robert.

"Lina, I'm so-…"

"Go away!" I screamed as tears began to stream down my cheeks.

There was no response from the other side of the door, but Evan's foot remained solidly between the door and its frame.

A few seconds went by before Evan said quietly, "I wasn't fair to you in the spring. It's true. It's not your fault that our parents made the decisions that they did. But you're not being fair to me now. Imagine if the situation was reversed. What would you do?"

I thought for a minute. I just spent the day convincing myself that I needed to stop keeping secrets. I told Frederick about his daughter because I couldn't stand how secrets parted people. But before today? I lied to Sam about my nightmare in order to not upset him. Heck, I still hadn't told him.

I lied to him about being the Allyen when I first found out. I'd probably lied a million times since I was born to all of the people in my life. Before today, I likely would have done exactly what Evan had done. The situation could have easily been the other way around.

"I've lost too many family members to count, Evan," I mumbled just loud enough for him to hear me. "I appreciate that you were trying to protect me, but we can't keep secrets from each other or our friends anymore. It'll destroy us even more than what damage has already been done!"

"So, can you forgive me?" Evan asked from beyond the door.

I let up on the door to allow it to swing open. Evan looked a lot like a guilty child from where he stood, but a moment didn't pass before I closed the distance and flung my arms around him. "Always."

Evan looked relieved when we parted. I told him to come get some stew, but I froze when I turned to see Sam as pale as a ghost still sitting at the table. He stared at his paperwork, dumbfounded, and fear began to bubble up inside of me when he continued not to move.

I asked hesitantly, "Sam? What's wrong?"

He looked up at me like he was trying very hard to remember how to breathe. "I-I think I know how Rhydin is involved in the war. You said Robert told you that Rhydin wants to 'liberate' Nerahdis?"

"Yeah," I whispered, my eyes darting from Sam to Evan

and back again. "He said Rhydin wants to liberate us from the Royals and restore peace. What's your point?"

Sam wet his lips. "The Liberator. The one going around warning the villages of imminent attacks to stop the violence. The people adore him now. I think Rhydin is the Liberator."

CHAPTER EIGHTEEN

"Alright, so here's what we've got," Rachel called us all to order a couple days later.

For the very first time, we all stood together in the same room. Xavier and Mira of Mineraltir, Frederick and Cornflower of Lunaka, Daniel and Lily of Auklia, all of the *Alyen nou Clarii* including the mostly-healed Bartholomiiu and Arii the Clariion, Cayce, Evan, Sam, and I. The Royal cottage was bursting at the seams with all of us inside huddled around the table. Yet, it also spoke to the gravity of the situation.

However, it didn't help that the room felt slightly like a pot that was close to boiling over.

Rachel continued, "We don't have much on this Liberator simply due to the fact that we didn't think he was a threat. But, my brothers and I have spent the last forty-eight hours going around Nerahdis gathering all the intel we possibly could on this figure."

"So, is he Rhydin or not?" Xavier asked impatiently, his

arms crossed firmly over his chest.

"I'm not one hundred percent sure," Rachel conceded, her red brow furrowed. "We have known for ages that Rhydin has been involved in this war somehow, otherwise King Adam and Queen Jasmine wouldn't be tirelessly ensuring that it continues. However, all the people we interviewed from the towns that the Liberator warned said that the person who contacted them was just a messenger. It was never the Liberator himself."

"If Rhydin wants to usurp the Royals, then why would he keep his identity a secret?" Frederick asked tiredly.

"If the Rhydin is the Liberator, he may have done so to avoid our attention," Rachel answered, "We thought the Liberator was a force for good, so we didn't worry about it."

Daniel cut in, "Well, he certainly succeeded if it truly is him."

"The important thing is that through our reconnaissance, we discovered that the Liberator isn't just swooping in and saving towns anymore. He's sending messengers to every town in Nerahdis now to deliver speeches, and, while we haven't been able to hear one in person yet, all of the people we've interviewed have mentioned how much they like and support him." Rachel grimaced. "Apparently, this guy is on some sort of campaign trail for something pretty radical for people to flock to him the way they have, although we're not completely sure what it is exactly. His next speech is actually in Lun in an hour, so we plan on attending to hear for ourselves."

Queen Lily angrily spoke, "Why did you call us all the way here if you are not sure that the Liberator is Rhydin? We cleared our schedules to come today!"

I couldn't help myself from rolling my eyes. This woman

was rapidly getting on my nerves.

Arii rose to his seven-foot height from where he lingered in the corner of the room. He spoke calmly, "Your Majesties, I thank you all for coming here today, but I ask that you remain in Lunaka until we ascertain the Liberator's identity. This figure is speedily becoming a person of interest if the population of all Nerahdis is swaying to him. After all, Rhydin desires to reclaim his rule as emperor. That task becomes much easier to attain if the people want him there."

I felt the blood drain from my face. I mumbled, "Do you think that was his plan all along? Begin a war with Duunzer, control every move of the Lunakan and Mineraltin armies through King Adam and Queen Jasmine, his Followers, and then warn the people before each of those moves to win them over to his side?"

Arii leveled his golden gaze at me. He spoke with a light staccato. "With Rhydin's ability to see the future" –he paused as he gave a heavy sigh– "I would be surprised if it was not."

"Well, Rhydin had no control over my army," Daniel responded nasally. "Say what you will about my pacifism now."

Frederick groaned and glanced at Daniel hatefully. "Daniel, Rhydin had free reign over Nerahdis with the Lunakan and Mineraltin armies because he never had to worry about the one army he didn't have control over. You only moved your army beyond your borders that one time. You played right into his plans because there was no one to stop his two armies!"

"At least my people are alive!" Daniel chirped.

"And your economy is in the toilet!" Xavier shouted.

"My kingdom isn't being controlled by Rhydin!" retorted Daniel.

"It's not our fault our kingdoms are! Besides, if you could control your kingdom, I wouldn't have spent the rest of my wife's life trying to help you!" Frederick raged, so far past the usual mediator I stared.

Xavier seethed, "And if Frederick had been home like he was *supposed* to, my son would not be *blind*!"

"*Stop!*" Rachel screamed as Daniel, Frederick, and Xavier hurled their angry words at each other from across the table. Xavier in particular appeared ready to start throwing more than just words. She looked at each of them disappointedly. "Get yourselves together! If you three fall apart now, Nerahdis is truly doomed." She turned to Daniel for one last remark, "Besides, it appears the Liberator was the source of the initial doubts in your leadership that now feed the chaos in Auklia. None of the kingdoms are without fault."

Mira placed a soothing hand on Xavier's shoulder, pushing down the arm that threatened to scorch the world. Daniel looked like he was boiling while Frederick was too angry and heartbroken to do anything but sink into the shadows. I glanced at each of them in succession before turning to Rachel and saying, "I want to go with you to Lun to hear the Liberator's speech."

Rachel nodded quietly. She looked drained when she finally adjourned the meeting. As soon as it was over, I crossed the room to find the Ranguvariian I hadn't seen since he leapt in front of me to block Rhydin.

Bartholomiiu was almost unrecognizable. His hair had grown out to his shoulders while the lower portion of his face and neck were horribly disfigured. Rhydin had grabbed him there, I remembered. I glanced at the jagged, white lines that ran across Jaspen's face. I had known for a while that the Ranguvariians couldn't be around Rhydin long without growing weak. But, I'd never known that just skin contact could be so horrible.

I tugged on Bartholomiiu's rainbow-colored sleeve. He moved his head slowly, and his eyes were pure white when he looked down at me. I couldn't help the smile that came to my face. "Bartholomiiu, I'm so glad you're okay! I never got to thank you for saving me. Are you back to stay?"

The Ranguvariian blinked at me. For the first few seconds, I kept waiting for the punchline. After all, Bartholomiiu had always loved jokes and laughing before what happened. As the seconds stretched on, my smile faded. The smallest of grins appeared on his face, but nothing else.

"Forgive him, Lina." James appeared from behind Bartholomiiu. "When Rhydin grabbed his neck, it seared his vocal cords, among other things. We couldn't undo any of the damage. He hasn't been able to talk yet, and we're not quite sure yet how much he can understand. He follows me everywhere now. We've been really close since we were kids."

I stared at him numbly. Bartholomiiu remained looking down at me like a tall tree. On that day, I had run off toward Sam without even thinking. Now, Bartholomiiu couldn't speak and had brain damage. It was my fault.

I forgot all the words that had come to mind upon seeing Bartholomiiu and instead inched forward until I had as much of him within my short arm span as humanly possible. James grinned sadly, but there was no response from Bartholomiiu. I let go abruptly and worked my way back toward Sam before my heart could shatter into a million pieces.

Sam eyed me cautiously as he juggled Kylar and Rayna but decided not to say anything about it. Instead, he said, "So, you're headed to Lun soon?"

I nodded numbly as I noticed that most of the Royals had dispersed to their separate rooms, although the tension in the room remained. Everyone was still so divided after what happened with Rayna and Taisyn, and it hurt my heart even more to see. Evan and Cayce remained in the room whispering to each other.

"Do you want me to come with you?" Sam gazed downward into my eyes.

A small smile cracked my face, and I reached between the two infants to grip Sam's lean form tightly. He tucked his chin against my head as I felt Kylar take a handful of my hair. "Sure," I answered, feeling ever so grateful that he could be here with me to save Nerahdis after being gone so long.

"What do we do with these two hooligans?" Sam chuckled as he pulled away, shifting our children in his grip.

"I know," I chuckled as I took them from him. I bounced across the room to where Evan and Cayce were sitting and proceeded to fill each of their arms. "Evan, it's time to embrace your duty as uncle!"

Evan looked at me wide-eyed, which then melted into subtle cheer. Evan had trod lightly around me after our blow-up about Robert, so I knew that he would jump at the chance to do me a service to make up for it. His voice was slightly scratchy as he spoke, "You trust me with them?"

I set my hand on his shoulder. "Of course! Thank you."

I gave Cayce a secret wink before I turned back around. I knew they would be fine in her care at least.

As Rachel and Jaspen moved toward us, Sam grinned and stretched his arms and shoulders, then straightened his Kidek bandana. He wasn't quite used to being a double-armed parent either. Rachel and Jaspen had both changed out of their brightly-colored, tribal ensembles into unassuming earth-tones.

Sam and I always wore regular Lunakan garb, so there was no need for us to change to blend in with our own people. Although, both of us did check to make sure that our feathers were tightly knotted around our necks to hide our presences from anyone who might be looking.

I found myself staring wistfully at my husband as Rachel took my arm and Jaspen took his. Aside from when we left the prison tower, the last time just the two of us had been transported by Ranguvariians was when we went to the Winter Ball shortly before Duunzer attacked a couple years ago. My heart fluttered, but it also mourned when we could actually do romantic things like that.

Sam made a funny expression when he saw me staring at him. His grin crinkled the new scar that framed the side of his face.

No sooner than Rachel and Jaspen opened the door to the cottage, the room flashed white. The wallpapered walls and the ornate, round table disappeared from view to be replaced by open, clear blue sky. Drying prairie grass sprang up between my feet, and the fierce Lunakan wind blasted my face out of nowhere. I breathed its scent of grass and soil deep into my lungs and opened my eyes.

We were on the outskirts of Lun, the only city in the western portion of Lunaka. I had never been to Lun before. The Rounan compound was self-sufficient and I was far more recognizable than Sam was, so Sam was always the one to travel on the few occasions that we needed something.

Soläna, my hometown and the capital of Lunaka, had been built downward to save it from dust storms and twisters. All the buildings were generally only one floor unless you were in the northern part of town where all the nobles lived.

Lun, which was closer to the mountains, had been built upward. As we approached Lun, it seemed that none of the buildings were less than two or three stories. In my naïve mind, the buildings nearly touched the sky. They were tall, built of a mix of wood and metal, and crammed next to each other like a child's building blocks while the wide, cobblestone streets were larger than any road in Soläna. It felt so open and jam-packed at the same time. It was so fascinating and different.

I was shaken from my musings rather abruptly as I noticed the pack of people hoarding through the streets to the center of the city. Their footsteps and chatter were deafening to my ears, and Rachel shoved my hood a little further over my face from behind. After all, we didn't need a repeat of the sort of hatred Evan and I received during our time in Kaiya, Auklia, and I was far more recognizable in my home kingdom.

Jaspen had parted from us once we reached the city limits since it would be impossible for him to blend in with his Ranguvariian height. Instead, I remained confident that he watched us from afar to make sure nothing happened. Rachel, Sam, and I subsumed into the massive Lun crowd and followed them to the center of the city as more people continually joined us.

Traffic came to a standstill in the heart of Lun, the calls of the shopkeepers silenced by the roar of the people. Carts, wagons, and buckboards stood motionless in the street, unable to progress through the crowd.

I gaped at all the people around us, and Sam and Rachel portrayed similar expressions. Whether this Liberator character was Rhydin or not, how could he have achieved this level of following? Everyone in the entire city and its rural outskirts combined had to be here! I could feel myself becoming more and more anxious with every minute that passed as we worked our way through the mass of people closer to the front.

Once we got as close as possible, or rather as close as we dared, I scanned the small platform that had been set up in the central commons. There were a handful of people already standing upon it, none of which were familiar to me.

One man in particular stood in the center of the stage who seemed ready to speak. He was middle-aged, but I couldn't decide if he was a noble or a commoner. His dress suggested both, but that couldn't be possible. I couldn't make out his face from our distance, but he definitely wasn't Rhydin. I'd recognize him no matter the distance.

I turned to Rachel and muttered over the roar of chatter, "Who is that? Is he the Liberator?"

Rachel's brow furrowed as she intently studied the man in the middle of the stage. "I don't think so. That's the mayor of Lun."

"The mayor?" I gawked. Why wasn't the mayor dressed according to his station? While this fact baffled me, I started to hope that this meant the Liberator wasn't Rhydin. Regardless of his overwhelming support, at least Rhydin didn't have all these people. As I inwardly hoped for this, the mayor of Lun began to speak.

"Fellow Lunakans! Thank you for gathering here today! I come on behalf of the benevolent Liberator who promises to liberate us all from the grips of those treacherous Royals! They have thrust us into this outrageous war which has cost all of us so much in terms of money and loved ones. Even the Allyens, who saved us from Duunzer, are hopelessly unable to stop this wretched war," the mayor's voice boomed, silencing everyone within earshot. "Our Liberator is an individual above any of our leaders, and I am proud to announce that he has gathered immense support in our beloved Lunaka, as well as our sister nations of Mineraltir and Auklia!"

"He," I breathed to Sam next to me. He met my eyes for the briefest of seconds before he turned back to the mayor. "He" could still be anyone, but I had been hoping for a "she" in there somewhere to thoroughly prove it wasn't Rhydin.

"Therefore, the time has now come!" announced the mayor. "Our dear Liberator has promised us from the beginning that he will stop this war and the Royals' abuse of us! He will end this war universally so there is no loser! Something that our *esteemed* Royals and Allyens have failed to do! And he has told me himself that this war will end *today!*"

My heart dropped into my stomach. How was this possible? Cacophonous cheering rang out among the masses. I squeezed Sam's hand tighter. They hated me for not accomplishing an impossible task, and it stung.

The mayor straightened his cravat and stood a little taller. He continued, "As I said before, I am so glad you all are here today. Because today, you will not just listen to me relay our beloved Liberator's message, but you will get to hear his words from his own lips for the first time!"

I took deep breaths as my insides twisted themselves into a knot. This was it. We would see the true face of the Liberator. *Please don't be Rhydin, please don't be Rhydin...*

A shorter man took the stage from one of the sides I couldn't see. He wore a clean, white tunic and some regular, faded trousers. Once again, I found myself surprised that this person wasn't more dressed up, but that thought was fleeting. I would know that dark head of sweeping midnight hair anywhere even without the all black ensemble and his usual golden flame crest.

My heart plummeted even deeper. Sam was right. It was Rhydin.

As Sam, Rachel, and I shared panicked looks, the crowd around us began to roar. The very same people who cowered before Duunzer and cursed its creation cheered, clapped, and stomped their feet in thunderous adoration.

My stomach recoiled. How could my people be so manipulated and clueless? And more important, how could we show them the truth when Rhydin had already won so many thousands of people to his side?

Rhydin held up but one thin, pale hand, and the crowd immediately silenced. Such power already, I thought to myself. He masked his normal cruel, bitter tone as he shouted, "People of Lun! Thank you for coming to see me today! I am so pleased to see you all are alive and well even with the Royals' constant attempts to prolong this war and ensure your suffering!"

The mass broke in and screamed curses against the Royals. Against the war. Against us.

Rhydin held up his hand again to quiet the discord, and my hatred began to bubble at this fake facade he was putting on to gain the people's favor. If only they all could have seen him atop Duunzer's head that fateful day rather than being stuck in the Darkness. This would be so different.

"Alas, my reasons for addressing you all, my faithful followers, directly today are of the greatest importance," Rhydin called throughout the commons. "Nerahdis has been trapped in this war for nearly two years! Yet, the reason it started was to discover the origin of Duunzer, the dark menace that ravaged our land! Our leaders have *failed* to do so, choosing to simply dredge on through this unending war! I can tell you confidently now the identity of Duunzer's creator to fulfill my promise of ending this war once and for all!"

"*Who?*" The crowd roared over and over again like a tumbling waterfall.

Rachel was holding her breath. Who was he going to blame? Even from this distance, I could see Rhydin's familiar smirk cross his face briefly. He was enjoying this.

He resumed with such a powerful voice that I wondered if he was using magic to strengthen it. "The Royals have kept a massive secret from us all! There is *another* Royal far more powerful than the rest who controls them just as they control us! *He* is the one who created Duunzer and sent it upon us to force us into further submission! This Archimage, as he calls himself, was supposed to cease to exist centuries ago, but he didn't!"

More angry shouting. My hands went cold at the word "Archimage." Dathian was supposed to be a secret to keep the people from freaking out. Now, Rhydin had spilled the beans, and it was happening. Panic rippled through the crowd like waves.

"Destroy them all!" screamed the mass.

"The Archimage is behind everything bad that has happened! Duunzer! The war! The Royals' abuse of us! He is like a puppet master pulling all the strings in the background!" Rhydin yelled passionately, although I was sure only we could see the triumphant gleam in his eyes. "King Adam of Lunaka and Queen Jasmine of Mineraltir are only pawns in his plan. I promise that I have personally met with them and have discovered that their allegiances lie with you, the people, and they want to be free of the Archimage's power! They deserve redemption while King Daniel of Auklia, I uncovered, is the

Archimage's *nephew* and is a part of his evil schemes!"

With that, Rhydin absolved his own people of crime and condemned my own. My mind raced to keep up with all of his radical claims, which were mostly false aside from a few true ones.

There was indeed a puppet master behind it all, and the Archimage didn't disappear like people thought. Dathian had mentioned he was once an Auklian prince, so it didn't surprise me that he and Daniel were related. Yet, there were so many false claims entangled with the truth. What on Nerahdis were we going to do to combat this?

"I promise you, once and for all, that today dates the end of this war, the end of the Royals' abuse, and the end of anyone who tried to hide the origin of Duunzer, including the Allyens! I *will* end this! I am your Liberator, *Rhydin!*" the dark sorcerer roared.

The crowd erupted into more cheering than ever. They chanted his name. *Rhydin! Rhydin! Rhydin!* An older woman in front of us began to cry tears of joy.

My heart hammered out of my chest as Sam clutched my hand so tight I feared it would break. Rachel rapidly spun on her heel and gripped my shoulder fiercely to turn me as well. The three of us squeezed through the mass away from the center of all the revolutionary lies. I only looked back once, and I immediately regretted it.

Rhydin's amethyst glare stared back at me.

As soon as we reached the edge of the crowd and found ourselves in an utterly empty section of Lun, Rachel yanked her hood off and signaled Jaspen with her bright green *matrii*. Once she finished, she began to pace and fret, "Oh, this is so much worse than we ever imagined. Rhydin had King Adam and Queen Jasmine start this war just for this purpose! To trick everyone into losing their faith in their leaders and make himself look like the best candidate to replace them!"

"What I don't understand is how he expects to end this war so no one 'loses.'" Sam threw some air quotes around the final word. "It's a blasted war, not a child's participation game!"

Jaspen suddenly dropped from the sky, his eyes brown with confusion. Rachel whipped around and began explaining the whole situation for him in Ranguvariian, far too fast for my foreign ears to even try to comprehend.

Even with Jaspen's leathery skin, I could see the blood drain from his face as Rachel spoke. He responded a few times with short, musical interludes, which I could only assume where questions to clarify certain things, but other than that, he remained silent.

Meanwhile, I inwardly reeled. Rhydin promised he would end the war today. But, how did he plan on doing that? While Adam and Jasmine were totally under his control, Daniel wasn't.

Besides, the whole point of the war when it initially broke out was that the people wanted to know who cast Duunzer upon them. Rhydin just told them it was Archimage Dathian, whether it was a lie or not. So, now what?

Once Rachel finished speaking to Jaspen, Sam moved closer to them, his hands jittery with nerves. "So, what's the plan? What are we going to do?"

"That would be a lot easier to answer if we knew how Rhydin expects to end the war now that he's made everything so complicated," Rachel moaned, crossing her willowy arms tightly across her chest. "All he did was basically redeem King Adam and Queen Jasmine by saying that they want free of the Archimage's control just as much as everyone else while condemning King Daniel and our Allyens."

Suddenly, it clicked. It struck me like lightning. I began to think out loud in case my logic wasn't sound. "When I saw Robert, he said that Rhydin wanted to liberate Nerahdis from the corrupt Royals."

"Right, we know that!" Rachel snipped, her patience wearing thin as time to fix things slipped through our fingers.

I met her blue gaze. "Robert said that's why Rhydin created Duunzer. To cover the land in Darkness just long enough to make sure all the Royals not following him and their loyalists were killed. The whole point was to remove all the Kings and Queens and the people who backed them so he could take power."

"And he failed," Rachel answered firmly, beginning to look at me cock-eyed.

"He did then," I responded, getting frustrated. I licked my lips before I got to my point. "But, how does he manage to usurp the Royals now? Without the help of the Darkness freezing everyone, who does he have to murder first in order to take his spot above the Royals? To take control of everything now that everyone loves him and approves of this person's death?"

I could see the moment understanding dawned over Rachel, Jaspen, and Sam. Rachel was almost inaudible as she choked, "Archimage Dathian."

CHAPTER NINETEEN

"But, Rhydin shouldn't even know where the Archimage Palace is! It's hidden with hundreds of charms and enchantments!" Rachel called from behind me as we walked briskly toward the edge of town. "Not even the Royals know, Dathian always summons them with his guards and transports them there himself!"

I whirled to face her angrily and shouted, "After the last few years, I think we all should know not to underestimate Rhydin! I'm sure he has ways of finding out even if he has to scour the whole mountain range."

"But Lina," Sam responded loudly as he trotted a couple paces to catch up to me, "What if it's just a big trap to lure you to the Archimage Palace? We don't know for certain if Rhydin wants to kill the Archimage!"

"Look, you know I don't like Archimage Dathian very much. Or, at all for that matter. But, besides us, he is literally the only thing standing between Rhydin and total domination over Nerahdis right now!" I whined desperately. "If Rhydin fulfills his promise to the people and kills him, the people will make him emperor tomorrow. We already know that he can snap his fingers and end the war, it's been his doing all along. It's Dathian's death that will seal the deal, and we can't let that happen!"

"Lina, will ya quit walking away from us for a second?" Rachel growled so darkly that I froze in my tracks. "I see your point, but what's your plan? We can't just waltz in there and ask him to stop! There's no magic arrow to foil him with one shot this time."

I shuddered in spite of myself. Jaspen, Rachel, and Sam all faced me, their faces twisted with worry and despair. She was right. We were never able to find the arrow after Duunzer was destroyed. While this terrified me, Rachel had reassured me that an Einanhi Duunzer's size needed at least a decade's worth of time to create.

After all, an Einanhi was merely an empty shell of magic given life, you couldn't just make one like Duunzer every day. Even Rhydin didn't have that kind of limitless magic, seeing as he waited three hundred years between the first time he created Duunzer to use against Nora, my ancestor, and the second. Besides, Rachel doubted he would resurrect Duunzer once more seeing as I had already proved myself against it once. No point in history repeating itself for a third time.

Even so, there was no magic arrow to simply hit Rhydin with and have him disappear. He could only be killed with Allyen magic, that was for certain, but as far as how to accomplish that... I had no idea.

Evan and I would have to duel him essentially, and that thought terrified me out of my mind. Besides, we all knew that Rhydin wouldn't be showing up at the Archimage Palace without several Followers and Einanhis as reinforcements.

I stilled my fingers from their anxious twiddle, gave my sash a little yank to tighten it around my waist, and folded my hands delicately in front of me. Taking a deep breath, I mustered my most even tone as I said, "We do have a plan. We go to the Archimage Palace and wait for Rhydin to show up. Then, we take him out. Before he can kill the Archimage. If he fails to kill Dathian and therefore produce evidence that the Archimage exists, the people will think he played them and he'll lose their support."

"How?" Rachel and Sam asked in unison as Jaspen stared in awe.

"Summon our allies," I breathed. "All of them."

We lost no time. Rachel and Jaspen transported us back to the cottage, and within minutes, the other Royals were briefed on the situation. Frederick, Xavier, and Daniel continued to glare at each other from across the table, and I desperately hoped that they could pull it together for the next twenty-four hours.

However, there was no mistaking the shock that entered each of their faces when we told of how many people were supporting Rhydin's rise to power on condition of his ability to end the war. Several hundred people were in Lun. Multiply that by the number of people in Nerahdis? It was staggering. And it had all happened right under our noses.

Everyone began to ready themselves without a moment to spare. Armor, chainmail, and clothing littered the floor of the various rooms of the cottage. The Royals shed their skins of fine materials and jewels, and donned war attire if they had it or chainmail and arm guards if they didn't.

Swords of different styles were sprinkled across the living room. Huge, double-edged broadswords for Lunaka, thin, one-sided blades for Auklia, and something that resembled more of a battle ax for Mineraltir. No shields though. I began to realize that today would probably be the most I'd ever used my magic in battle. To defend and to wound. Even more than with Duunzer.

Evan and I found ourselves a few pieces of armor to strap to our arms and shoulders, but I didn't want to be too weighed down. I tightened my trusty boots that had walked with me through every battle and ensured that my locket was still safely clasped around my neck. I would need its amplification more than ever. I remembered how Rhydin smashed my spells with one hand when I'd tried to fight him without it during the battle with Duunzer.

I planted a firm kiss on both Kylar and Rayna's heads, who both slept through the chaos, and dearly hoped that when I saw them again, the world would be a safer place for them to grow up.

As Sam and I hustled out the door with Evan and Cayce on our heels, Frederick and Princess Cornflower, his youngest sister, were in the heat of an argument. The thirteen-year-old appeared half-dressed between her scarlet gown and a few pieces of armor, and she stamped her heel hard into the ground. "Frederick! Don't leave me here with the babies! I can do so much more to help at the Archimage Palace! I'm an aeromage, not a nanny! Please-…"

Frederick set his hands on her shoulders and overpowered her voice as he said, "Cornie, I need you here. These children are the future if we fail today."

Cornflower groaned loudly, whispering something hatefully that I couldn't hear. Then, she chucked the few pieces of armor that she had managed to put on across the room, and stomped away toward where Kylar, Rayna, Taisyn, and Dominick slept in the corner. Frederick watched her go wistfully, then he followed us out the door and bolted it shut.

Outside, I gasped. In the twenty or so minutes that we had been in the cottage since we returned from Lun, a dozen or so Ranguvariians had assembled to transport us to the Archimage Palace.

There were male and female Ranguvariians, all of them leathery-skinned, freakishly tall, and with pointed ears and a variety of eye colors according to the emotions that each of them was respectfully feeling. They all wore different colors decorated with the same tribal design that I had seen Rachel, Jaspen, and her brothers wear, and some of their hair were filled with braids. I had never seen so many Ranguvariians together in my entire life.

"Lina, meet the rest of the *Alyen nou Clarii*! All of them have watched over you or Evan at some point in your lives." Rachel grinned at my wide eyes and gestured to the rest of her people. "It's time to go! Grab a human and rendezvous at the Archimage Palace! *Iiba Alyenes uny raniin*! Long live the Allyens!"

A chorus of "*Iiba Alyenes uny raniin!*" erupted around us. Various Ranguvariians thrust their fists into the air, and a few finished sharpening their blades with a big flourish. I felt my heart flutter in humility. Rhydin may have tricked all of Nerahdis to follow him, but the Ranguvariians' loyalty would always be to the Allyen.

Evan wore the same expression when I revolved toward him, and he nodded at me. We were ready. The Allyen twins were unified to fight Rhydin together, as it was always meant to be.

One Ranguvariian warrior was left behind to watch over Cornflower and the children, but the rest divided themselves among the humans and took each of them by the arm. I took a deep breath as Rachel reached toward me.

Glittering wings filled with the feather shards I knew so well spread around us all, and as I exhaled, Rachel took a firm hold of my upper arm. The world blinked white for only an instant as I tried to calm my racing heartbeat and twiddled my locket. We could not fail.

When the world cleared again, the edge of the mountains greeted us. Their rocky faces stood out in sharp contrast to the drying prairie beneath them, and the constant Lunakan wind swept any possible loose piece of gravel a world away. All of the Ranguvariians jumped into the sky with their passengers rather than letting us go, and it was mere moments before we were high among the slate peaks.

At one point, I mustered enough voice over the rippling air to ask Rachel how the Ranguvariians knew where the Archimage Palace was if it was such a big secret. She responded that they had always known. The mountains were actually their territory and had been so for far longer than any human had been in Nerahdis.

I gazed in awe as we approached a certain section of mid-range peaks, and, as Rachel led us around to another angle, the vague shape of the Archimage Palace revealed itself from its camouflage.

It was fascinating how well its builders had managed to make it blend in with the rugged scape of the mountains, although I did catch a peek at the gorgeous stained-glass windows that captivated me when we were here last. The ones of the First Three Kings lined up side by side, perfectly equal, with the larger, round depiction of whom I could only guess was the First Archimage.

The Ranguvariians swooped downward in a formation not much unlike a flock of geese and glided across the large drawbridge that was raised to complete the palace's disguise. A sense of childish glee washed over me when Rachel kicked the huge, stone door open without bothering to knock. She grinned at me, knowing how much I rather hated Dathian after his degrading comments about Sam. Our band rapidly entered the acres' long throne room and rushed across the navy-carpeted, deep midnight floor to the other side.

Dathian promptly rose from his black and white marble throne, bedecked in all the regalia of an emperor as a look of intense anger crossed his pale face. He roared, "What is the meaning of this?"

I grumbled, getting ready to come up with a snippy remark, but Rachel beat me to the punch. She stooped into a low bow, as she called across the cavernous hall, "Your Excellency, excuse our rude intrusion! However, we expect Rhydin's arrival at any moment to kill you! We cannot allow this to happen."

"Oh," Dathian breathed, his navy eyes darting among the twenty-or-so of us. "Well, in that case…"

The tall man instantly scooped up his immaculate robes and galloped away from the scene. I shook my head in fury. How dare he!

"Typical," sneered Rachel as she rolled her eyes.

Sam glanced at the hatred in my eyes and questioned, "Boy, what did he do to make you mad of all people?"

I shot him a dark look and shuddered. "You don't wanna know. You'd hardly want to stay to defend his sorry life."

"But now I'm curious," Sam chuckled.

"Later, dear," I said as I shook my head.

As a few of the Ranguvariians began to lift a massive bolt into its place to bar the front door, several people jogged into the throne room. My nerves lifted at first, expecting an attack, but they soon went limp.

They looked like they belonged to two different families, older men and women with fierce lines in their faces along with a slew of young people, all dressed in plain, gray uniforms with aprons. None of them gave us any sort of acknowledgement before Dathian's servants rapidly slipped through the crack in the door before the sound of the lock thundered through the abandoned palace. I shuddered. They knew what was coming wasn't good.

Behind them marched half a dozen soldiers dressed in the same heavily-gilded, silver and navy garb as the soldier who summoned me to the Archimage Palace for the first time so long ago. All of their helmets were closed to hide their faces behind reflective masks. They also each bore different kinds of weapons, but all of them looked razor sharp and shined in the dim room.

The Archimage's guards stomped to join us in our formation, and I forced myself to be grateful that we at least had six more helpers even if the Archimage himself and the rest of Nerahdis had abandoned us.

Once everything had stilled, my eyes turned upward to the blue mist that hung across the whole room. The mist that swirled endlessly even though there was no breeze and allowed Dathian to see anyone and anywhere in Nerahdis. It was churning more rapidly than normal, and I wondered if it was linked to Dathian's anxiety.

When I glanced down, I was met with the sight of the future Three Kings not looking at each other. Frederick was tucked into a corner by himself, his grief plainly written on his face, while Daniel sat on the short trio of stairs leading up to the dais and the Archimage throne with Lily, his wife, a couple feet away from him. It was easy to see the anger in their body language, as well as the clear divide between them. I began to wonder if they would ever recover.

Xavier and Mira were in yet another corner, quietly whispering to each other in far more serious tones than I once could have considered possible for the red-haired prince. I ardently hoped that the three men would separate their disparaging feelings for each other from the much more pressing need to stop Rhydin. If they couldn't work together...

Evan was striding toward me when I felt it. My hand absentmindedly reached for my locket as Rhydin's presence invaded my senses. A timeless darkness that brought to mind all the cruel things he had done. To me and all of Nerahdis. All of the blood he had shed. My heart stumbled under its weight and chill. Sam squeezed my hand hard.

A whole string of musical words and commands unraveled from Rachel's lips, and upon hearing them, the other Ranguvariians began to take their positions. They held up their various weapons, sharp and decorated with colorful tassels, prepared for anything.

As Rachel drew her own blades, she switched back to Nerahdian. "Be ready. Time is of the essence. The longer this battle goes, the more likely it will fail due to our inability to be around Rhydin's magic too long!"

I remembered how Rachel, Luke, and James struggled to help me during the battle with Duunzer. They began the fight swords blazing, weaving around its head in the air, and ended it limping along on the ground with barely enough energy to remain upright. There was a time limit on this fight, and the clock was already ticking.

"*Anae-mous, maten-tous!*" Rachel shouted, and her voice echoed back along the room as all the other Ranguvariians returned the chant. She whispered to me afterward, "It's a soldier's blessing. 'Go together and return to our people safely and victoriously.'"

Time seemed to slow as we all faced the massive door, waiting. Rhydin's presence was undeniable, yet we continued to wait. As the seconds stretched on with no noise beyond the barricaded door, I snuck a glance at my brother. His confusion mirrored mine. If Rhydin was here, why hadn't he attacked yet?

The Ranguvariians fidgeted nervously, obviously feeling the presence that could destroy them if time took too long. I touched Evan's shoulder and closed my eyes, trying to hone into Rhydin's presence more directly.

As I focused, I felt my magic shifting. Instead of the massive door ahead of us, my magic swept to the flank of the throne room where a large hallway connected the north wing of the palace.

Impossible. The front door was the only entrance.

I scurried down from the dais and across the room to the wooden door of the northern hallway. Pretty much everyone in the room turned their heads and watched me go, glancing between me and the barricaded door several times. The window to the hallway was slightly above my head, so I hopped up to get a look down the hallway.

Rhydin was striding toward the door on the opposite side, back in his regular, dark attire emblazoned with his hollow, golden flame with the red orb in the middle. He was surrounded by a sea of black-clad Followers. His purple eyes became like little fires when he glimpsed my face in the window, and with a smirk, he lifted one of his sickly, pale hands.

I didn't have to guess what was coming. I dropped like a sack of potatoes, rolled away from the door, and screamed to anyone who was listening, "Get out of the way!!"

People dove left and right, but only seconds passed before a gigantic beam of purple devoured the hallway door and anything else in its path with the roar of a hundred twisters. Smoke and debris spread throughout the room as a few people coughed. I hid behind the tiny remnant of the door as Rhydin slowly entered my line of sight. Triumph filled his eyes as his army of Followers and Einanhis flooded into the room around him.

Immediately, the sounds of war reached my ears. Clangs as blade met blade and booms as magic met magic. However, Rhydin stalled where he was, his back turned toward me as he surveyed the battle. All in a matter of seconds, I stilled my shaking fingers by gripping my sword tighter and touching my locket one last time. *Don't fail me now.*

I sprang from my hiding place, my sword aimed to kill. Rhydin rotated eerily and met my blade faster than my mind could process, and we exchanged a few blows before I threw a golden orb of magic at him. He easily dodged it, and a wicked grin graced his face.

Rhydin laughed like this was easy and sneered, "Surprised to see me, Linaria? I know this palace better than any of you combined."

"That's the only victory you'll get today," I growled as I caught a glimpse of Evan over Rhydin's shoulder.

Evan zoomed forward, slashing at Rhydin's head, but as I watched him, Rhydin dodged and simultaneously charged a quick, violet ball of energy that knocked all the air out of me. My body flew a few yards away, but I was back on my feet in seconds.

Before I could manage my way back to help Evan, another figure in black leaped in front of me. Allyen magic mixed with

Rhydin's darkness, I sensed. I barely raised my blade in time to block a strong blow, and Robert's Allyen eyes met my own. Anger filled me, and I found myself hitting harder and harder.

As we bounced off each other, Robert rubbed his moustache and reached toward me. He shouted, "Put down your sword, Linaria! It's over. Join us, and I will make sure that you survive the change of power!"

Given the moment, my head oscillated to catch up on the rest of the throne room. We were vastly outnumbered. Each of the Ranguvariians were battling at least five Followers each. It was easy to hear where all the Royals were, although I couldn't quite decipher their yelling and arguing from here.

Sam was dueling both Kino and Eli, and my heart jumped into my throat at the sight of blood trickling down his forehead. He dropped his sword, grabbed the two of them with his Rounan magic, and knocked them together.

Several of the Ranguvariians were still in the air, although a few of their shard-like feathers were beginning to disappear. There was still a chance if we moved quickly.

"After everything you've done? After what you did to Taisyn? Never!" I yelled as I hurled another brutal ball of magic at my father. It knocked one of his legs out from under him, so I took the opportunity to sprint back to where Evan was fighting Rhydin for his life.

With the two of us slashing at him from opposite sides, the smug grin began to fall off of Rhydin's face. Confidence bubbled in my chest as my locket glowed lightly, empowering every move I made. For about thirty seconds, I felt like I could see the light at the end of the tunnel. Victory was within reach.

Oh, how I wish now that could have been the case.

When I left Robert for Rhydin, Frederick had flown forward to take my place and give us our chance. His height gave him an advantage over Robert, but the man was an Allyen and required all of his concentration.

Out of the corner of my eye, I could see the bob of a blue head nearby, Daniel, but he and Frederick never once looked to the other for help. It was like watching lone buoys in a tumultuous ocean, struggling to stay afloat yet unwilling to admit the need to work together.

A couple lanky, black-clad, and blank-faced Einanhis whirled right past Frederick, who was barely meeting Robert blow for blow, aiming for Daniel, but I was forced to turn away before I saw the outcome.

A female shout penetrated my ears as Kino nearly dropped on top of me. Rhydin's Follower slinked around all of my moves like a cat, and my arm burned before I ever saw her raise her sword to cut me.

Another Einanhi appeared behind me, and my head spun like an owl's searching for the nearest help, but the few I saw were embroiled in their own fights. I channeled my magic and thrust my hand at the Einanhi. It suddenly gave a shudder and dissolved into sand as I swung my other sword-bearing hand at a surprised Kino.

As soon as she crumpled to the ground, I spun on my heel to find Rhydin once more, only to see him standing silently where he had been sparring with Evan moments before. My brow furrowed in confusion until I saw Evan a few feet away also busy taking on Einanhis.

Frustration simmered inside me. Where was all our backup? Hadn't we shown up at the palace with a dozen Ranguvariians and a handful of Royals to allow us to focus Rhydin?

I lifted my blade to engage Rhydin once more, but that evil smirk reappeared on his face as he tipped his head to the left, almost like he had popped his neck. I stared at him for a second until I saw the flash of a sword out of the corner of my eye.

I turned in the nick of time to stop Kino from killing me from behind, and as I pushed against her blade with my own, my eyes couldn't help but trace her armor. The wound I gave her was still there, but it was no longer bleeding. If Evan and I couldn't focus on Rhydin, he was going to be able to heal every Follower we cut down!

I swung at the weakened Kino once more, but when I turned again, Rhydin was nowhere to be seen as three more Einanhis pushed toward me. A colorful, shard wing flickered in front of me as the three created beings fell over, and James beamed before he continued flying and diving around the throne room.

Relieved, I jogged over to my brother and scanned the room once again. Where in Nerahdis had Rhydin gone? Eli pounced on me before I had another chance to look, the reds and oranges of the setting sun glinting off his gigantic glasses.

CHAPTER TWENTY

T he sounds of the battle in the throne room became incrementally muted as Rhydin walked, thinking about how much he wished he could capture one of those blasted Ranguvariians so he could conduct experiments on it. It still plagued him that he could not sense the filthy creatures, but his mind was soon occupied by the architecture around him.

Nearly three centuries had passed since he had stepped foot in this palace, yet it seemed as if the place was as timeless as he was. Everything was exactly the same. How fitting, the sorcerer mused. Except for the addition of the navy carpets and banners, Dathian's color. Rhydin would have them burned.

He passed through the hallway noiselessly, his black boots nearly indistinguishable from the onyx floor. He knew where Dathian would be, that disgrace of an Archimage who shamed the title. There was only one place he could hide in this labyrinth of a secret castle.

Unfortunately for him, Rhydin knew this palace like the

back of his hand. He couldn't forget it even if he tried. Too much had happened here. It was permanently ingrained in him. Just as his aging had ceased, everything else was frozen too.

As Rhydin turned into a new hallway, his eyes trailed over the details. The dark color of the floor lightened as it reached up the marble columns on either side, transforming into pure white at the ceiling as it did throughout the palace.

It was symbolic, Rhydin thought. Indeed, the Archimage Palace was where light and dark mixed. Today, his darkness battled the light of the Allyens, and three hundred years ago it had been the same.

Everything found its beginning here, Rhydin mused as he passed portraits of every Archimage Nerahdis ever had. There had been many of them by now. After all, it had been nearly three centuries since Emperor Caden had been killed.

Rhydin still hated the man, but he regrettably had nothing to do with his death. He probably would have, but he had too much ignorance in him back then. It was far better to be the way he was now, even if there was still one remnant linking him to that past.

Even though Nerahdis was as good as his through his own cunning, Rhydin looked forward to the day where he could end the cycle. Sever the last connection he had to the ghost of his past and destroy the Allyens' power to stop him all in one blow.

All he needed was the two halves of the locket. Then, he would truly be unstoppable with his full powers at his fingertips. Nerahdis had seen nothing compared to what he would be capable of once he had the locket, and once he did, he would rule in peace for the rest of time. No one to stop him like last time.

Perhaps, today would be that day.

Rhydin paused in his triumphant musings and glanced at the portrait some imbecile had placed in the spot reserved for the First Archimage. A rendition of King Joshuua of Mineraltir's spindly daughter who had been second in line for the throne.

Rhydin's memories were fuzzy from the era before he purged the ignorance from himself, but he remembered when they made this unfortunate girl Archimage. A ridiculous move by hare-brained Royals who were out to ruin the continent just as Rhydin had warned Emperor Caden before his death.

No matter. Nerahdis would be in his far better qualified hands soon, and he would remedy all the foolish things the Royals had ever done, just as he was always meant to do. Including the ludicrousness of making it appear that this frail, thin-faced princess was the First Archimage. It was blasphemy.

While Rhydin didn't plan on reestablishing his empire in the same palace that held the final fragment of his past that he wanted to destroy as soon as possible, he planned on setting the record right before sealing it away once and for all.

An involuntary shudder wracked Rhydin's body as he turned into the room next to the portrait of the second Archimage that the world claimed to be the first. The room was a small study, one that the servants never came into because it was so tiny and out of the way.

Books lined the dusty shelves against all four walls, and myriads of papers were strewn across every surface available. It was dark, but Rhydin snapped his fingers and the lanterns around the room lit themselves. He was no pyromage, but someone of his power could manipulate most elements to some degree.

A puff of wind pushed against him from the study, and Rhydin felt the pull of his magic inside him, his entire body really, toward the source. Rhydin scowled and muttered, "Of course, you would be in here. However, you are even more of a fool than I thought if you thought it would be that easy to steal your magic back from me."

Nonetheless, Rhydin cast a vague protection spell around himself before he walked into the study, papers scattering in his wake. No need to give any sort of hope to the ghost of his past.

Rhydin skirted around the heavy, oak desk in the center of the room to a corner obscured by a small side table with only a pot remaining from a plant that had long since died and dissolved into centuries-old dust. He smirked when he noticed that the papers had been cleared from the floor behind the table.

With a flick of his pale hand, a trap door previously indistinguishable from the rest of the black marble floor lifted up with a breath of stale air. It revealed a miniscule hole only large enough for one person, maybe two if one didn't mind not being able to move. The shine of two eyes stared back up at Rhydin. In fear.

The sorcerer smiled.

My ears went deaf. Too many crashes of explosive magic and peals of metal swords to count or even keep track of. Einanhis surrounded Evan and I as we fought back to back, desperately trying to meet each and every attack.

I couldn't hide my cries of pain when I failed anymore, even as I scanned for any opportunity to break away and find

Rhydin. There were no longer any Ranguvariians flying above us, and I wondered how many were still alive on the floor. Our time was nearly out, and it was taking everything I had to preserve my own life.

As I parried another blow from yet another blank being created by Rhydin's magic, Jaspen suddenly dove into the fray surrounding Evan and I, dispatching two of the Einanhis. I took a moment to breathe air into the deepest reaches of my lungs before my attention was snatched away by one of the remaining Einanhis entangled with us.

Rachel came forward out of the corner of my eye to help, but Jaspen abruptly yelled at her, "*Rahchii, anae!*"

"*Tenste da?*" Rachel stammered in confusion as she met an Einanhi's blade, her icy blue eyes flicking from her opponent to her husband.

"*Machliis anae! Vaeste!*" Jaspen rattled off once more and added in Nerahdian, "Please, *Rahchii!* Are future Clariion, you!"

Rachel fiercely shook her head. "I'm not leaving you! Any of you!" Her eyes met mine from across our separate duels.

Jaspen grunted, the scars on his face wrinkling, but only a few seconds passed before a blinding light burst throughout the throne room. We took advantage of the distraction to eliminate the rest of the Einanhis around us, but when I looked up, shock entered my system.

Above us, Arii himself had appeared, the seven-foot-tall Ranguvariian leader, his eyes a fierce color of dark brown, nearly black. His colorful wings were grander and brighter than any other set I had before witnessed, and he was flanked by three new Ranguvariian soldiers.

My spirits began to lift as the split-second thought that he had brought us reinforcements washed over me. It didn't take long for the wave to pass and the realization that he had only brought the bare minimum set in. He wasn't here to help us win. He was here to get us out before we died.

Almost instantaneously, one of the three warriors swooped downward and collided with Rachel, who was standing in the open. Rachel kicked and screamed, but before a second could even pass, the two of them disappeared in a burst of light. Jaspen gave a sigh of relief as I noticed the remaining two Ranguvariians maneuvering themselves above Evan and I.

No!

I sprinted two steps before a single call silenced the tumultuous throne room. Everyone turned their heads. The Ranguvariians, the Royals, the Einanhis, the Followers, the Allyens. My ears rang with the sudden quiet after what felt like hours of noise. There, on the dais, Rhydin stood in front of the solitary, marble throne holding a dagger to Archimage Dathian's neck. His deep blue eyes were as wide and frenzied as the Auklian ocean during a storm.

In a manner of seconds, I surveyed the frozen room. The Royals were nowhere in sight. There were only a couple of the Archimage's guards left. Exhaustion and blood lined my brother's face next to me. Sam was across the room, still standing but looking like he could collapse at any second. He was standing over Cayce, who appeared to be knocked out.

Luke and James joined Jaspen, all three of them absolutely ragged. They reminded me of plants that had been without water for days, tipping on the precipice between life and death. They had been around Rhydin's magic far too long.

So much of my own body hurt and bled that I couldn't distinguish the pain from separate wounds anymore. I knew then and there that the only thing keeping me upright was the magic amplification coming from my locket. But, I had to try.

Giving up had never been in my nature.

I leapt into action. I swung my sword one last time to clear a path before it slid out of my numb, slick fingers. Arms reached out and grabbed me. Legs appeared in my path to trip me. Yet, I hurtled forward to foolishly try to do anything I could to stop the inevitable.

After I had gone a few yards, I really did end up tripping over something and falling to the hard, marble floor. As several Einanhis grabbed me to keep me from going any further, I got a good look at what I'd tripped over. Whom I'd tripped over.

Daniel, lying dead and forgotten. His ocean blue hair was unmistakable. My heart fell to my toes.

"It is finished, Allyens!" Rhydin shouted across the room as he heaved Dathian's chin higher. He lifted the dagger victoriously in his hand. "You are outnumbered and hopelessly outmatched! *All* of Nerahdis supports me! You cannot stop what's meant to happen here."

Unable to do anything else, I squeezed my eyes shut so I wouldn't have to see.

Ten seconds passed before I heard Rhydin grumbling. My eyelids flew open as Rhydin screamed, "You filthy Rounan *scum*! You are only delaying the unavoidable!"

Rhydin tried to shove the dagger toward Dathian's neck again and again, but it was frozen in place. It was like Rhydin's arm was handcuffed to the ceiling. My head snapped back to where I had seen Sam earlier, and, sure enough, both of his arms were outstretched as he frantically tried to keep his invisible hold on Rhydin.

Dathian squirmed in Rhydin's grasp, too terrified to move but too panicked to hold still. His fingers flew over and over a small item in his grip.

The sorcerer growled once again, "Let go, or I will kill you where you stand! I will murder every last one of your unnatural people!"

It was difficult to perceive what happened in the following seconds. Abruptly, the dagger seemed to shake loose from Sam's hold, but then the unthinkable happened. As fast as lightning, the dagger turned and carved a jagged mark across Rhydin's pale cheek, aimed downward as if it was headed toward his neck.

A collective gasp traveled around the room, from those on our side and those who were not alike. To my intense confusion and horror, no cherry-red blood seeped from the wound. Nothing ever came.

Instead, as I looked closer, the cut along Rhydin's cheek and jaw appeared more like a crack in cold marble than a gash in warm flesh. The whole room gaped as Rhydin shook with rage. Dathian's brow furrowed as he clung to his tiny object in hope.

But, in a matter of seconds, Rhydin reached out toward the room, caused a dozen Einanhis to collapse as he repossessed the magic he had given them, and bellowed, "This is the day Nerahdis falls!!"

The dagger reappeared painted scarlet. Dathian crumpled to the ground in a heap of regal, navy and gold robes without so much as a sound. The blue mist above us dropped like rain, pattering over our heads, before it vanished completely.

A wild grin spread across Rhydin's thin face, sending a few more cracks into the strange cut in his cheek. Dathian's remaining two soldiers turned and hightailed it out of the room. Rhydin ran his hands through his hair as he laughed with pure elation. Then, he pointed the dagger at my brother and I, cackling, "I have won, Linaria and Evanarion! I have fulfilled my promise to the people of Nerahdis, and my empire is as good as reborn!"

Hatred spread through me like wildfire. I caught Evan's eye from where he stood behind me, and the flame of fury burned there too. He sprang and cut down the motionless Einanhis that held me, and the two of us rushed toward the dais, my magic burning in my fingertips, aching to be used. We were within ten yards of him when Eli and Robert blocked our path.

"It is too late to stop me now!" Rhydin laughed as he wandered over to Dathian's throne. "If you strike me down, all of Nerahdis will hate you! I have already won! Nerahdis is on my side, as they always should have been. If you destroy me, all of Nerahdis will come after you. *This* is what the people want! The Allyens didn't end the war. *I* did!"

Evan shouted back, "The people don't want what you're offering! They don't know the truth!"

"The people want to be *ruled*! They are the very ones calling for my coronation!" Rhydin sneered darkly as he fingered the marble throne temptingly, "The people want *peace*. And peace they shall have for the rest of time under my reign."

"And who shall have peace?" I growled as I shook my head from beyond Eli and Robert's physical wall between us and Rhydin. "The Rounans? The Ranguvariians? Anyone with magic that is not yours? Peace isn't peace if the people lose their freedom. They don't know they've just sold their world to a dark magic-wielder who will never age, but you can't hide your true identity forever! They will discover your deception and cast you out!"

Rhydin chuckled, "By then, my reign will be far too established for those imbeciles to even lift a finger against me."

The room fell into silence for a few moments. I stared hard at the floor, having no idea what to do at this point. Part of me wanted to charge over to Rhydin and kill him where he stood, if I could even get through Eli and Robert in my weakened state. The other part wanted to run far away.

As I thought, my eyes wandered to the massive, stained-glass windows behind the throne. The three smaller ones down below of the First Three Kings. The giant, round one above of whom I had always guessed to be the First Archimage. The pale complexion, the midnight hair, and the blue and red chunks of glass that hadn't properly melted together where the eyes were supposed to be.

I looked at Rhydin a moment. Then back. My mind began to spin and put pieces together. His desire for control over all of Nerahdis. His knowledge of the other entrance to the Archimage Palace and where Dathian would be hiding. His age. His amethyst eyes.

Blue and red. They should have mixed together upon melting. Blue and red made purple. Dread and ice seeped down the back of my neck.

I licked my lips, dearly hoping it wasn't true. My voice faltered as I decided to bait him. "Who do you think you are that you can just waltz in and tear up the order of things again? The First Archimage is probably turning over in their grave. Why are you doing this?"

Rhydin shook his head mockingly from side to side and gave a snort. The crack in his face chipped further. It appeared I had hit a nerve, which I'd never known Rhydin to have before. He planted his feet in front of the throne and spat ferociously, "I *am* the First Archimage!"

All the color drained from every single person's face in the room. It appeared even Rhydin's Followers hadn't known this information. Rhydin paced the front of the room like a ferocious tiger, his tantrum far from over.

"That fool, Caden, helped me create my power to keep his idiot sons in line. If only he knew he actually equipped me to be a far greater emperor than he ever was!" he growled. "Being Archimage after your precious Emperor Caden's death wasn't enough to save Nerahdis! It was my *duty* to lead Nerahdis from the depths his sons drove it to as an emperor myself! Yet, I only ruled for three, measly, perfect years before *Nora* ruined everything! Therefore, I must still deliver Nerahdis from you treacherous Royals and Allyens who continue to allow corruption! That is *why* I must do this, you *foolish* girl!"

Before another second could pass, Rhydin raised both his hands. I felt his profound use of magic right before a massive crash resounded behind us. Evan and I turned just in time to see a liquid wave of amethyst magic sweep inside the throne room through the front door. It filled the room rapidly, but there was no evading it. The wave swelled around my ankles and within seconds was above my waist.

All of the Ranguvariians jumped into the air, but one of the soldiers who had come with Arii to retrieve us wasn't quick enough. He let out a fierce roar as Rhydin's magic enveloped him, and he dropped dead instantaneously.

I whirled around to find Sam as the purple liquid washed over me, and he was still several meters away. I tried to reach for him, but the bright wave began to dull in color and harden into a fudge-like consistency before becoming like glue. Wiggling fiercely, I tried with all of my might to free myself, but it was no use.

My various wounds began to sting and throb even worse

than they already had, and the tight enclosure made me more aware of where they all were. Robert and Eli looked with proud, wide eyes at their master's amazing feat of magic. They could still move through the purple glue effortlessly.

Rhydin lowered his hands and began to stride towards us. "Now, Evanarion and Linaria, I will bid you adieu to reestablish my reign once I retrieve your halves of the locket. I must take care of one more matter of business before I leave this palace for eternity." The sorcerer looked up and down the hall as if just the sight of it could make him vomit.

Seconds. I had seconds to stop him from winning something. The sound of fluttering wings reached my ears. Arii was flying toward us, his wings rapidly deteriorating around so much of Rhydin's magic, which reduced the other Ranguvariians to clinging to the tops of the marble columns.

I acted on instinct. I reached for Evan right next to me and latched onto the leather cord around his collar. Snapping it, I looped my own necklace over my head as fast as lightning.

Rhydin saw me moving and hurried forward, but he was too late. I chucked both halves of the locket high above my head with the last of my strength. Arii instantly snatched them out of the air and disappeared in a burst of light.

"No!" Rhydin growled as Arii vanished. Fury blazed through him. He hustled toward us with his dagger drawn.

My eyes squeezed shut. This was it. This was how it would all end.

Familiar Allyen magic washed over my senses. When I opened my eyes, I expected Evan to have done something, but instead, Robert stood between us and his master.

Rhydin glared at his Follower with hatred, the ugly crack in his cheek gaping emptily, but Robert's grasp on Rhydin's wrist was firm. He spoke low, "Master, you promised. You have won. Leave my children be. I still must have the chance to turn them. Their power will benefit you just as mine does."

"If you were not my right hand, you would be dead," Rhydin snapped. With the swift nod of his midnight head, every single Follower and Einanhi vanished into a puff of purple smoke. Rhydin passed a quick, pale hand over his cheek, leaving it flawless once more, then glared at Evan and I, unable to keep the grin off his face as his body slowly dissolved. "The next time you see me, I shall be your emperor once again. Permanently."

As soon as Rhydin fully disappeared, the thick, dark purple glue vanished without a trace. Without anything to hold me up and bereft of my magic-amplifying locket, my knees immediately hit the floor. Evan collapsed next to me, and the next thing I knew, Sam's face was hovering above mine along with three anxious, exhausted Ranguvariians.

"Lina? Lina, talk to me," Sam whispered. I felt his hands travel over my arms and legs, and I heard the sound of fabric being ripped before pressure appeared on top of the sources of all my pain.

A Ranguvariian shard feather floated hazily over my head, and as music filled my ears, my physical pain became ever so slightly better. However, nothing could fix the emotional pain of knowing that we had failed.

After a few minutes went by, I could lean forward even though the pain still threatened to knock me out. Sam grasped my hand in relief and pulled me into his embrace. I gripped him tightly as if that was the only thing keeping me awake.

I looked around the ruined throne room. The blood of each of the Three Kingdoms of Nerahdis littered the obsidian floor. There were cracks in the stone where swords had hit and scorch marks absolutely everywhere magic had fired. The

navy strip of velvet carpet had been ripped up and soiled. One of the marble columns had fallen across the throne room, shattering everything in its path. The amount of destruction was too much to take in. I tried to turn away, but ruin was everywhere I looked.

Someone had covered the bodies left behind. They included at least a dozen Ranguvariians, Daniel, and Dathian, but I was unsure of the rest of them. Queen Lily was nowhere to be seen, but I was told that someone saw her flee the battle.

As Luke worked to heal Evan, James was a few feet away cradling a still unconscious Cayce. The fact that he too dangled a feather over her sent relief flooding through me that she had to be alive. As soon as Evan was able, he crawled over and lay next to her.

Frederick, Xavier, and Mira stood before me then. The only Royals left, I thought with pain. One of Frederick's arms was bent at a sickly angle, and Xavier's entire right side was burned with magic. Mira looked a little better for wear, but it appeared that Xavier was the only thing keeping her upright.

I worked to stifle my anger. If they could have just worked together, this battle could have turned out differently. But, I bit my tongue. We had been outnumbered from the beginning. So, instead of chastising them, I chose my words carefully, and I didn't care if they stung a little. "If we hadn't been outnumbered, do you think we would have won?"

The three Royals stared at their toes. Frederick was the only brave one. "I don't know, Lina. And I apologize for that. If we'd had more time to-..."

"If we'd taken more time to put aside our differences, Dathian would only have been dead sooner," I remarked sternly. "I dearly hope that you all will be able to forgive each other in the time it will take for the people to realize Rhydin isn't what he seems and trust us again. We'll never defeat Rhydin without the help of the people now."

Frederick and Mira, the Lunakan siblings, stared at each other. An unspoken conversation seemed to fly between them, but Xavier continued to stare at the floor emotionlessly. He glanced once or twice at Daniel's body a few feet away.

Daniel was gone. Xavier seemed unwilling to even look at Frederick. I found myself suddenly hoping that this failure wouldn't cause even more discord between us all. Otherwise, we truly would be lost.

Tears welled up in my eyes, the gravity of the situation weighing on my heart as well. My voice warped as Sam held me tighter in silence. "How could we let this happen, Frederick? How could we fall so far?"

The golden-haired prince looked away, unwilling to see me cry. "Our focus was on the new Allyen child, so Rhydin was able to work undetected. As emperor, he won't be able to do that anymore. Everyone will know his face now. Moving forward, we will have the advantage of working behind the scenes."

I nodded and sniffled, trying to pull myself together. "Did you know he was the First Archimage?"

Frederick continued to look away, so Mira answered, "No. None of our histories mention it, even in Lunaka Castle. The historians must have wiped that era clean for some reason."

Remembrance swept through me. Arii had said that the people of Nerahdis had changed their histories in order to forget the terrible era where Rhydin was in power. I mumbled, mostly guessing, but I knew it was probably true, "Because the First Three Kings were ashamed of their failure in allowing Rhydin to become Archimage and therefore become emperor the first time."

Mira blinked widely in surprise, but then wilted. Xavier and Frederick were too absent-minded to make a response. Xavier silently supported Mira with his one good arm while his bum hand remained a fist, and the two walked away without another glance to anyone.

My eyes lingered over their forms, wondering where they would go. Somehow, I didn't think anyone would be heading back to live in the Royal cottage after this. My attention wandered back to the lump under someone's cloak that used to be Daniel. I croaked, "What are we going to do about Auklia? How will we gain their trust again without Daniel?"

"I don't know, Lina," Frederick sighed sadly.

A light blinked in the dark room, which had been steadily growing dimmer as the sun went down outside. There were bags under Arii's eyes as his towering frame crossed the shattered, bloodied floor. Evan and Cayce, who were both nearly healed to the point of walking unassisted, came to join Sam and I as Arii smiled a sad smile. "You should be applauded for your quick thinking, Allyen Linaria. Rhydin was defeated at least once today."

His long, leathery fingers unfurled to reveal mine and Evan's halves of the locket. The round, silver, amber-studded exterior and the flat, transparent interior. I reached for mine hesitantly. My fingers trembled at the touch of its cold metal, which warmed instantly with my touch. Energy coursed through my veins as it amplified my magic once more. I gripped it tightly as if it was life itself, and Evan mirrored my expressions. I turned back up to Arii. "What do we do now?"

Arii took a deep breath and sighed. The moonlight reflected across his silver crown. "Rhydin will not be able to hide his true character for long. Someday, the people of Nerahdis will need you both once again and will be willing to join our fight. We need only wait until that day inevitably comes. However, the Ranguvariians and Rounans already do need you."

I nodded more to myself than anything. Another question popped into my mind. "Why didn't Rhydin bleed?"

"That is something that I will be looking into thoroughly," Arii murmured, his eyes dropping to the side as they melted into a deep yellow. "I have never seen such a thing in all my years."

I looked back up to Sam, a hint of a smile cracking my face. "That was good thinking on your part too. When you grabbed the dagger and cut Rhydin with it."

Sam's face flushed slightly. His hand reached up and steadied his bandana, his nervous tick. "Uh, Lina, I'll admit I was the one who tried to stop the dagger from killing the Archimage. But, cutting Rhydin instead... That wasn't me."

My brow furrowed, and Arii chuckled, "Perhaps, Dathian's helpful 'ghost' is on our side."

After that, the throne room rang with silence. As Luke and James each placed a hand around Evan and Cayce to transport far away, I began to wonder if we even knew what we were up against.

Rhydin wasn't just a random dark sorcerer out to take over Nerahdis anymore. He was once the First Archimage. The first leader over all the Royals after Emperor Caden's death. He once twisted that position to become the next emperor by usurping the thrones of the First Three Kings.

Now, he had convinced everyone that he was going to free them from political corruption and seemed to truly believe that himself. When cut, he did not bleed, only cracked like stone. What happened three hundred years ago to turn him into who he was today? I wished I could ask my ancestor,

Nora Soreta.

The one remaining Ranguvariian who had arrived with Arii to rescue us moved forward and looped her arm through Frederick's. As they vanished, Jaspen took my husband's arm, ready to do the same. Sam gave my hand a squeeze and planted a peck on my lips before he allowed Jaspen to take him far away from this wretched place.

With that, Arii and I were the only remaining people in the Archimage Palace. The servants had all fled before the battle, and the guards had all deserted after the murder of the one they were supposed to protect. Death lingered in the air as Arii promised me that he had people en route to bury the fallen.

As I stared up at the stained-glass window and single, marble throne for what felt like the last time, I realized there was a faint presence in the room with us. It was so vague, I couldn't read anything about it aside from the overwhelming feeling of sadness.

I glanced at Arii only once, but he didn't appear to feel anything. He had once said that there was perhaps more to this palace than everyone thought, whether the presence was a ghost or not. Slightly creeped out, I rapidly reached out and grasped his arm.

"Ready?" Arii asked pleasantly.

I nodded, ready to rejoin my little family for whatever amount of peace we could have before Rhydin could schedule his coronation.

After our departure, the palace was left completely darkened. A lonely cry of agony echoed through the empty palace walls.

CHAPTER TWENTY-ONE

Early Autumn 16th, Year ~~35 of King Ad~~ 1 of Emperor Rhydin's Reign

It happened even faster than I imagined it would. Today is a new holiday as far as the rest of Nerahdis is concerned. "Liberation Day." The day the war ended. The day that Rhydin became emperor and "liberated" Nerahdis from the Royals while actually enslaving it to him. Archimage Dathian was murdered only a week ago, and the people have already practically shoved Rhydin onto the throne.

Sam and I have stayed far away from Lun for the past few days, where they celebrate in the streets and toast the "young" emperor's health. It physically hurts to think of them all so happy when I know it will turn disastrous at any time.

THE WAR OF THE THREE KINGDOMS

At home in the compound, no one strays out of doors. The air is filled with a funeral dirge. The Rounans know perfectly well what is going on, and it makes me wish all the more that they were on speaking terms with the people of Gornish descent who are partying.

King Adam and Queen Jasmine have been pardoned of all their terrible crimes. Rhydin has convinced everyone that they were merely following Dathian's orders and are actually good people.

Meanwhile, Auklia dissolved into chaos for the week they spent without their rulers. Queen Lily was never found, and since Daniel was an only child with no heir, the people of Auklia have embraced Rhydin's leadership all the more to save themselves from falling apart. With the release of all their prisoners of war, their economy is already improving. Of course, Rhydin is taking credit for this too.

When the Ranguvariians buried Dathian, they found the object that I saw him twiddling with right before Rhydin killed him. It was a small gold frame in which was a painting of a young woman with hair the color of emeralds.

Arii brought it to me a few days ago to ask if I had seen her before, which I had not. Considering the facts that there is no heir to replace Daniel and that Dathian was his uncle, Arii is now scouring the Auklian family tree to discover if this woman could be the rightful heir to the throne. A person we desperately need if we ever hope to sway Auklians to rebel against Rhydin and help us.

In the meantime, our little group has pretty much disbanded for the meantime in order to hide from Rhydin.

The Ranguvariians feel very confident that Rhydin won't waste much time to come after us while the people love him and hate us so much, so we have all split up just for the time being. Until the people discover him for who he truly is, that is.

Frederick returned to the cottage long enough to collect his sister, Cornflower, his son, Dominick, and his belongings, but then disappeared. I think the Ranguvariians have an idea of where he is, but no one else is allowed to know in case anyone is captured.

Likewise, Xavier and Mira have taken Taisyn underground as well. The two groups didn't speak before going their separate ways, so I hope every day apart will them some good.

As of now, Sam, Evan, Cayce, and I are still in the Rounan compound, but Arii has made it very clear that we need to make a plan for when Rhydin comes for us. The compound has always been protected by a windchime created from several Ranguvariian feathers, so it seems safe to assume that Rhydin doesn't know where we are currently. We know this is only temporary, seeing as Rhydin hates Rounans far too much to not begin hunting them down.

Sam is putting off deciding when we will leave and where we will go for as long as possible because he does not want to admit that it will mean leaving his people. Rachel has suggested Caark as a destination, but I hate the thought of leaving Lunaka again. I want to stay so badly, so I can be here when my people discover they need me again.

The only hitch with staying is Kylar and Rayna. If we stay, then it will put our children, the future Kidek and Allyen, in danger. Plus, I'm not sure the Ranguvariians would even allow us to stay and are instead giving us the illusion of a choice.

Sam and I are still going back and forth on what to do, so each day I only hope that Rhydin will not come the next day. Rachel and her brothers never leave my side for that reason, ready to transport us anywhere at the first inkling of danger until we can make plans to leave.

Instead of working on that decision, my thoughts rebel and churn over other subjects: Robert's defense of Evan and I. My sister, Rosetta, and how she is faring in the midst of Rhydin's Followers. The strange, miserable presence I sensed in the Archimage Palace. How we will ever find this mysterious, green-haired woman that Dathian cared for so much. How long it will take for the people to see Rhydin for who he is and turn their loyalties back to us.

It is a waiting game, and I've never been very good at waiting. I watch Rhydin's every move from afar. He is the center of the news now, and I watch for any possible slip in his benevolent facade. Nobody can pretend to be perfect forever, and I always hope that I can detect a flaw, a hint at the true person he is.

If that happened, I can show the people who he really is and the decision to leave can be avoided altogether. Then, we can begin recruiting people to our cause to gain the numbers and strength we will need to defeat Rhydin once and for all.

Meanwhile, Rachel fills my head with reports that the Ranguvariians and the Rounans alike are scattering into the mountains so that Rhydin can't find them, and that Rhydin is building a brand-new palace in the shadow of Caden's Peak, overlooking Caden's Plain.

Concurrently, I focus on practicing my magic and enjoying every possible moment with Sam, Kylar, and Rayna. After all, it could be tomorrow that we are forced to choose between our people and our family once again.

Rhydin is wrong. His dark reign will not last if we have anything to do with it. The war of the Three Kingdoms may be over, but the war for Nerahdis has only just begun.

END OF BOOK TWO

ACKNOWLEDGMENTS

This book has been in the works for a very long time, and there are several people who deserve recognition here!

More than anyone else, I would first like to thank all the readers who loved *The Allyen*. I have heard so many wonderful things from you all about the first installment in this series, which made me all the more excited to get Book 2 finished! My readers' support has blown me away and makes my writing career possible.

As always, my first shout-out goes to my super cool husband, Olin. You also make my writing possible, and you don't mind listening to me read my books aloud to you before they've been edited. You rule!

Secondly, I must thank my entire immediate/extended/in-law family. Whenever any of you travel to see me at a book event or purchase my books, y'all make my day. Not every author has a super awesome family who supports her, so thank you! Your efforts do not go unnoticed.

Of course, I must thank all of the poor souls who convert

my sporadic writing sprees into something grammatically correct and worth reading. To Rachel Evans, the one who has been there from the beginning and who continues to enlighten me on Ranguvariian mysteries. To Daphne Evans, who lets me know when I write something totally illogical and gets all those commas where they should be. To my fellow writer, Hannah Robinson, who keeps me sane and shares in all my writing joys and struggles. Also, my mom, Cynthia Riley, who keeps me consistent. This book would not be in print without you all!

Last but definitely not least, I must thank Magpie Designs, Ltd. for yet another gorgeous cover! You're an absolute miracle-worker. Also, thank you to L. N. Weldon, who graciously updated the fantastic map of Nerahdis for Book 2. I may or may not still be geeking out about it.

Once again, thank you, faithful readers! Y'all rock, and I am so pumped to share the next installment of *The Story of the First Archimage* Series with you all! Find my author page on Facebook or visit my website to stay in touch on future publications!

Visit my website to learn more!
www.michaelarileykarr.wordpress.com